Cobwebs in Time

Cobwebs in Time

a novel by

Lois Fenn

Crow's Nest Books

British Library Cataloguing in Publication Data
A catalogue record for this book is available from the British Library

ISBN 978-0-9542884-2-6

Typeset by Amolibros, Milverton, Somerset
www.amolibros.co.uk
This book production has been managed by Amolibros
Printed and bound by T J International Ltd, Padstow, Cornwall, UK

Dedication

In loving memory of my dear husband Ralph

Acknowledgements

As, in my world of fiction, my own family ties are strong, and I would like to thank my family for their continued support, particularly in the field of computer literacy, which often appears quite alien to me.

My daughter Lisa and her husband Fred are close at hand for urgent consultations, my daughter Karen is an invaluable ally in computer skills, my son Andrew provided the original photograph for my book cover design~ my daughter-in-law Kathryn (Kate) points me in the direction of marketing avenues, and my son Ian links me with web-site 'know how'. My grandchildren, Vicky, Angela, Christopher, James and Daniel keep me in touch with youth, and my three great-grandsons Connor, Samuel and Joshua point to the future with index fingers seemingly programmed from birth to activate a 'push-button' world. From childhood evacuation to all of this. What huge webs time weaves!

My thanks to Jane Tatam of Amolibros for editing and typesetting and for her invaluable advice.

Humber

Push time back. So soon already
The old pier is abandoned. Down this ramp
Cars, cycles, motorbikes, lorries, vans
No longer trundle into their jigsaw places
On the ferry's deck. The gibing wind evilly
Whistles round rusting columns and girders, through
Emptinesses where once gangplanks connected
The swaying boats and Yorkshire; and the muddy water
Laps drearily against the jetty's stone.
Gone for ever are the *Castles* –
The *Lincoln*, the *Wingfield* and the *Tattershall* –
Into marine museums, or as posh eating places
Moored up by the Embankment.
And where now
Are the gaunt packet-boats that came before them?
Brocklesby, Immingham, Killingholme,
Tall-funnelled and smoky and grim, with raucous hooters
That would scare the pants off Satan?
A fog-horn at Salt End, way out in mid-stream murk,
Bleats as if to say 'They may be here,
I'm not telling. If they're not, go on to the beckoning
Finger of Spurn, if you think you can fool the sandbanks,
And ask the kittiwakes there; but I'm not telling.'

But here am I, telling
How on hot summer afternoons, when the malodorous
Fish Dock corrupted the air in the squalid streets,
The Dray horses, jingling their brasses, clopped
On granite setts that led down into the Hoss Wash

1

And splashed away the dust and sweat when
The welcome tide was high. I am telling too
Of riverside smells – the pirate-story whiffs
Of tar and black tobacco and paint; of the too-ripe
Smells of squashed plums and oranges outside
The importers' warehouses. I show you the dance
Of apple-wrappings round the maypole of the wind,
The beauty of sun upon oil iridescent
On dirty pools before it is swallowed
In the river's gullet.
The other night I dreamt
I was with Charon in his dinghy, crossing
The Humber. He was bemused – he hadn't even
Collected my obol – and looking up at the Bridge,
'You know,' he remarked, 'a bridge is sometimes a cheat.
Pretending to be a shortcut. True enough
It can pass from place to place, but perhaps never
From time to time, unless all time is one.'

An extract from the poem 'Humber' written by the late Dennis Winterburn, a good friend and mentor, in which he recalled his childhood memories of his native city, Hull, in the 1920s, and linked them with changes made during the latter years of the century.

Reproduced with the kind permission of his daughter Mrs Pamela Arney.

Prologue

Leigh 'watched' the conversation between his mother Sarah and her friend Julie. He had a strange way of visualising letters and numbers, seeing them dancing around in front of his eyes, and imagining them to have personalities or colours. In fact, he was a strange child altogether. His senses had become heightened since his near-death encounter with meningitis, while the tragic death of his young sister Lucy, who had sadly not been so fortunate, had left him in a state of shock and a need to retreat into his world of fantasy.

He fuelled this fantasising with a huge appetite for reading. He couldn't remember a time when he did not read and his level of attainment now, at the age of seven years and seven months, far outstripped the levels of his peers.

As he turned his head, looking from one adult to the other, he ignored the dancing words and studied the faces instead. His mother's blonde hair and fair skin contrasted sharply with her friend's dark looks. Her full wide mouth, coated with a cerise-coloured lip gloss, shimmered against the whiteness of her teeth. She threw back her head and laughed. What was so funny, he asked himself? Should he think it was funny? He was always in trouble for day-dreaming and not sharing in other people's lives. He decided to laugh in a comical way like the dummy at the fairground in the glass box, which rolled around, making loud noises each time someone fed the machine with a coin. His mother stopped laughing and glared at him, and he drew away from the hatred in her eyes.

Julie giggled nervously. 'He's a strange little kid, isn't he? Who does he take after? Where does the red hair come from?'

Sarah didn't answer, and Leigh wanted to defend his hair. It was not red. His toy tractor was red. The door across the road was red.

The kids at school called him Red deliberately to annoy him. He pretended not to care and hated the teacher who defended him. She treated him like a casualty, he thought. She said that his hair was like marmalade, and that made them snigger all the more. Silly old crow! That teacher! He didn't like teachers. But Grandma Hannah is a teacher, his father reminded him one day. Well, she was not in this country. He had only seen photographs, although, apparently, he had been to England when he was a baby.

The conversation between the two adults had recommenced, and Leigh rested his elbows on the table and pressed his fingers against his ears, in and out, distorting the words into unintelligible bursts of sound. Then he pushed his nose up with his little fingers and crossed his eyes. The adults didn't seem to notice him and he fancied that such distortions of his face could make him invisible, even his clothes. He had read about something like that in a story but it couldn't really happen, not if everything one touched vanished like clothes and then it would be furniture, the house, the town, the world, the universe! 'Wow!' he exclaimed, crossing his eyes again and focussing on the end of his nose.

'Bye Leigh,' Julie laughed. 'You'll stay like that! God! What beautiful blue eyes and those lashes! Girls would die for them! He's too pretty for a boy.'

Sarah waited as her friend's car glided away towards the freeway, her mouth hoisted up in a smile. Leigh, standing in the doorway, watched the mouth, seeing it suddenly moving down at the corners into a different shape. He fancied that it was like a pink banana. He dared not look at her eyes. He knew that they were regarding him coldly; cold blue stones. He prayed to become invisible now, not caring if the whole world was to vanish with him. But he remained in the hallway and she was still there, closing the door.

Only half an hour had passed since Julie left but for Leigh the whole concept of time had changed. He would describe it as a nothing kind of time when past, present and future merged into emptiness. He strained his eyes against the dim light, fancying that someone was hiding in the folds of the curtain; a tall thin soldier perhaps, or was it Lucy? She was always hiding. He pulled the sheet over his head, smelling the tangy lemon of the fabric rinse; smelling the sweat on his body. He could still feel the pressure of her fingers where she had dug them into his arms, shaking and shaking, rattling his brain into muddles of fear. He could still hear her voice. 'You horrible child! Showing me up like that. She thinks you're an idiot. Too pretty for a boy. A horrible boy!'

Leigh had watched the glossy lips twisting and writhing with hysteria. He longed for them to smother him with kisses; longed for them to call him baby. She had started to shake him again and he desperately tried to control the flow from his bladder, praying that a tell-tale dark patch would not spread beyond his shoes into the pale blue carpet. But it did, and he waited for his next punishment, bed with no food or drink until morning.

It was getting dark. The sounds of traffic and people in the road beyond his window seemed strangely dispossessed, in another world. He strained to hear the sound of his father's car engine. He could recognise it from two blocks away.

There it was at last. He pulled back the covers and ran to the window. Now he could see the familiar shape pulling into the drive. The car door slammed to and his father became silhouetted in the brightness of the security light. Leigh ducked behind the curtain, suddenly feeling vulnerable. Would she tell his father? What would she tell him? A loud banging on the front door startled him and he shrank down to the floor as his father shouted, 'Sarah! Come on! You've got the latch down. Let me in. It's freezing out here!'

Leigh crawled to the bedroom door and listened. He visualised his mother standing at the top of the stairs. Was it his heart beating so loudly or hers? Ah, they were talking to each other now. His shoulders relaxed as he heard familiar sounds of activity in the kitchen. Perhaps everything would be all right soon, he thought. Perhaps they could go back to how it used to be. But that was impossible and he knew that it was his fault. If he had not contracted meningitis, then Lucy would still be alive. His mother had told him this many times. A sudden scream sent him tumbling back into bed to huddle once more under the blankets. Muffled sounds of shouts and bangs, the slamming of a door and the sound of a car engine left him trembling with fear, but it was the return of the silence that stretched his senses to their limits.

'Leigh!' That was his father's voice. 'Have you had a drink or anything to eat?'

The child cleared his throat. 'No. We got sent to bed early. I mean I did. Sorry, Daddy.'

Mark Clayton put his head around the bedroom door. 'Oh for God's sake,' he muttered. 'Is this ever going to end? Do you want anything?'

They couldn't just miss Lucy out, Leigh thought. They could still pretend she was here like he did, except that he was not pretending. They wouldn't understand that. 'Don't be scared, Lucy,' he whispered as he followed his father down the stairs. There was no sign of his mother and he consumed the raison cookies and gulped down the hot chocolate in frantic expectation of her return. An hour later, settled back once more in bed, he learnt that his mother had gone to stay with her friend Laura for a few days, which apparently would do her good. 'We'll have a little holiday as well,' his father promised.

Leigh and his father waited in a room in the tallest building the child had ever seen. However, they had only travelled three floors up in the lift, and the surrounding buildings blocked out the view of the sky; row upon row of windows reflecting each other in a kaleidoscope of patterns.

Leigh swung his legs and stared at the woman who sat at the reception desk typing in sudden bursts and then glancing sideways at a sheet of paper. The second hand ticked steadily around the clock face. Two-forty-five, Leigh said to himself with a little glow of satisfaction. That was an easy one. His father looked at his watch and shuffled his feet. The receptionist glanced in their direction. 'Sorry to keep you waiting,' she said, continuing with her typing and offering no explanation for the delay.

Leigh had no idea why they were there. 'To see a doctor,' his father had said. Was he sick again or was it something else?

At that moment, a door on the opposite wall opened, and a woman stood in the space raising a hand to attract their attention. Leigh studied her appearance. She reminded him of a mouse; long, pointed nose; round, little ears, which stuck out through her light brown hair, and rounded, narrow shoulders. He could imagine her being in a story with little animals dressed up like humans.

'Mr Clayton…and this must be Leigh,' he heard her say in a squeaky voice. He put his hand over his mouth to hide his grin. 'Would you like to join me?' She nodded her head towards Mark and then glanced at the child. 'Not you, dear, at the moment. I'll speak to Daddy first. Mrs Burton will be there if you need anything.'

Leigh settled back in his chair. So, it was his dad who was sick, he thought. He looked all right but you never could tell with grown-ups. Mrs Burton had stopped clicking on the keys and was thumbing her way through sheets of paper. The sound of his father's voice came from the other room. Leigh concentrated all of his ability on observing the sounds, the words appearing to him like cartoon language in bubbles. Now he visualised them sliding under the door.

'It all began with meningitis,' he heard his father say. 'Leigh was a normal little six-year-old – very sensitive, mind you, but now that sensitivity is hyper and his imagination is driving him into a world of fantasy. His sister Lucy caught the bug a short time later – the vaccination didn't seem to work – I don't know why – she died and Leigh can't accept it. Mind you, he's always been that way inclined. Night terrors and things.'

'Perhaps it is not fantasy as we understand it. It could be a form of autism,' the doctor replied. His father repeated the word 'autism'. 'Although it usually comes to light earlier, but we still have a great deal to learn,' she continued. 'Still, it's worth investigating. What about the relationship between Leigh and his mother?'

Mark Clayton didn't reply immediately. Mrs Burton began to type again and Leigh struggled to pick out words – difficult birth—didn't want a boy—blamed Lucy's death—depression. Mrs Burton walked over to the filing cabinet. She didn't seem to be hearing the conversation. Leigh wasn't surprised. Adults were not good at listening.

'A complete break,' he heard the doctor say. 'Get the child away, and sort out the relationship with your wife. The shock of losing a child can be devastating, especially for your wife, who really as you say, wanted a daughter. Perhaps one day she may have another daughter when the wound has healed. So let me spend a few minutes now with Leigh. I will tape the session so that you can listen to it later.'

✳

'She hardly got a squeak out of him,' Leigh heard his father say. 'That was a waste of money. Jesus! A hundred dollars for that! These shrinks certainly know how to charge.' Mark Clayton was in the entrance hall speaking on the phone, whilst Leigh was sitting at the kitchen table with a banana milk shake and a macaroon. So his mother didn't want him, he was thinking. She only wanted Lucy. Well, she could do without him. If she didn't love him, then why should he love her? But he did love her. 'Is Mummy coming home?' he shouted.

'What? Just a minute, Julie, Leigh's calling.'

Leigh stared towards the door. It was Julie on the phone, not his mother. 'Nothing, Daddy,' he shouted. He jumped down from the stool, knocking the milkshake over in his confusion. A little voice in his head clamoured, 'Must clean it up! Must clean it up! Mummy will be cross.' But it wasn't Mummy. It was Julie on the phone. Where was his mother? His thoughts raced backwards and forwards, visualising his mother's blue eyes and her friend's dark brown ones.

Mark put his head around the door. He looked relaxed and cheerful. 'Leave that, son,' he said. 'It's only milk. I'll clean it up later. Come on. Let's have half an hour in the park before it gets dark. Then you could do with an early night.'

An early night, Leigh thought. He knew what that meant. His father wanted to get him out of the way.

Later, as he lay in bed pleasantly tired after kicking a ball around for a good hour, he thought about the doctor's questions. Did he have playmates? Were they invisible? Where did they live? Was Lucy one of them? He kept saying no, or shrugging his shoulders. He could see Lucy standing looking at him. It was quite funny really. He giggled. If only they knew. Lucy always was a naughty girl, but he was the one who got the blame. It was not really Lucy's fault, he reasoned. His mother had encouraged her and punished him. Now he understood why. His mind became fogged by sleep but his sense of hearing remained on alert. At first the sounds of a door closing and of muffled voices collided with his dream, and he struggled to make some sense of it, until the dream state thinned away, leaving behind the dark room and his singularity.

Now he listened, hardly daring to breath. Had his mother come home? He half hoped that she had, but the fear was returning. Had his father mopped up the spilt milkshake under the table? He could hear them in the bedroom. He climbed out of bed and slowly opened the door. He could hear different sounds now. They had talked about it at school. Were they trying to make another Lucy? His thoughts returned to the milkshake, and he decided to go down and check the floor. The staircase was dark, but the kitchen light was on. He was out of breath with tension by the time he had tiptoed down the stairs and reached the open kitchen door. There was a clean cloth on the table and he crouched down to look under the hanging drapes. Just as he thought, the pool of milk was congealing on the kitchen tiles. He stood up and reached over the counter to the roll of kitchen paper and crawled back under the table, the drapes of the tablecloth enclosing him in a kind of tent.

The sound of the front door opening and closing, and footsteps in the hall froze his actions. He could hear a quiet tread on the stairs followed by a silence broken by giggles from his parents' bedroom. The soft tread of feet returned down the stairs. Leigh pressed himself into a tight ball. It was his mother. He recognised the sound of her breathing. She had come into the kitchen. He could see her feet as they reached the knife drawer; the sharp knife drawer, which he was not allowed to open. Her feet were now at the door and now once more climbing the stairs. He heard the creaky seventh step and counted each one that followed. She was at the top now.

A huge sense of dread flooded his mind as he realised that he had witnessed this before in his worst nightmare, and he waited for the screams.

1

"Take time to dream. It is hitching your wagon to a star.
Take time to love and be loved. It is the privilege of the gods.
Take time to look around. It is too short a day to be closed in.
Take time to laugh. It is the music of the soul."

English prayer

Hannah Clayton regarded the sleeping child with tender compassion.
The innocence of childhood so apparent in the relaxed expression,
the fine complexion, the gentle breathing, induces such a feeling
of tenderness even between strangers. Indeed, Hannah did still feel
a sense of strangeness in the company of her grandson Leigh. She
mentally reproached herself, as she had done many times since they
had been given the shocking news of their son's death. Mark's
marriage to an American girl and his consequent departure to begin
a new life in the United States of America had led to family
estrangement, encouraged not only by the sheer geography of it but
by a change in his lifestyle and character, which led to
misunderstandings. Still, she thought, she herself could have made
more of an effort. Jack could have as well, she reasoned, in a sudden
attempt to dilute the guilt. How was she expected to cope with the
demands of family life and organise the daily management of their
flourishing garden centre? But then it doesn't take long to write a
letter. She was reminded of her feelings when she was evacuated,
waiting for letters from her mother, and of her own accusing

thoughts. With the selfishness of a nine-year-old, it had never occurred to her that the air raids were making life a living hell, and survival was the only thing on people's agenda. She couldn't imagine now how bad life had been. No one these days, living in such comparative luxury, could even begin to visualise it. She had some vivid memories of the year before she was evacuated. Her father was not required to serve in the defence of his country until the late summer of 1941, and both her parents had been reluctant to sign the evacuation papers. She was an only child and they were afraid to let her out of their sight. The air raids in May had been a nightmare. Hannah remembered hearing the whistle of bombs and then the seconds of silence before they hit their target. People still talked in Lincolnshire of how Hull burnt, lighting up the sky in a red glow, which could be seen all over the county. And here she was, she thought, her mind back in the present, making excuses, and comparing her troubles with those of her parents. Still, as old Auntie Ella would say, 'All the chickens come home to roost.'

The aeroplane gave a sudden judder and her heart missed a beat. She looked out along the wing of the plane, which was vibrating in a frightening way. It was huge, enough for a car park. She mentally divided it up into parking slots, an exercise, which momentarily took her mind off the supposed fragility of the structure, but another judder set her heart into a flutter of fear. She closed her eyes and took a couple of deep breaths. It was the fear of flying that had coloured her decision not to travel to the States, even when Lucy was born. She hoped that Mark had understood that her excuses were genuine on that score. If she was honest with herself, it wasn't the only reason. She had never really been reconciled to Mark's marriage. In her opinion, Sarah was just not right for her son. She spent hours on her appearance and even in that short time of knowing her, Hannah felt that she had no affection for anyone. She wasn't surprised that Mark had been unfaithful. He had always been such a caring boy, but he had changed so much, and had become almost a stranger.

The arrival of the police had changed that bright sunny day a month ago, into the blackest day ever. Death comes in many guises, mostly unwelcome, even when life has slowly and painfully drained away, but murder presents a terrible image. The word itself, the wounding savagery of cold intent, indeed the whole concept scars one's thoughts forever. What had it done to this child? Did he understand how his father had died and that his mother had taken her own life? He had not spoken of it, in fact he had hardly said a word since their re-union, and she dared not broach the subject. He seemed to be in a world of his own, twisting his face into strange grimaces and sometimes crossing his eyes. She could remember, as a child, being fascinated by children who squinted. You didn't see that so much these days, she reflected. It used to be quite commonplace. She would stare into the mirror with her eyes crossed in order to see what it was like to have such an affliction. Was her little grandson doing the same thing?

Her thoughts drifted back to the funeral, a nightmare in itself, with the long delays before the body was released, and the red tape that followed, in order that their son could be returned to his final resting place in Norbrooke churchyard. During that dreadful day, she couldn't focus her mind on her son. She couldn't visualise his face, or any time when she had shared the same space with him. All she could focus on was her pain. During the weeks that followed, time seemed to be standing still. Today was still yesterday and tomorrow was of little consequence.

Jack's leg was the final straw. Fancy, she thought, after all the momentous happenings, it was Jack's accident, which had propelled her out of the quagmire of bereavement. And now, here she was, on the return flight from Chicago, all legalities signed and sealed, and she and Jack pronounced legal guardians of their grandson Leigh. It had all been pretty straightforward. Sarah's parents had no wish to take on the responsibility of a child. Hannah had never met them, but she did know that they had no other family apart from Sarah, and enjoyed extensive travel, which precluded the company of a small child. Apparently they saw little of Leigh and even less of Lucy. 'Terrible grandparents we all turned out to be,' Hannah muttered.

She was glad that Jack was not with her. It had been an adventure, in spite of the circumstances, encouraging her to reflect on the state of their marriage and her dependence on Jack. They were in danger of merging into one entity in order to preserve the union, and she had taken a back seat in many issues over the years; such passivity chipping away at self-assurance. She began to think of other people's marriages and comparing them with her own. Most of her friends had a good social life; cheese and wine parties as they called them, bridge evenings and theatre outings. She didn't care for wine or for cheese for that matter. They had never aspired to bridge, the weekends were their busiest times, and theatre just didn't appeal to Jack. How dreary we must seem to others, she mused. Yet did she really want to change her life? Well, she just needed to have her own space sometimes. That was it, she decided.

Poor Jack! She imagined him still hobbling around on his crutches. What a shock they had all had when the tractor wheel suddenly sank into the well shaft. Who would have thought that a well that size could have been boarded over and forgotten? She gave a shiver as she thought of the children playing in that area when it was an overgrown patch awaiting development. As the news had spread, Hannah heard similar stories. It seemed that Lincolnshire was full of forgotten wells.

Simon, their second son was a blessing, solid and dependable like Jack. In fact, he was getting more like Jack in looks. He had an instinctive rapport with nature. Yet Mark had always been Jack's favourite and his father had never really forgiven him for leaving the family environment. Jack's accident had given Simon the opportunity for some hands-on experience during his eight weeks break from his employment as a junior lecturer at the local horticultural college. The whole family had moved in to Willow Cottage. Simon's wife Marie, was so amenable and Alice, their nine-year-old adopted daughter, was bright and creative, stirring the now half-buried teacher instincts within Hannah. Alice would understand Leigh's periods of introspection and fantasy. But the twins were a different kettle of fish. Five-year-old Karl and Kirsty, their biological grandchildren, obviously were not physically identical, but nevertheless they had a shared essence and readily closed ranks against an intruder. They bore no resemblance to their mother Rachel,

Hannah's and Jack's elder daughter, apart from the colour of their hair, which was a rich shade of brown. Their eyes were like their father's, deep set and the kind of brown that always seems to have a hard shine, and which could glitter with aggression. They had square jaws, not a family characteristic that Hannah recognised in the Flynns or the Claytons, although if she was being honest, she had little idea of Jack's lineage. It was just that they obviously favoured their father's side, and consequently they often seemed to Hannah to be the intruders. She struggled to give them a fair share of her love but each time she encountered an alien trait, she couldn't help having reservations which were fuelled by Rachel's comments such as, 'Oh, they take after his mother!' Or 'That's just how Steve would react!'

She sighed. Life had seemed to be so simple in those early days at Willow Cottage with her young family. They'd gradually restored the cottage to how she remembered it during her foster parents' ownership, returning the ambience of 'old world' living, but with added modern amenities. The previous owners had decorated it in a style that was totally out of character. She let her mind wander through the cottage, room by room, seeing it once again through the eyes of that young evacuee who she now referred to as 'she', when she recounted her own story to herself. How surprised 'she' had been at the size of the place. Her parents' little terraced house had the minimum of required space, but here there were unnecessary rooms; an old back kitchen with a pantry where large hams hung wrapped in muslin, sharing space with shelves of bottled plums and pears, and jars of jam; a small walk-in cupboard known as the Glory Hole, like an Aladdin's Cave; a large wooden rack which was lowered on pulleys from the ceiling to be used on wet wash days after the sheets had been put through the wooden mangle, which stood in the corner; the scrubbed top table and old pot sink with the well used wooden draining board; the quarry tiled floor. The front kitchen, entered by steep stone steps from the hallway, had blue painted cupboards and was the hub of the house with its solid fuel stove and old world comforts. It had always smelt of cooking, particularly of Ella's scones.

Hannah mentally wandered through the little doorway, and up the winding stairway to the 'kitchen' bedroom where Ella used to sleep. What a joy it had been to find the little cellar below this bedroom. It was green with mould in those days but how 'she' had loved the musty smells of age, reminded of the secret passages in her favourite fantasies. The small, so called music room, which housed a piano and a large collection of books, was another favourite place in her childhood. She and Jack could hardly wait to put back the bookshelves, and rip out the pseudo-gothic plasterboard arches, which were so out of place in this small cottage room. The main staircase led up from the hall and gave access to a further three bedrooms. In those wartime years, the high feather beds were necessary to combat the cold, when condensation used to freeze on the insides of the windows in beautiful patterns, the work of Jack Frost, 'she' was told. Now, central heating was a great comfort, and modern beds replaced the old fashioned high bedsteads with their creaking springs. However, the furniture in hers and Jack's room was antique pine, set against Wedgwood Blue delicately patterned wallpaper. It was this space that housed her collection of treasures, as she called them. The family called them knick-knacks or even clutter if they were feeling self-righteous about their modernity, but Jack let her indulge in her excesses, and ducked to avoid the crystal mobiles that scattered rainbows across the ceiling on sunny days. Of course, the 'pièce de resistance' as Aunt Kate, her foster mother, had called it, was the living room, with its minstrel's gallery and large inglenook fireplace, and 'she' had spent many hours sharing the gallery with the cat, her head buried in a book, lost to the world.

Hannah knew that Leigh would love it. She could visualise him caught up in the daydreams of Willow Cottage, with Alice to share in his fantasies.

She stared out of the aeroplane window at the white banks of cloud glistening in the sunlight, and had a sudden picture of all the energy of people's thoughts rising up like balloons and floating away. She closed her eyes and began to drift with her own thoughts into a quiet dream, where Leigh was a baby again and again, coming in and out of her life as though time didn't matter. This was a favourite kind of fanciful dream, and there was no need of recall as the captain's voice brought her back into consciousness.

The events of the next few hours hurried along in a logical procession, without any major problems. By the time they reached Willow Cottage, the sun had long since disappeared behind the horizon, and the familiar light at the front door was a welcoming sight. Leigh leaned forward from his slumped position in the back seat of the family car as Hannah announced, 'Willow Cottage,' in the theatrical kind of voice she reserved for visitors. Simon carefully steered the car up the driveway into the gravelled forecourt, which was fenced off from the public parking area at the side of the property. Things had changed since Leigh's last encounter with life at Willow Cottage but of course he was not aware of this, as he would have no recollection of his first and only visit when he was a baby. The low, whitewashed cottage always looked attractive at this time of night, when the light from the outside lantern illuminated the climbing rose around the porch, and the shadows along the path around to the back gave it an air of mystery even to the initiated. Leigh squinted through half-closed eyes, immediately attracted to the quaintness of the building. It was how he had envisaged an English country house. His father had described it to him once, and he remembered some of his mother's rather scathing comments about the primitive way of living in an English village. But any opportunity to explore visually these new surroundings further was taken away by a flurry of excitement. The front door was flung open and three children spilled out, closely followed by a dog and two women, and the words 'careful' and 'slow down, don't shout', clamouring between the tubs of asters and the colourful border of dahlias.

Hannah knew that Leigh was pretending to be sleepy. She remembered doing the same thing herself as a child when she wanted to shelter from probing curiosity. 'Not now, children,' she said. 'We've had a long journey. I'm sure all that Leigh needs is some supper and a good sleep. We'll save all the excitement for tomorrow.' She cast a quick glance at Rachel. She could really do without Karl and

Kirsty today. She had not expected them to be here, especially as apparently they were all invited tomorrow to celebrate her birthday. Simon had let the secret out on the way back from the airport. She had sighed at the prospect. Barbecues were not her idea of a good time, and she would only be fifty-six; hardly a milestone, not like the dreaded sixty. She knew that they all meant well. It was their youthful way of trying to jolly things up, but inevitably she would feel duty-bound to help in the preparation and in the clearing up, especially with Jack firing on one cylinder so to speak.

She glanced across at Rachel again, noticing the tight pressure of the lips and the hardness in her eyes. If only she could turn the clock back to the days when her daughter was young and carefree. She was such an attractive young woman, with her dark curly hair and deep green eyes, so like her maternal grandmother in a photograph taken before the outbreak of the Second World War.

Marie had already picked up on the tension. With one hand tightly grasping the collar of a black and white, rough-haired collie pup, she pointed with the other hand in the direction of a door at the end of the entrance hall.

'I'm sure Leigh will need the toilet, Alice,' she advised her daughter.

The twins stared at Leigh, their brown eyes darkening even more with curiosity. Kirsty said something behind her hand and they both giggled.

'Daddy's here,' their mother announced and Hannah relaxed a little as the headlights of Steve Palmer's car shone in the driveway. She desperately needed space, and where was Jack? 'Where's your Dad, Rachel?' she called.

'He's escaped as usual. Too many small fry.' Rachel still sounded sulky.

It was true. Jack was not good with small children. Still, Rachel did know that. He had always been the same, only developing a more meaningful relationship with his own children as they matured. He really had not wanted a large family. One would have been enough. Too many memories of his childhood, she supposed. Perhaps it would be different now with Leigh as the only child on a regular basis. But Leigh would be a permanent reminder of Mark. Would Jack be able to cope with that?

After supper, Leigh was settled down in the small room off the kitchen. He was intrigued by the narrow, twisting flight of stairs, which led beyond a door in the corner of the front kitchen. Hannah explained, as she always did to visitors, that it was traditionally the maid's room, and in the past it was recognised to be the housekeeper's room until she had married and gone to Hexham. Alice was using it whilst her parents were helping out. She welcomed the company of her young cousin, feeling isolated from the main bedrooms and sometimes a little nervous, especially as the cellar lay directly underneath. More often than not the sounds of voices in the kitchen went on until quite late, and that night she and Leigh strained to hear the adult conversation as they huddled against their hot water bottles.

Rachel and the twins had left before supper. Simon and Marie settled down to hear Hannah's account of the procedures in Chicago and her vivid descriptions of air travel. Apparently, Jack had retired for the night, and Bobby, the boisterous puppy, was released from the old back kitchen to share the large shaggy clip rug with the long suffering tabby cat, Tiger.

Leigh stared into the space that surrounded him. It was the blackest space he had ever known. It must be the blackest place in England, he thought. Back at home on the outskirts of Chicago, the pollution caused by street lighting and the illumination of high-rise apartments used to filter through his bedroom curtains. Admittedly, he had gained no comfort from that half-light, which invoked fears of lurking, shadowy beings, but he longed to return to them now. Fears were tangible at home. Anything would be better than this kind of blindness. He had not had an opportunity to become familiarised with the lay-out of the room, only to be aware of a narrow curtained window on the opposite wall. He took some comfort from the sound of the steady breathing coming from his right. Alice was soundly asleep. He liked Alice. She had a gentle quality that he found reassuring after the abrasive nature of his sister. But there were other sounds, not reassuring; creaks and shuffles like small creatures moving around in the fabric of this ancient building. He dare not begin to imagine what they could be, and tried to think of something good, but there didn't seem to be any good thoughts any more.

Suddenly, the blackness that surrounded him began to vibrate. The air was charged with a force that he recognised, and he sat up in bed, straining his senses to their limits. 'Is that you, Lucy?' he whispered. He knew that it was not his sister. Over the last few weeks he had come to recognise her spiritual presence, but he desperately needed comfort. There was a flash of light and he became aware of a small boy standing next to his bed. The voice that had always talked inside his head told him that this was Nigel, a long-dead tenant of Willow Cottage. He learnt also that Nigel's parents were Kate and Harry Churchill and that he had died when he was very young, little more than a baby. 'I would be fifty-seven years old in your time,' the voice continued, 'but time comes and goes and I quite prefer being the same age as you.' This silent communication was two-way. Leigh asked for news of Lucy and his parents. 'The Mooncat will help,' Nigel advised. 'Alice will show you.' The solid stillness of night returned, and Leigh pulled the sheet over his head and huddled into his own space.

Hannah was aware of the faint light creeping into the room. She had slept soundly for a few hours but the difference in time zones and the consequent jet lag had disrupted her sleep pattern, although she was no stranger to insomnia at the best of times. It had become a familiar enemy as her body shuffled into post-menopausal symptoms. The so-called change was often treated as a joke by men, who did not understand, or by younger women, who could still be flippant about the advancing years. She remembered Mrs Heron in those early days of teaching, bringing it up in conversation as an excuse for every failing; every creak and memory lapse. It was no joke now. Nothing could ever be a joke again. A sob caught in her throat, and she swallowed hard, protecting Jack from her grief. Then, conversely, she felt a surge of resentment. How could he sleep? Snoring as soon as his head hit the pillow! 'Typical man,' she muttered. But then Mark was a man – but Mark was her son. That's a whole different ball game, she thought.

Yet, she should be glad of this day, the completion of fifty-six years and the first day of life with her grandson. Alice had taken on the role of first grandchild even though she did not appear on the scene until Leigh was nearly two years old, and she was turned three. Hannah's thoughts reached back to Simon and Marie's sadness at yet another miscarriage, and their decision to adopt. She herself was so lucky to have no complications. 'Breeding like rabbits,' she had heard a customer comment in their village shop when it became obvious that she was pregnant for the fourth time. That seemed like another lifetime before they moved to Willow Cottage to run a garden centre. Thinking of the comparison with rabbits took her mind even further back to the night after she was reunited with Jack. He had appeared as the White Rabbit in a vivid dream, and she had been Alice in Wonderland, falling and falling in love, or was she going round in circles and getting nowhere? How many years ago was it? Twenty-four from fifty-six – crikey! Thirty-two years! That was when the Mooncat had come back into her life and with it her renewed interest in the paranormal. Yet somehow these days the magic had disappeared. She had lost that feeling of being on the edge of something. She could never explain what she meant by that. It was always so fleeting; a sudden realisation of the truth, which was taken away like a puff of smoke. Jack described it as being away with the fairies and these days she seldom talked about it. She knew from little comments that Alice, with her long straight hair and blue eyes like the original Alice, was always in a wonderland of imagination. She reminded Hannah of herself as a child, although during those wartime years she had never been allowed to grow her hair long in case of nit infestation, and in spite of no family relationship, strangers made comments like, 'You can see where she has come from.' Hannah wanted to point out that Alice was fair-skinned like her mother Marie, but she couldn't be part of the deception. Oh, family relationships could be so complicated, she said to herself.

'Well, this won't get the baby a new dress,' she muttered, voicing one of her mother's favourite expostulations against the passage of time. 'Jack, are you going to make a move? The forecast was good. It could be the last busy Sunday.'

Jack grunted, and turned to bury his face in the pillow.

'I can hear that dog yapping in the back kitchen. I thought we agreed not to have any more dogs now that we have the little children around,' Hannah continued, determined to get some response from her sleepy husband.

'Well, he's another orphan in the storm. How could I leave him at that rescue centre? He'll be a good dog to have around the place once he matures. Besides, children and dogs grow up happily together. I noticed an immediate bond between them, and Tiger doesn't seem to mind.'

'I expect she soon established who's boss around the place. One lash of her paw soon puts dogs in their place.'

Hannah pulled the covers back and staggered into the bathroom. Her limbs were stiff after the long journey and she was tempted to crawl back into bed and leave the work place to the younger ones. However, after a shower and a vigorous rub-down with a big fluffy towel, which she guarded jealously for her personal use, she felt that her flagging spirits were becoming energised, although her limbs were somewhat lagging behind. She decided to dress for the special day, choosing a figure-hugging, powder-blue blouse, and a well-cut pair of trousers, which gave her the freedom not to wear tights. Not that I'm ashamed of my legs, she thought, but she hated them being encased in nylon. Normally, ankle socks teamed up happily with jeans and a tee shirt.

She gave Jack another shake and hurried down the stairs. From halfway down she could hear the sound of voices coming through a gap in the partially closed doorway, and she stopped to listen. She heard Alice announce, 'This is the Mooncat. He's magic.'

'I know,' Leigh replied. 'My dad told me about him. He gives us special dreams that come true, doesn't he?'

'Yes. I don't understand it, do you? How can we dream about something which hasn't happened?'

'But what if it already has?' Leigh replied. 'I think it doesn't really matter. Everything seems to get mixed up. Do you know someone called Nigel? He is on Lucy's side, not ours. Do you know what I mean? Well, he's in this house.'

'Do you mean he's a ghost?'

'No! You can't talk to ghosts and I talked to him for ages.'

'I didn't hear you.'

'Well, it's kind of silent. Sort of in my head. Anyway, he used to live here, and would be very old by now. Fifty-something I think.'

Hannah flinched at his idea of old age and decided to make her presence known. She could feel the goose pimples rising on her arms and guessed that Alice must be feeling disturbed. She pushed the door open and went down the stone steps into the kitchen, with a flurry of energy, as though she was dispelling anything, which could be hanging in the air.

'Did you sleep well?' she asked.

'Yes, thank you, Grandma,' they answered in unison, in the kind of sing- song voices that children seem to think go with the good manners demanded by adults. They were looking at each other and Hannah knew that they were wondering how much she had heard.

She clattered the cereal dishes onto the tea-plates and put a packet of cornflakes in the middle of the table. 'Here you are, look—milk and sugar. Make a start. I'll just sort out cups of tea for everyone.' In spite of her vigorous stirring of the atmosphere, she could still sense the tension.

'So, what do you think then?' she asked Jack later, as they sat on their own in the living room. She had spread some sheets of paper out on the coffee table, and Jack had carefully read through each one.

'Well, all it boils down to is that Leigh was affected by his illness and the death of his sister and now…well, all the rest of it.' Jack raised his hands in a silent gesture. It was obvious that he was not prepared to discuss his son's death, but Hannah persisted, hurrying the conversation on.

'But don't you think that he is an exceptionally gifted child anyway? Do you think he does communicate with Lucy?'

Jack sighed. 'According to the experts, he is a lonely child who invents playmates. He doesn't have to invent Lucy, does he? But it doesn't mean anything. It's just a game I think.'

'But what about him seeing Aunt Kate's little boy Nigel? Don't you think that's amazing? You know, things begin in childhood. Look at that woman in Tilham. Apparently, she heard voices when she was a child, and she described people from the past who she couldn't possibly have known. Children do seem to have a sixth sense. Look how I was when I was a kid, having dreams coming true. Don't you believe in it any more? It seems to wear off as we grow up. Time is very strange, isn't it?'

'Oh for goodness sake, don't dwell on this time thing. You are either looking back with regret or looking forward with fear these days. Mark must have told him. You've talked about things for years. Anyway, let's get on. The first customers are arriving.'

Hannah knew that the barrier, which Jack seemed to put up between them occasionally, was back. She couldn't understand him sometimes. Of course his leg had been painful and it was not easy using crutches, but he had been resting quite a lot, and it wasn't as though she was asking him to look after Leigh. She sighed. Where had all the dreams gone? Did life have to be reduced to the mundane, with no flights of fancy?

She had always puzzled about baby Nigel ever since Ella had told her of his tragic death at Willow Cottage. She had assumed that the ghostly cries which she had heard a number of times when she was growing up belonged to him. But then when Mark and Sarah came to stay that summer six years ago, there was no mistaking that it was really Leigh's cry that she had heard, and not Nigel's. How could she have heard a voice from the future and why did she? She was back with 'time' again. She sighed. She didn't seem to be able to get anywhere these days. She had always tried to understand the puzzles of life and death, reading long books on different philosophies, and savouring words of wisdom. Now, Leigh was going to be a constant reminder of her dear Mark. Was time the great healer? Perhaps Jack was right. Time would always be a mystery.

❄

The sunshine had encouraged a number of people to visit the garden centre, although it was the end of the season. There were always those looking for bargains and trade was brisk until the gates were locked at four-thirty. Steve, Rachel and the twins arrived at four o'clock to help with the barbecue just as the telephone rang in the hall.

'It's for you, Mum…I don't know. Somebody with a loud voice.' Rachel stood with her hand cupped over the receiver, pulling a disapproving face. 'Shall I say you're not here?'

Hannah shook her head, reaching forward and staring into the phone as though the voice would materialise into a recognisable form. Seconds later she knew who it was. 'Hannah! Happy Birthday! I have been looking for you everywhere,' screamed her old friend Sally Blenkin.

'Happy Birthday to you as well!' Hannah was yelling now. 'Never mind you looking for me. I knew you were wandering around Australia. Your brother Gavin told me but no one seemed to know whereabouts. So, where are you now?'

'In Hull, of course. You didn't think I would be ringing from Australia, did you? I'm staying with Gavin and his family in Anlaby. Is there any chance of you making a break for it?'

'I've only just come home from Chicago.' Hannah emphasised Chicago and Sally sounded suitably impressed.

'Oh very adventurous for you! Look,' she continued, 'I'll have to go. They're taking me out to celebrate. I'll catch up with you later.'

The phone clicked, leaving Hannah open-mouthed in the middle of an OK.

'Who on earth was that?' Rachel asked.

'An old friend from Hull. We are both fifty-six today. It's thirty odd years since I last saw her and she suddenly pops up like a rabbit out of a hat. I'm sure I must have told you it was because of Sally that I was reunited with your father. I would never have gone back to Cragthorpe if she hadn't encouraged me. I can't believe that she's suddenly back in my life. I wonder if she is still writing or if she has settled for married life and a family.'

'Oh! She's the one in the photo album. The glamorous writer with the long blonde hair. I wonder what she looks like now?'

Probably still glamorous, Hannah thought ruefully as she caught sight of herself in the hall mirror. She ran her fingers through her short bob in an attempt to fluff it up. Her naturally blonde hair was becoming finer over the years, and had a faded look at the temples, which sometimes took on a greyish hue. Sally could always make her feel dowdy even in the old days. She had sounded very surprised that her country friend had been anywhere south of Nottingham, never mind Chicago. Still, she wasn't doing so bad, she thought, patting her stomach and running her hands down her hips, which fitted neatly into her new cream trousers.

Later, the promised balmy weather had warmed the night air, and the clusters of candles on the tables, their light illuminating the flagged area on the south side of the house, gave shadowed glimpses of faces animated by laughter, or pensive in recall. The scene seemed to hang, caught up in time like a snapshot, as Hannah stood watching from the shade of the greenhouse. A telephone bell shrilled through the buzz of conversation and broke the spell.

'Telephone! Where's Mum? It'll be for her again.'

Hannah stepped across into the old back kitchen and through into the central hall. Could it be her younger daughter Emma? It was a shame she couldn't be here. Perhaps it was Sally returned from her jaunt. She quickly realised that it was neither of them as she strained to hear the quavering voice of Auntie Ella.

'Have I got it right? It is your birthday, isn't it? I get in such a muddle these days. Have I dialled the right number?'

There was a crashing sound and Hannah's eyes widened with anxiety. 'Ella!' she shouted. 'Are you OK?'

'Oh dear! I dropped the phone. Can you hear me? I'd better put it away.'

There was a click and then a return to the dialling tone.

Hannah stared into the receiver. Should she call back? She

envisaged Ella jumping at the sound and perhaps stumbling in her panic to answer it. Someone should be looking after her, she thought. She had no one to care for her since Jim had died.

Rachel and the four children had followed Hannah into the house. 'Was it Emma?' Rachel asked.

'No. It was Auntie Ella. She sounds very confused. We'll have to do something about her, and about this dog. For goodness sake get down. I must say your dad has excellent timing. He could have waited until Leigh was settled in.'

'Who is Auntie Ella?' Leigh asked Alice as he gathered Bobby up in his arms, ducking his face away from the enthusiasm of the licking tongue.

'She used to live here and do the housework, when Grandma was a little girl. She comes to stay sometimes. She's a nice old lady. Like an old granny really. You know, like you see in fairy-tale books.'

'Perhaps we can get Ella into a local nursing home and then we could keep an eye on her,' Hannah said, looking across at Jack as she rejoined the barbecue.

Jack returned her gaze with a long steady gaze of his own, almost accusing, she thought. 'Transplanting doesn't always work,' he suddenly remarked. 'The soil might not be right or the climate.'

Hannah followed the direction of his stare towards Leigh and for a moment shared his feelings of misgiving. She recalled a friend describing herself as the jam in the sandwich being squeezed from both sides, and she knew the feeling.

She sighed with relief, as half an hour later everyone decided to call it a day. Steve and Rachel made their excuses, and Simon volunteered to clear up. Hannah had been ordered to sit down and she didn't argue. She watched Simon, thinking how much he resembled Jack with his dark hair and intense green eyes. Mark had been a cross between Jack and her father with that extra bit of Irish thrown in.

'You've caught the sun, Simon,' she called.

'I think it's the heat from the barbie,' Simon laughed. 'We had a few burnt offerings, didn't we? Still, you're worth some sacrifices. Although you look done in. Perhaps it wasn't such a good idea.

You must be feeling the effects of jet lag. Dad looked worn out as well.'

Of course, Hannah thought. Jet lag was the problem. She would cope with everything after another good sleep. It was nothing to do with Leigh, Ella, the dog, or even being fifty-six.

Simon sat down next to her on the bench and put his arm around her shoulder. 'Leigh seems like a nice little kid,' he said. 'Very polite. Not at all what I expected. Still, it's different in the films.'

Hannah yawned. 'Sorry, my dear. I can hardly keep my eyes open. Bless you! Your dad can't get over Mark, you know. Anyway, thanks for helping.'

Simon took his arm away and stood up. 'It's hard to compete,' he muttered as he bent to pick up a stray paper plate.

Alice said goodnight and turned off the light. The blackness seemed like velvet at first, smothering the air, but Leigh, reassured by the happenings of the day, could now relax into a more pleasant reverie than on the previous night. Admittedly, he had some misgivings about his new surroundings. The twins had given him sly pinches when they thought no one was looking, calling him Ginger Nut and Yankee, or jealously tried to draw Alice away from him with silly excuses. He ignored them, afraid to retaliate in this close family atmosphere, although once or twice he wished that Lucy was there to support him. She would have sorted them out, he thought grimly.

Now, as he stared into the darkness, he was aware of being watched. It was a familiar feeling of late because Lucy had frequently shared his night space since her premature entrance into the spirit world. It could be frightening even though he knew it was Lucy. The fear of this unknown world made his skin prickle.

'Where are you, Lucy?' he mouthed. She had made no contact with him for over a week. He knew that his parents were on the other side. Sometimes he wished that he was there too. But perhaps now that they were both with Lucy, they wouldn't bother about him anymore.

As he relaxed into sleep, he had the strange sensation of floating away from his body and up to the ceiling. Suddenly he knew that he could leave the confines of Willow Cottage and move into a world where anything was possible. He became aware of high hedges and a narrow pathway like a tunnel. A door opened at the end of the path, and an old woman dressed entirely in black waited for him to arrive.

She beckoned him in. The rings on her fingers sparkled with jewels of all colours and her black shining hair hung down to her waist. He found himself in a cosy room full of cats: black, grey, ginger, tabby, long-haired, short-haired, with large eyes which caught a reflection of a blazing wood fire. In the corner he was not surprised to see the Mooncat. He walked towards it and as he reached out to touch it, it vanished and Lucy stood in its place.

'Now Lucy, be a good girl and give Leigh the message,' the old woman said. 'You mustn't tease him.' The dozens of sequins on her black dress sparkled like stars in the sky.

Lucy giggled, and pointed her toe forward like a ballet dancer, before telling him that their parents were not at liberty to communicate. They had arrived safely, but there was much they had to do. All would be settled in good time. She began to fade away, to be replaced by the Mooncat once more.

The old lady wagged her finger at Leigh and he backed away towards the door. There was a flash of light and he found himself back on the other side of the closed door. No matter how vigorously he rattled the latch, it made no sound. He tried to shout, croaks gurgling in the back of his throat as he returned to his body in his bed and to the thoroughly alarmed Alice.

'Are you all right?' she asked. 'You've been dreaming. Gosh, you didn't half scare me!'

'Sorry,' Leigh muttered. 'It was Lucy in a house with an old woman. I think she was a witch. Do you still have witches in this country? There were cats everywhere. I've never seen so many cats. The Mooncat was there as well, but it changed into Lucy.'

'I told you it would work, rubbing the Mooncat's head. Did Lucy say anything or was it one of those silent kind of dreams?'

'Er, nothing much.' Leigh yawned. He didn't want to discuss his parents with anyone else. He slid back down under the covers. Were they being punished, he wondered? Had they gone to Hell? He was not sure whether he believed in Hell. People sometimes said, 'Go to Hell,' when they were angry. His mother once shouted it at his father. He sat up again, directing his voice towards Alice through the darkness. 'Have you ever seen a witch? This one was all black except for her face and hands. Black hair, a long black dress that sparkled as though it was covered in stars, and I think even her shoes were black. She had rings on her fingers. Oh they were all different colours, all shining like the rainbow.'

His description sent shivers down Alice's spine. She pulled back the covers and left her bed. 'Move over a bit,' she whispered. 'I'm freezing.' They both cuddled together, silently contemplating Leigh's strange out-of-body encounters, until Leigh drifted back into a deep sleep. Eventually, Alice returned to her own bed, shivering once more between the cold sheets. She was a tender-hearted child and worried about her little cousin. She had picked up some details of his past experiences from carelessly spoken comments. Should she tell her grandmother about Leigh's dream? She didn't want the twins to find out. They were too young to understand and in any case they seemed intent on hurting Leigh. Perhaps it wasn't a good idea to rub the Mooncat's head. Sometimes Grandma called it the Magic Mooncat. What if it was a witch's cat? Alice decided to put it back in the cupboard when no one was looking. She lay awake for a long time, reassured by Leigh's steady breathing, but tensed up against the other noises of the night, her mind caught up with witches, cats, Lucy and Nigel.

2

*"Time is a sort of river of passing events, and strong is its current.
No sooner is a thing brought to sight than it is swept by, and
another takes its place, and this too will be swept away."*

Marcus Aurelius

'I'm really worried about Ella,' Hannah said, as she struggled back
into bed after putting the customary seven o'clock cups of tea on
the bedside tables.

Jack sighed. 'You're always worrying about something these days.
If you've got to worry, why not worry about us?'

He means I should worry about him, Hannah thought, irritated
by his criticism. That wasn't fair. She was always concerned about
him, especially just lately. Was this about Ella, or was it really about
Leigh? Ella had never been a problem in the past, happily spending
time at Willow Cottage during those lonely months since her husband
Jim had passed away. But then she didn't have dementia; a little
forgetful at times but not this irrational behaviour that had shown
up in recent telephone conversations. Ella was the only aunt she
had, and then she wasn't really her aunt. But did it matter? Did
flesh and blood matter? She worried about Alice sometimes. In her
opinion, Simon and Marie were leaving it far too late to explain to
her that she was adopted. Could she have any memories of her
unhappy past? She never gave any indications of it. After all she
was barely three years old when she was put up for adoption.

Hannah thought of her own childhood during the World War Two evacuation policy and then in the years which followed, after the death of her mother and the rumoured death of her father. Life had been wonderful with Aunt Kate, Uncle Harry and Auntie Ella. But then it had all gone wrong, and flesh and blood did matter after all.

'I'm only thinking of you.' Jack interrupted her thoughts, putting out his hand to pat her gently on the back. 'I'm not complaining.'

'As if you would,' she laughed. The awkward moment had passed and with it any further discussion of Ella's future.

Hannah could hear Simon and Marie on the move. Alice was back at school today. It was quite a long journey for her while they were all staying at Willow Cottage but her father would be back into his own routine the following week when the new term began at the college. Marie planned to check up on their own property after dropping Alice at school. Hannah hoped that they would be able to cope without Simon. He had been a godsend during the last six weeks. Jack had always managed with one full-time employee and a weekend lad, and now, with his leg on the mend, he should be able to cope. Hannah did her share in the finance department, taking payments at the till and keeping the accounts in good order, although gardening was her greatest pleasure; a pleasure she indulged in the tending of the flower beds around the cottage.

However, such indulgencies would have to be shelved for the time being. She had decided to keep Leigh at home for a while, and revive her own teaching skills. According to the medical reports, he needed very careful handling and she had discussed the matter with the local head teacher.

As she showered and dressed, she began to plan her future actions. It would have to be without Jack's co-operation, she thought. This week, while Simon was still helping out, would be the only chance she would have to drive up to Northumberland and bring Ella back. She would take Leigh with her. It would be a good opportunity to relax him away from the family and it would simplify life for everybody else, she said to herself, with thoughts of Jack's recent impatience. The trip to America had given her a sense of freedom, which she was loath to abandon. If she could face all that, she could face anything.

It had been a long drive up to Hexham. Hannah had forgotten just how tense long car journeys made her feel, even as a passenger. Jack usually took the wheel when they travelled together and consequently her confidence in driving skills had suffered. The traffic was a nightmare with major road works along the A1 causing lengthy tailbacks. Leigh was not good company. He seemed miles away with his hands over his ears, pressing them hard as they overtook articulated lorries, or were overtaken themselves by motorway maniacs, as Hannah called them.

She was beginning to have second thoughts about Ella. Perhaps it wasn't such a good idea. It could be months before she was settled into a nursing home, even if they could persuade her to make that move, and Leigh certainly had issues which would not go away overnight. Jack was right as usual, she thought as she pulled the car to a halt at some traffic lights. He told her that she was too old for this Florence Nightingale act. But then fifty-six wasn't old, for goodness sake! She tapped her fingers irritably on the steering wheel, waiting impatiently for the lights to change.

Everywhere seemed different since the last time she had been here; one-way streets and pedestrian areas. Still it must be more than five years since they had visited Ella and Jim. An old, recognisable shop caught her attention, and she settled back into the driving seat, comforted by the sight of other familiar buildings along the sides of the road.

Hannah was not sure whether Ella understood her intentions. She had said 'yes' at the right times during the telephone conversation last night, and repeated 'tomorrow—Tuesday' several times, supposedly confirming that she would be at home. They were heading out of Hexham now and Hannah pulled into a lay-by to study the map. Leigh hungrily ate the last ham and tomato sandwich, washing it down with the remains of the mineral water. At least all the disruptions in his life had not affected his appetite. Hannah smiled at the idea. With her experience of boys, it would take an earthquake to do that.

'Auntie Ella is getting very old,' she said. She had not broached the subject of Ella's dementia before, not wanting to disturb the child, especially after the irrational behaviour of his mother. 'She may say some strange things and get muddled, but don't take any notice just leave her to me. If it's nice, you will be able to play outside.'

Leigh nodded, rubbing his hand across his mouth.

'Here,' Hannah continued, passing over the map. 'See if you can work out the way to Peth Head. This is the first time I've driven along here. I'm usually in your seat and looking at the scenery. I can't keep stopping and looking at the map. It will take us for ever. Or I'll drive into a ditch or something.'

She wasn't really surprised to find that her grandson was a very good map-reader with a remarkable sense of direction, and twenty minutes later they pulled up in front of The Linnels, Ella's cottage. Ella was peering through the window, but as Hannah waved, she ducked out of sight. They made their way to the front door along a path bordered now by roughly dug soil. Hannah rapped her knuckles on the half-glazed door. There was no response. 'Come on, Ella. Answer the door please,' she said. She knocked again and tried the knob, turning to speak to Leigh. He was nowhere to be seen and she exploded into impatience. 'Oh for goodness sake!' she yelled. 'Where's the wretched child gone? Leigh!'

'I'm round the back, Grandma. The front door is locked and the key is lost.'

Hannah found Ella, all smiles, in the back yard standing with her arm around Leigh.

'Kate! I didn't expect you,' she said. 'And you've brought Nigel. Hasn't he grown?'

'No Ella. It's Hannah and this is Mark's son Leigh.'

Ella looked from one to the other. 'You've all changed,' she said. 'Didn't Harry come with you?'

Later, after Hannah had made up the single bed in the spare room and pumped up the airbed, which she had brought with them, she called around to see the next-door neighbour, Mrs Thorpe, who was 'keeping an eye on things' as she described it. 'She's not safe to be left,' she said. 'She wanders you know. She was out in the garden at two o'clock in the morning digging up potatoes. She keeps cooking them every day for someone called Harry. She seems to have forgotten about Jim.'

Hannah thought briefly of the past. She always suspected that Ella and Uncle Harry were sweet on each other. His anger against her when she married Jim would make sense if that was the case, but then Kate wasn't happy about it either. Perhaps she felt closer to Ella than as a paid companion; maybe as a sister. How complicated relationships could become.

'If you don't mind me saying,'—Mrs Thorpe's voice broke into Hannah's thoughts—'there isn't really much of any value furniture wise. Do you want me to ring up some house clearance people?'

Hannah backed away from the urgency in this woman's voice. It was Ella's home she was talking about. All the bits and pieces she had dusted and treasured over the years. God, this is harder than I expected, she thought. 'We'll see,' she said.

In a way, it was a blessing that Ella seemed to be in another time. She helped to pack her personal belongings in that efficient way she'd always had when she was housekeeper to Kate and Harry Churchill. Sometimes Hannah answered to Kate and occasionally she became Hannah again. In the end, it didn't really seem to matter.

Leigh was wonderful with Ella. He seemed to understand her perfectly and settled her down to sleep each night, reading out loud from one of her books in his Yankee voice as the family called it. Ella took no notice of the unfamiliar accent. She herself had lost a lot of her native Lincolnshire over the years, a sing-song 'Hexham Shire' flow of words now escaping readily from her tongue.

They all walked each afternoon down to the Rowley Burn at Peth Foot. The water gurgled amongst the rocks, gathering into deeper pools where the flow was restricted, before leaping on again, as it overflowed in its ultimate journey to the sea. It reminded Hannah of one of her favourite pieces of music, *Voltava* by Smetana. She was introduced to it during her teacher-training course and always thought of the little fast-flowing river close to Ella's cottage, each time she played the tape. There were so many happy memories in this corner of Northumberland. Memories of Ella's middle age, when she was the only close 'relation' Hannah thought that she had, and then wonderful holidays, introducing the children to the wild scenery and the breathtaking coastal views. They'd camped nearby in a farmer's field where there was a constant supply of milk and eggs and very often a shared meal in the big farmyard kitchen. Those small patches of recalled contentment gave this brief interlude in her life a timeless quality, where problems did not exist and her spirit floated in a rosy hue.

Leigh was creating his own memories, which, no doubt, would stay with him forever. He watched the dippers bobbing on the platforms of rock above the splashing water. He threw sticks into the burn and followed their progress downstream, aiming small stones to free them from ensnaring weeds or other obstacles. Always Ella was at his side, back into the joys of childhood, clapping her hands with excitement when his aim was good, and each small vessel bobbed merrily along on its way. Her cheeks were rosy, and her eyes were bright, reminding Hannah again of a robin, a memory so clear in the days of her own youth. But then, back in the confines of her cottage, her aunt could relapse into a kind of vague melancholy, constantly repeating herself or heading for the garden, intent on digging up potatoes.

Dear Ella. How cruel old age could be. But then she'd had a long life. Poor Aunt Kate had never really reached old age, Hannah thought as she headed for bed.

They had planned to return home on Friday. With reservations, Hannah had agreed for Ella's furniture to be sold and the money to be sent on. It seemed pointless to consult the old lady. She just couldn't make such life-changing decisions any more and the landlord was given notice of the ending of her tenancy, and all debts squared. However, all of her little treasures and her clothes were going with her to Willow Cottage, and they had filled two large suitcases. Studying her photographs of post-war years, when she herself was a teenager, brought a lump to Hannah's throat. It was another lifetime, and one to which Ella had returned.

✳

Marie ran a comb through her long hair, and looked hard at her reflection in the cloakroom mirror. She couldn't wait to get home and back into her own routine. She was fond of her in-laws, and tried to make allowances for Simon's sake. Life had not been easy for any of them and she sympathised for the loss of Mark although she had never met him. It was all about the generation gap really, she thought as she patted the dark shadows under her eyes. She'd noticed it more yesterday with the arrival of Auntie Ella. Hannah and Jack readily slipped back into the 'make do and mend' era and needed no encouragement to get on their high moralistic horses. Marie felt like a teenager in their company, guilty of too much youthful optimism. Oh now I'm being mean, she thought, just because Hannah had mentioned Alice's adoption. She was right of course. Alice would have to be told but it wasn't that easy. At the time, they'd promised Alice's mother that they would never tell her daughter what she had done. The trouble was it had not been a normal adoption with the usual anonymity. Alice had been nearly three years old when Molly Petch had found it impossible to look after her. Being a single mother at the age of fifteen had presented many problems, especially as she herself was an orphan and the only relative she could rely on to give her any assistance while she completed her education was her maternal grandmother. At the age of eighteen, she was offered a place at drama school as a promising young actress. Unfortunately, her grandmother had been taken seriously ill and suddenly Alice became a problem.

Marie was staying with one of her sisters in Ireland at the time, recuperating after a third miscarriage and coming to terms with the news that she was never likely to conceive again. Everything seemed to happen so quickly and, even now, Marie was not too certain of the legalities. The priest had been involved, which was no problem to Marie (she was a practising Catholic) and Molly had signed a paper to say that she would never make a claim on Alice again. It was then that she had asked Simon and Marie not to tell Alice. 'Why make her unhappy?' she'd said.

She and Simon had discussed it recently, and, if we are honest, Marie thought, we really don't want to risk Molly claiming back her daughter. Not that she could, she reassured herself. It had all been signed and sealed, hadn't it? Well, she would fight it in a court of law if necessary.

'Marie! Are you making your will in there? We're ready to go.' Simon rattled the knob of the cloakroom door.'

'Sorry. Just coming.' Marie turned the tap on, and lathered soap through her fingers. There was no rush to do anything, she decided. Perhaps when Alice was older. Eighteen would be ideal, and then she could make up her own mind about things.

3

"The golden moments in the stream of life rush past us, and we see nothing but sand. The angels come to visit us and we only know them when they are gone."

George Eliot

Life soon settled down into some kind of normality. Jack was now coping with work in the garden centre, albeit relying more heavily on the full-time employee Mike Cross than he had done before the accident. Hannah dealt with all the daily finances, working at the till, and cashing up and banking each day, yet still managing to give Leigh his daily lessons, and keep an eye on Ella. The days were getting shorter. It was now the slackest time of the year. Chrysanthemums filled the long greenhouse, many destined to end their days in wreaths, which Jack made for local funerals. Hannah had disliked the pungent smell of these flowers ever since she was a child, when Uncle Harry used the long greenhouse for this same purpose. He could lay his hand to anything in those days, although he was a builder by trade. She remembered how all the wreaths were laid out on the back gravel, and sprayed with water to keep them fresh and ready for a particular funeral. Nowadays, she was spared this display of grief. The local funeral director collected the orders and delivered them to the cemetery or crematorium. She'd always associated winter with grief, beginning with her mother's and grandparents' deaths in the air raid, Aunt Kate's death from a heart attack, and her father's death from the effects of war wounds and his battle with alcoholism. Now, although the most recent death had a place in late summer, she couldn't bear to admire Jack's skills each time his services were in demand.

Ella seemed to be a little more rational as she settled down at Willow Cottage, back in the house she had loved for nearly twenty years of her life. But still Hannah had to answer to the name of Kate, and Jack was plied with food under the alias of Harry. There were a number of near catastrophes in the preparation of meals, and Hannah, from time to time, seriously considered picking up the phone to contact the social services.

However, Leigh continued to smooth things over, sitting with Ella when she became confused, and reading to her in a voice that was quickly absorbing the local accent. They were such an odd pair, Hannah thought as she watched them sharing a game of snap, something Ella had done with her as a child.

She and Jack had decided to continue to educate Leigh at home for the duration of the autumn term. He still had periods of introspection, especially after a disturbed night. Hannah didn't question him about his night-time experiences. She was afraid to tip the balance, and Jack agreed with her that the trauma of the last few months was not going to be healed for a long time. It was all part of a grief that had affected the whole family; each member sensitive to moments of recall, but not always sympathetic to each other's consequent mood swings.

Simon, Marie and Alice, now established back into their own routine, were regular visitors at the weekend, Rachel, Steve and the twins spent more time with Steve's parents, who lived close by in the same village. The latter took great pleasure in indulging Karl and Kirstie. They had no other grandchildren and, in their eyes, the twins could do no wrong. Hannah and Jack had no wish to compete and Rachel, their mother, became caught up in the middle, her loyalties being stretched in all directions. Consequently, their occasional Sunday visits some times ended in frayed tempers.

On one particular Sunday, about two weeks before Christmas, the whole family had gathered to celebrate Ella's birthday. Jack and

Leigh had gone in the car to collect the cake from a friend, who Hannah described as a dab hand with marzipan and icing sugar. Alice was disappointed to find Leigh missing when she arrived. The twins tried to monopolise her attention, irritating her with the telling of silly jokes, which she had heard so many times before that she wanted to scream.

She decided to walk along the lane to meet the car, and have a ride back with Leigh. She knew that the twins were following and turned round quickly, catching sight of them before they jumped to one side giggling and squealing.

'You are little pests,' she yelled. 'Don't come any further. I'm going to wait for Granddad at the crossroads. There won't be enough room in the car for you. And it's rude to pull faces. No wonder Grandma gets fed up with you.'

'Don't tell us what to do. Anyway, she's not your grandma.' Karl's face twisted in malice, his dark brown eyes sparkling as he plucked up the courage to play their ace card. Ever since he and his sister had overheard their mother and father discussing Alice's adoption and criticising Simon and Marie's reluctance to disclose her status to Alice, they had been desperate to come to Willow Cottage and confront Alice.

Alice stopped walking and spun around again. 'Of course she's my grandma. Stop talking such rubbish and go back.'

'No, she's not then,' Kirstie jibed, her resolve strengthened by the boldness of her brother. 'You're adopted, so there.'

The truth hit Alice like a bombshell. Yet it was immediately recognisable; the little looks; the hesitations; the changing of the subject; the half-truths; all gelling into sudden comprehension. In one way it came as a relief. She had wondered whether somehow she was not a normal baby, and that that was why she often felt at odds with the world, wanting to escape into a fantasy world instead. She needed no more proof now, but was obliged to listen to Kirstie's crowing voice as she elaborated.

'We heard our mum talking to our dad. Your mum isn't real and neither is your dad. So Grandma is not yours either. You've got a different one somewhere. She might be dead, even. So there.'

They both ran off giggling towards the back path to the house. Alice stared after them, not really angry with them over their revelations. They had only played a small part in the deception. No, her anger was travelling much deeper than that. They had all lied to her. Even Grandma had lived the lie.

She walked slowly away from the house towards the crossroads. A huge sense of loneliness swept over her, but she no longer sought the company of Leigh and her grandfather. She turned down a narrow path, overgrown with cow parsley gone to seed, but still escaping the ravages of winter. The vegetation had grown tall with its nearness to a ditch filled by the heavy summer rains that year, and she could scarcely see over the top of it. She welcomed its protection, weaving her way slowly along the rutted path, avoiding puddles of water, which had gathered during a recent storm. The path led to the edge of an escarpment known locally as The Cliff. A seat had been positioned here, with a view of the vast plain towards Nottinghamshire, in remembrance of a parishioner whose name few people could recall now. It was seldom used, almost hidden by long grass and stinging nettles. On a previous visit, Alice had beaten back the nettles with a stick, creating a narrow path. She noticed this time that somebody else had been there. Several cigarette ends were littered around the legs of the bench. She stepped over them and climbed onto the plank, stretching herself full length. She loved to lie on her back and stare upwards. Today, little grey clouds seemed to be rushing angrily across the sky in the direction of the village, where they gathered together into threatening blackness. Alice closed her eyes, pressing against the tears, which, nevertheless spilled out and pooled into the hollows of her face.

'You beat me to it,' came a deep voice. 'This is my favourite place for a sit-down.'

Alice's eyes flew open and she pressed her hands on the seat, pushing her back into an upright position. She recognised the man, who stood behind the seat. He used to work at her grandfather's garden centre. It was a long time ago and she couldn't remember his name. She said hello out of politeness.

'Have you been crying?' he asked.

Alice quickly rubbed her eyes, embarrassed to share her grief with a comparative stranger. 'No,' she said. 'I've got dust in them, or pollen or something. They get itchy.' She declined the proffered handkerchief and scrambled to her feet. 'I'd better be getting home. Tea will be ready.'

'I don't want you to go just yet.' The man reached forward and grasped her right wrist. 'There has to be retribution, you know. God has sent me a sign. Don't make a sound. I don't want to hurt you.'

He began to pull Alice along, keeping a tight grip on her wrist. She struggled to escape, and tried to shout for help, but her voice seemed to stick in her throat, coming out in hoarse croaks as he grabbed her long hair, tugging her head back in a violent jerk.

'I said I don't want to hurt you. Now do as you are told. It's him I want to hurt.' The man spoke the last words quietly, as though he was addressing himself.

They were stumbling along the path away from the village towards a plantation of fir trees known as The Triangle. A blue van was parked just ahead of them where the path joined a cart track. Alice began to cry again and tugged at her wrist, her fingers going from red to purple as he tightened his grip. She tried to drop down to the ground and he lurched forward, almost going his length. His voice became angry. 'Look. If you carry on like this you're going to hurt yourself. You've done me a mischief, I think. That leg's not been good since I caught my foot in a rabbit hole.'

Alice could hardly make out his gabbled words as he pulled her to her feet. She turned to look behind, pushing at her hair, which streamed across the front of her face. Perhaps the twins were still following her, but there was nothing but emptiness, everywhere a feeling of desolation; a gnawing feeling, which seemed even to be inside her stomach. Moments later they reached the van and Alice was pushed into the back amongst young, freshly cut fir trees. Her heart was beating so fast that she could scarcely breath. The engine burst into life and the van lurched forward, bouncing in and out of ruts and potholes, throwing the child from one side to the other. Then they appeared to have left the track behind and were travelling along a metalled highway. Alice could hear the sounds of other traffic passing them, and tried to work out where they were. The small rear window had been painted black on the outside. She could see light through streaks in the paint but it was impossible to get her bearings.

Suddenly, the van lurched around a sharp bend and they were back on a rough track. Again Alice was thrown against the trees and she cried out in pain. Blood began to trickle from the deep scratches on her legs made by the roughly cut trunks of the little trees. The man was driving the vehicle quite slowly now, and she could hear no sounds beyond the chugging of the engine. After another sharp turn, they came to a halt, and the hand brake was pulled on. She strained to hear his actions; his feet crunching on dry leaves and twigs; his voice as he muttered something to himself; his heavy breathing, and then the clicking of the back door lock. She tensed up, ready to make her escape. Daylight entered, dimly exposing the inside of the van, and then beyond the body of her captor, she was aware of trees amongst dappled light and shade. She had no idea where this place could be.

Grasping her wrist again, the man pulled her out of the van. 'I don't want to hurt you, duckie. Just be a good girl and we'll get along fine.' He sounded quite jovial now, but his change of tone did not reassure the child, and she looked fearfully beyond him to a derelict building. The guttering was hanging away from the wall, and the only visible window was boarded up. Trees crowded around it, and a tangle of briars and brush caught against her legs on either side of the path, as he dragged her to the front door.

She could make out no details inside at first, He had closed the door behind them and thin strips of light, which entered through the cracks in the boarded window, were soaked up in the volume of blackness.

'Sit on this chair,' the man ordered, pushing her across the room towards a smoke stained brick fireplace. 'I'm sorry. I'm going to 'ave to tie you up, duckie. Tell me if it's too tight. I don't want to hurt you.'

He picked up a length of thin rope, which was draped over the back of a neighbouring old armchair. Alice had the strange feeling that all this was waiting to happen, as though she was in a dream. Why was the rope there? Did this man know this morning that she would be his prisoner? She wished it was a dream, and she could wake up and leave it all behind. She was too tired and too afraid to struggle. He tied the rope around her waist, and looped it behind the wooden back of the chair, securing it in a knot beyond her reach. By the time he had finished, he was out of breath. 'God, I could do with a drink,' he gasped. 'I expect you could as well. I'll just have to get the trees put away. I have to hide them, you see. There's a lot of thieves around.' He grinned broadly at his joke, revealing crooked teeth stained with nicotine.

Zacchaeus Pound, or Zacc Pound as he was known, returned to his van, which was parked in a small clearing amongst a group of silver birch trees. He loved these trees, and glanced at them fondly, as their silvery trunks caught the late sunlight streaming through the wood on this winter afternoon. He opened the doors of the van to reveal the six small fir trees that he had chopped down earlier. The sight of the sap oozing from the thin trunks saddened him, and he apologised to each one as he dragged it out of the van and laid it on the ground.

'Well, Christmas is Christmas,' he muttered. 'And money is money.'

They'd fetch a good price at the market. As long as I can dodge the police, he thought. There's always somebody who'll rat on me.

He pulled some boxes away from the side of a shed, revealing a rotting door. It swung back on its own, creaking on its hinges, exposing more fir trees stolen on the previous day. He stacked the others in one by one, pushing them together in the confined space, and then wedged the door shut with a plank of wood. Finally, the boxes were stacked up on the outside to hide the door. Zacc trusted no one, sometimes not even himself. Consequently, he went into a kind of overkill and his behaviour was becoming more and more obsessive. Yet, he never prospered.

He stood back and did a rapid calculation on his fingers. Adding up money was one of his strengths. Eighty-five pounds! He whistled through his teeth. Then his mind wandered to his latest acquisition. How much would he get for her? They'd be sorry when they couldn't find her. 'Revenge is sweet, sayeth the Lord,' a small voice chanted in his head. 'Yes, revenge is very sweet,' he repeated out loud. He wouldn't listen, would he, he thought? That Jack Almighty Clayton. Well, he would listen now. She wasn't his kid. He knew that. But she was his granddaughter and he'd still cough up. How about a hundred pounds? He could do with a hundred. Or would that be enough? He'd stolen a tax disc for his van, and dreaded the police taking a close look at the details. He had no insurance, and the MOT was two months overdue. What about a thousand then? His eyes sparkled. That would be chicken feed to them Claytons.

He pulled his tobacco pouch from his pocket, and took out a paper and a thin strand of dark tobacco, dextrously rolling a thin cigarette between his fingers. He flicked impatiently at the wheel of the cigarette lighter, drawing down a feeble flame into the shaggy end of his roll-up. He had to get this right, he thought. Used bank notes, that was important. He wasn't quite sure why, but that's what it always was on the telly. So where would they leave the money? Should he ring them with instructions? It would have to be from the call box in the next village, and it would mean disguising his voice somehow. Perhaps, he could send a note instead. Cut words out of a magazine and glue them on a piece of paper in a message. I'VE GOT YOUR KID. PAY UP OR ELSE. He visualised it and grinned at his cleverness. But then he would have to post it, and the mail was slow at Christmas. In any case, he had no paper or envelopes, not even a stamp.

'Oh Christ!' he exclaimed, turning his gaze upwards in an act of contrition for his blasphemy.

He shrugged his shoulders, and took his mind back to the fir trees. Everything could wait until tomorrow after he'd sold them. Now, what should he do with the kid? He'd better feed her, and give her a drink. That would do for now. She couldn't escape and Jack Clayton would have all night to suffer.

She seemed a nice little kid, whatever her name was. Did she know his name? The thought suddenly struck him. He'd recognised her, but it was over three years ago since he was sacked. Surely she would have been too young to remember.

He tossed the glowing end of the cigarette down and trod it into the damp earth. He would ask her when he went in. But what if she did remember him?

'Oh bloody Hell,' he cursed. He stood and stared into the gathering gloom. After a few moments of thought, he decided that he would explain the situation to her. Tell her it was to be a secret. Tell her to say that he had looked after her when she had got lost. That should do the trick. But then his thoughts returned to the money. He'd forget about it. Well, the thousand anyway. A hundred would do as a reward.

He breathed more easily now, and stared across at the derelict building, where he had been squatting for several weeks. He guessed that it had been a gamekeeper's cottage back in the days when the old hall was still standing, and the local gentry had high stakes in the countryside. It had no mains facilities, but it served his purpose; all part of the 'ducking and diving'. Yet he longed for home comforts.

His mother had died two years ago. That had been an unpleasant year, beginning with his dismissal from Norbrooke Nurseries. He'd told his mother that he had been unfairly sacked, whereas he was caught pocketing money from sales. They wouldn't believe that he was sparing customers from a long walk back to the cash desk, and that he intended to hand the money in before he went home.

His mother, who spent many hours reading her bible, believed in her son's innocence, and had declared that retribution must be made. Such was her religious fervour that Zacc began to believe in his innocence, and in the need for the future fulfilment of her wishes.

He rolled another cigarette, and began to walk along a narrow path, which wound its way through the trees. It had become his custom to do this each night, keeping a sharp eye out for the law and a sensitive ear for wildlife.

''Where ever is she?' Marie's voice was shrill with anxiety.

'She'll have wandered off and forgotten the time. You know what she's like when she is in one of her day-dreams. You were with her earlier, weren't you?' Simon turned to address the twins. 'How long ago was that?'

Neither of the twins answered, looking at each other in a kind of agreed silence, which they often did, Hannah thought. She had an uneasy feeling that they knew more than they were prepared to say.

Jack came back into the living room, shaking his head at their questioning looks. 'I've rung the Scotts and the Wrights. Their kids haven't seen Alice at all today. Is there anybody else she may have decided to look in on?'

'Is it time for tea yet?' Ella called from the kitchen. 'I'll butter some bread.'

Hannah jumped up and ran into the kitchen. 'No, Ella,' she said. 'You sit down. We're waiting for Alice.'

'Where's Harry?' the old lady asked. 'Where's Harry?'

'Oh, for goodness sake! Leigh – Leigh! Come and talk to Auntie Ella, please.'

The sound of raised voices drew her back into the living room. She found the twins in tears and Marie and Simon glaring at Rachel.

'They've just said that Alice sometimes goes along the path to the Cliff, wherever that is. I don't know why you couldn't have said that in the first place. She may have had an accident.' Marie's voice was both anxious and accusing as she pulled on her coat and headed for the door. Simon followed close behind.

'I'll come as well,' Hannah called. 'Rachel. Keep an eye on Ella. She is very confused. Jack. You'd better stay near the phone.'

She hurried along the path, which led to the back lane. The other two waited for her to catch up.

'You go with Marie,' Simon said. 'I'll try the village. It'll be dark soon. It's best that we spread out.'

'Where is this path?' Marie asked. 'I don't think I've ever been to the Cliff.'

'It's about halfway down the lane. It's very overgrown these days. I didn't know that the children went down there. There's the entrance look, just past that ash tree.' Hannah was speaking in short bursts as their footsteps quickened.

They noticed that the grass was trodden down near the ash tree and turned to follow the narrow path through the cow parsley.

'Look. There's an old seat there. Oh my God! That's a steep drop!' Marie's voice rose in hysteria.

'Alice! Alice! Are you down there? Oh, answer me, Alice, please.'

Hannah had walked on along the path. Suddenly, she gave a cry, and stooped to pick something up.

'What is it?' Marie shouted.

'It's a hair band. Did Alice have one? Blue with gold sequins?'

'Yes. That's Alice's. She chose it especially for Ella's birthday. Oh, what is she playing at? There's nothing up here. She wouldn't have gone to that plantation, would she?'

'I don't know why she would. Let's go a bit further. There's only a track beyond it and I don't know where that goes to. It looks like the main road over there.'

They were almost running now, stopping only when they reached the plantation. They noticed the signs of recent tree felling; the raw oozing stumps and disturbed earth. The tracks in the wet earth indicated that a vehicle had turned here and continued along the side of the plantation. They followed the tracks, calling the child's name and picked their way further into the plantation stopping and listening for any response. The silence of the place was eerie. They continued to call out. Only a slight echo of their voices answered them and then the silence returned. There was no sign of life, not even of a bird, and after standing for a few seconds and looking towards the boundary, they returned to the muddy track, and followed the tyre imprints across the field. They had ceased to call Alice's name and were no longer able to verbalise their fears. By this time, they had reached the main road and the end of the track, and, without communicating their intent, they turned, and hurried back towards Willow Cottage, with the mutual hope that they would find Alice there safe and sound.

Simon was waiting for them at the gate. He shook his head at their questioning looks and their hearts sank.

'I'm going to call the police,' Jack said when he heard about the recent activity at The Triangle plantation. 'It'll be dark soon. Alice would never stay out as late as this.'

Rachel suddenly came into the hall, holding a twin on each side. Her face had gone very red. 'It's these two,' she yelled. 'They're going to get a good smacking.'

Steve stepped forward to protest and Rachel released her grip on their hands. They ran to their father, their faces twisting in fear.

'Now what?' Steve, as always, was ready to protect his children against the in-laws.

'Well, they've only upset Alice by telling her that she's adopted. They think she has run away and now they're scared they will get into trouble. I'm sorry Marie,' Rachel turned to her sister-in-law. 'They must have heard us talking about it. We were worried that you were leaving it too late to tell Alice but it was none of our business. Still, she may be hiding in the house or garden.'

'I don't think so,' Hannah said. 'We found her hairband on the path along the Cliff. She wouldn't just leave it there. Her hair would be in a mess without it.'

'She really liked it. It was special for the party.' Marie's voice was shaky now.

They could hear Simon talking on the phone in the hall. 'The police are on their way,' he said as he came back into the living room. 'You all have another look in the garden before it gets dark. If she was upset, she may have not noticed that her hairband had come adrift. She could be hiding. I'm going to take another look along the Cliff path. I'll take Bobby with me. You never know, he may pick up her scent. Are you coming, Steve?'

The darkness came down quickly on this December day, and Alice began to shiver with cold. She had struggled, without success, to free herself from her imprisonment in the wooden framed chair, and when Zacc returned from his stroll in the woods, she was crying with frustration and fear.

'Don't cry, duck,' Zacc said. 'I'll light the fire, and then I can untie you. I'll be in and out getting wood. You don't want to be running away out there. It's not safe after dark. Anyway, you'd get lost. By the way, do you know who I am?'

'Yes. You used to work for my granddad. I can't remember your name.' Alice rubbed her eyes. 'You showed me a slow worm under a sheet of corrugated iron in the garden. Don't you remember? I thought it was a snake but you said it was a lizard.'

'Oh yes. A slow worm is a legless lizard. Not many people know that.' Zacc's face beamed with pleasure at her recollection of him. 'I bet your teacher doesn't know,' he said. 'I bet I could teach all of them a thing or two about Nature Study. I don't suppose they've seen a slow worm.'

He'd already forgotten why he'd asked her if she remembered him. Nature study had been his favourite subject at school, and during one half an hour each week, he was the star pupil. What a lot he could teach this child if she was his daughter, he thought.

'What's your name, ducky?' he asked.

'Alice. Like Alice in Wonderland.' She always said that when introducing herself.

'That's a nice name. Mine's Zacc. Short for Zacchaeus. And Pound. In for a penny. In for a pound. That's me. Do you know who Zacchaeus was?'

'No. I've never heard of him.'

'Haven't you? Fancy that! He was in the bible. Don't you sing about him at Sunday school?'

Alice shook her head. 'I want to go home,' she said, the tears beginning to roll down her cheeks once more.

Zacc took no notice. Instead, he began to sing in a hoarse voice.

'Now Zacchaeus was a very little man and a very little man
    was he.
He climbed into a sycamore tree for the Saviour he wanted
    to see.'

He suddenly stopped singing and cleared his throat, looking hard at Alice to see whether she was laughing. He was remembering now how the other children always giggled when they sang that song, emphasising the words 'very little', and pointing their fingers at him behind the teacher's back, as she played the tune on the old upright piano in the chapel school room.

Zacc only reached five-feet-two inches in adulthood, a little man in comparison to his peers, and extremely little compared to the majority of the younger generation.

'My mother said I was special. That's why she gave me a bible name.' He felt obliged to be on the defensive, even though Alice was far from laughing. Her face was becoming pinched and blue with cold and the tears continued to roll down her cheeks as she thought of her mother, who was not her mother after all.

'Sorry, duckie, you're cold, aren't you? I'll get a good fire going.' Zacc went outside, returning a few minutes later with an armful of sticks and a couple of stout logs. In no time at all, it seemed, a fire blazed in the iron dog grate, the door was locked, and a heavy bolt was pushed into place at the top, before Alice was freed from the constraints of the rope. She crouched close to the hearth, watching the pan of oxtail soup, which balanced between the front rail and the burning logs. She shouted to her captor when it began to bubble furiously, and Zacc hurried over with an old basin and an earthenware mug, which he had found in the cupboard. Normally, he would visit a roadside café or get a bag of chips, only keeping a tin of beans, or in this case some tinned soup, for an emergency. He had few possessions, having sold the contents of his mother's house when she died, and sleeping rough in his van for a long time before he had found this place.

'They won't know where I am,' Alice said quietly, not wanting to upset Zacc after he had given her the soup. 'I won't tell them about you. I promise.'

'So why did you run away then? You were running away, weren't you? I used to do that because I didn't want to get locked in the coal shed. It wasn't dust in your eyes, was it?' Zacc's attention reluctantly returned to the business of kidnapping. He could quite happily enjoy the companionship of this child always. In spite of the fact that very often he had loathed his mother, he had missed the closeness of another human being since her death.

In spite of the strangeness of the circumstances, which now drew them together, Alice needed his reassurances. She told him about the twins, and how she had discovered that she was adopted. 'I don't know who my real mother is, do I? Or my dad. And Grandma isn't Grandma anymore.'

'Well, isn't that strange? How alike we are. I was adopted as well. My real mother dumped me in a waste bin, so my mother told me.' Zacc didn't know whether he believed that. His adoptive mother could be so cruel. 'It was very dark in the coal shed you know. I could hardly breath. Perhaps my real mother was nice. Still, they've all passed over to the other side. Mustn't speak ill of the dead.'

He stared into the fire, recalling how he'd often wished his adoptive mother dead, and sometimes thought of murdering her. He never could of course. He feared retribution too much for that. Hell fire and damnation. Was she in Hell? But then she wanted revenge for him. She must have cared. 'I'll get it, Mother,' he muttered. 'Don't you worry.'

After a long silence when both man and child stared into the flames, he continued, 'Fancy you being adopted then. So were you on your way to look for your real parents? You could stay with me, you know. But I would need some money. Your grandfather owes me a thousand, but five hundred will do. Do you think he's got that much money?'

Alice didn't answer and Zacc returned to his musing. What if they didn't care? Would they even pay one hundred? And how could he make sure that she wouldn't betray him?

'Once I've got the money, duckie, you can go home. Mind you, you must tell them that I've looked after you. Given you supper and kept you safe and warm. You mustn't tell them who I am, or the police will come after me. You wouldn't want that, would you, my duck? They never leave you alone, you know. Questions, questions. They do your head in.' He stopped and stared as a white cat suddenly appeared near Alice's chair.

'Jesus!' he yelled, casting his eyes heavenwards and putting his hands together for a quick apology. 'Where did that come from?'

The cat opened its mouth as though about to mew, but no sound emerged. It rubbed against Alice's leg, yet she did not feel any contact. She bent down to stroke it, only to see it leap away and then vanish. Zacc grabbed the torch and began to shine the light around the room. There was nowhere a cat could hide. The only furnishings, apart from a wall cupboard, were the two chairs and a wooden box with a candle pushed into the neck of a beer bottle standing on top. The beam of light illuminated clumps of black dust-filled cobwebs, which had gathered in the corners, and areas where the plaster had parted company with the walls and ceiling. The wallpaper below the picture rail was stained with both rising and falling damp, although in its original pristine state, it apparently displayed exotic birds not native to these parts.

'I hate cats,' Zacc muttered. 'Bloody things. They kill all the birds. Thousands of them, they do.'

'What about the rats and mice?' Alice commented. 'I like cats.' She looked under his chair, shuffling her feet on the old cracked linoleum, as Zacc waved the torch about.

'It must have run in when I was doing the fire, but God knows where it's gone to now. Sneaky little things! I 'ate them. We'll just pretend we don't care. It's probably smelt the soup. You see, it'll come crawling and fussing back.'

He relaxed into his chair, and within minutes he was snoring. Alice studied his face, now that he was no longer aware of her appraisal. His hair was black and greasy, combed back from a low forehead. His eyes, she knew, were different colours, one brown and one green. That was the first thing she had noticed about him, together with his habit of blinking more than was normal. He was wearing an old navy bomber jacket and some rather dirty jeans going threadbare at the knees. His legs and arms were short, but she knew from his earlier grip on her wrist, that he was very strong. He reminded her of a gypsy, rather swarthy with a dark complexion. She remembered a gypsy woman calling a few weeks ago selling pegs and lace. She'd said that she had too many children to feed and they would go hungry if no one bought her pegs. Perhaps his mother was a gypsy, she thought, and had given him away because she had too many children. Perhaps that was why her mother had given her away.

Her mouth was very dry. The soup had been too salty and she needed a drink. Zacc had offered her a can of beer and she had refused it. She'd seen a closed door in the opposite wall, when Zacc was looking for the cat. Maybe it would lead into a kitchen, with a back door or a window. She picked up the torch and tip-toed past the sleeping Zacc, waiting until she was well away from him before she directed the light at the far wall. The door swung open as she turned the knob, to reveal a very dirty room. A tin bath was propped against the wall and a chipped enamel bucket occupied the centre of the room. There was no sign of a tap. She sighed and moistened her lips with her tongue. She could only assume that there was a pump somewhere or perhaps a well like the one her grandfather's tractor had toppled into. Her grandmother had told her about life without taps and bathrooms and for a moment she was caught up in a fascination of 'the olden days' as she called those years. She returned her attention to the white cat. Where could it be, she wondered? There was no sign of an open window or another door where it could come in or go out.

She shivered, and returned to her chair. Comforted by the heat from the fire, she fell into a deep sleep, exhausted by the unhappiness of the day.

'I know it seems the last thing on our minds, but we ought to try and get some sleep, don't you think?' Jack suggested nervously. He could hardly keep his eyes open. They had walked all around the village again and along the Cliff path calling Alice's name, accompanied by a group of friends from the village, who had been alerted by Jack's telephone calls. The police had stayed for half an hour, taking down details, and giving reassurances concerning runaway children who usually came home again when they were cold and hungry. 'But Alice wouldn't do that,' Marie had protested. The older of the two officers gave a nod and an 'OK', implying that he was usually right and Marie hated him in that moment for his apparent arrogance. However, they did walk with Simon along the path to The Triangle plantation, noting the recently felled trees and photographing the tyre tracks, with a view to questioning the farmer if it was a case of theft.

Rachel, Steve and the twins had long since gone home, although Rachel would have preferred to stay. Leigh had settled Ella down in bed. She was not aware of the missed birthday celebrations or the comings and goings of the family. She seemed to be enclosed in a bubble where only her own physicality mattered, and her mind drifted around in the past, apparently making sense of her surroundings. Now, at two o'clock in the morning, she slept soundly, together with Leigh, who was lying beside her under the bedspread.

The conversation between the four adults had become reduced to the occasional solicitude, and Marie stared in disbelief through swollen eyes at her father-in-law, frowning at his suggestion that they should try to sleep. 'You all do what you like,' she snapped. 'There's no way I can sleep, and you can't, can you, Simon?'

'Well, I don't think it will help Alice if we're all worn out,' Simon replied, patting Marie on her hand. 'I know how you feel, but we can take it in turns to keep awake. Someone should be here to answer the phone. I think I'm going to have another search in the garden and up the lane. Try and close your eyes for a bit, Marie.'

Marie scrambled to her feet, and hurried to the door. Simon followed her, looking back to shake his head, half in apology and half in desperation, it seemed to Hannah, who turned to speak to Jack.

'You go to bed, my dear. You look absolutely exhausted. You've been on your feet for such a long time. Marie doesn't mean to be angry, does she? She just doesn't know how to be. I'll come up as well when Simon gets back, and leave them together. Although I think I'm past sleep now. We'll find her. I'm sure we will.' Hannah knew that she was saying too much and talking too quickly. It was the only way she could cope.

Jack struggled to his feet, and walked unsteadily to the door. He had never been right since he broke his leg, Hannah thought. He had always been so fit, and now this was really getting to him. 'I'll give you ten minutes to use the bathroom,' she called.

By the time she followed him into bed an hour later, he was sleeping soundly and she lay on the top of the duvet, not bothering to undress, feeling that sleep was impossible.

Dear Alice, she thought. She was such a lovely child, but Marie and Simon should have told her before about the adoption. Now Alice would be reading all sorts into their reluctance to tell her. Such avoidance of the truth made the relationship between them very fragile. It was a difficult issue. Still, perhaps it would have been at any age.

Her thoughts turned to her other grandchildren. Why were the twins so spiteful? Was it jealousy, since Leigh's arrival? Or did they feel less loved? She recognised that both she and Jack found it difficult to embrace them. There seemed to be an invisible barrier, a coldness, which she could not explain.

Steve had always been difficult to get on with, and his parents' attitude didn't help.

Her thoughts wandered to her other daughter Emma. She was another cause of worry; brief phone calls and letter cards with the minimum of news. She had promised to come to Willow Cottage for a few days at Christmas, instead of her usual flying visit on her way down south. Both she and Jack had agreed not to interfere. She needed freedom to develop her own way of life, and young women had so much confidence these days. She wouldn't appreciate her old-fashioned mother constantly at the end of the phone and she did seem to be having an exciting life in Hull, not in the back streets, which she herself had known as a child.

Oh Alice. What's happening to you? Her mind was dragging her back into the agony, in spite of her unconscious effort to divert her thoughts. It was the not knowing that was dreadful. If any man hurts that child I'll kill him, she thought, with an uncharacteristic vehemence.

An image of Tom Porter's face suddenly loomed up in her memory, and she was back in her childhood, when she was evacuated to Eastfield Cottage with Tom and Elsie Porter. She could understand now, how Elsie must have felt when she had found Tom in the wrong bed. She remembered her own fear as she crept out of the house and hid in the barn, waiting for Elsie's return from the Women's Institute meeting that fatal night. And then how she had drifted into sleep and the candle had set alight the straw. It was only years later, when she learnt that Elsie herself had been abused by her own father and had become pregnant, that she could understand why the poor woman had left her husband to die in the burning barn. Hannah had never told anyone of how Elsie had pushed Tom into the fire. It had been made quite clear to her, that, as she had caused the fire with the unattended lighted candle, she was just as guilty. This guilt feeling had stayed with her for the last forty-seven years. Now, the memories rose vividly to the surface with the fears for Alice's safety. Bastards! Bastards! Bastards! Her mind kept on repeating the word and she knew that she had plumbed the depths of her own vulgarity.

Her breath had quickened, and her heart was beating far too quickly. She tried unsuccessfully to think of something else, but her thoughts would not let go. Could history be repeating itself in some strange way, she asked herself? Everyone said that Alice was like her, not only in looks, but also in her sensitivity and imagination. And yet she was no relation. She felt this new guilt rising again. Alice must have felt betrayed when she learnt of her adoption, yet if only she knew how much she was loved. Perhaps one day she would understand.

'Oh, please God, don't let anything happen to her,' she prayed.

She stared into the darkness, her eyes aching yet defying surrender into closure. Eventually, after Jack had settled down into a deep quiet sleep, stillness seemed to descend upon the house, dulling her brain, and she felt the consciousness slipping away, and with it the anguish.

'Wake up, duckie. I'm off now.'

Alice was roused from a sleep, deep and dreamless, as her body attempted to recover from the traumas of the last eighteen hours. For a few seconds, she stared into the face of Zacchaeus Pound without recognition. Then, as realisation of her surroundings grew, she shrank away from his grinning face. An observer, ignorant of the circumstances, would recognise the fear, not only in the child, but also in her captor. His voice was hoarse and barely audible.

'I won't be long and I'll bring you some crisps and fizzy pop. I bet you like fizzy pop, don't you? I always did. Sorry, I'll 'ave to tie you back up.'

Alice crossed her arms across her chest, pushing her hands under her arm pits. She began to tremble with both fear and with a chill that had stiffened her limbs, as the heat from the fire had diminished during her period of sleep. 'Please. I want to go home,' she whispered. 'I won't tell anybody about you. Please.'

'I'm sorry, but I can't take any chances. My mother wanted Jack Clayton to be punished. And so, God rest her soul, she'll be satisfied.'

He pulled Alice's arms back behind her and she didn't resist. She knew that she could not compete with his strength, and the look in his strange, odd eyes frightened her into total submission.

'Right. I'm going to get these trees to the market. That's the first thing to do and then I'll sort out this other matter.' He was muttering to himself now as he walked towards the door. 'Perhaps I'd better put the blanket round her. It's turned cold in here.' He stopped and stared at the fireplace. 'I hope that old biddy's not out with her dog. Bloody dogs! Frightening all the birds. As bad as cats.' He turned back to Alice and pulled the old blanket off the other chair. 'That'll keep you warm, duckie, and I think I'll 'ave to keep you quiet, just for a bit.'

He pulled a brown, hand-knitted scarf from around his neck, and, holding it between his hands, he leant across in front of Alice. She gasped in alarm, her eyes wide open above the stained ribbed wool, as he pulled it across her mouth and tied the ends together at the back of her head.

Alice heard the key turning in the lock and she sank back into the chair. He had seemed so different last night and somehow, sitting in the firelight chatting, had been a kind of strange adventure. But now, in the light of the day, it was more like the most frightening nightmare she could imagine. Her breathing was laboured behind the confines of the scarf. She could smell and taste its greasiness and the coarse fibres irritated her nostrils as she breathed in through her nose. She twisted her head to look for any signs of the cat, but the air hung in solitude around her. Suddenly, she thought she heard sounds coming from the outside, and she tried to shout. Only low moaning noises escaped from behind the brown woollen gag. The silence returned and she sank back for a while into total despair.

As she calmed down and settled her thoughts into some kind of logical pattern, she decided that she would make an attempt to escape when Zacc returned. She could run fast, and, now that it was daylight, she was not so afraid. Would they be out there looking for her? How far from home was she? Had the twins told anyone why she was upset? The police would find out. Zacc was afraid of the police. She had promised not to tell them if he let her go, but now she wasn't sure. It was different this morning.

'Grandma! I've got something to tell you!'

Hannah woke up to find Leigh pulling at her hand. She sat up, rubbing her eyes and looking around. 'Whatever's the matter, Leigh? What time is it? Are you ill?'

'No, Grandma. It's about Alice. I've had a message from Nigel.'

'Oh goodness me. Have I been asleep? Have they found her? Pass me my dressing gown. Oh, I didn't mean to sleep. Where's your granddad?'

Leigh pulled again at her hand. 'Please listen,' he yelled. 'Why doesn't anyone listen to me? I rubbed the Mooncat's head last night. I saw the old woman again. The one in the black dress.'

'Do you mean Mrs Knight? Have you seen Mrs Knight?' Hannah's voice was shrill with excitement.

I don't know what she's called. She lives in a house full of cats. The Mooncat was sitting on the windowsill. The last time I was there, it changed into Lucy, but this time it was Nigel, the little boy who used to live here.'

'It is Mrs Knight. Fancy! After all these years!'

'Grandma, listen! Nigel gave me a message. He said we should look for Christmas trees and something about a penny, or was it a pound? Oh I wish I could remember. It's starting to vanish out of my head.'

'Calm down, darling. Is Granddad downstairs?'

'Everybody's downstairs. You're not listening to me. They don't listen either. I know it's important.'

Hannah pushed her arms into her dressing-gown sleeves. 'I am listening,' she said, 'and they'll listen too, when I'm with you.'

'Why did you leave me in bed, Jack?' she asked as they went down the stone steps into the kitchen. 'You knew I didn't want to sleep. What's happening? Have the police been in contact?'

'Nothing yet. I was just going to bring you a cup of tea.'

Leigh tugged at Hannah's dressing gown, as she sank down into the old armchair next to the range. Jack passed her a cup of tea and she took a sip before asking him if he remembered Mrs Knight.

'Of course I do. How could I forget her? Is this about Leigh's dreaming again? I don't think we've got time for it at the moment.'

'She was the owner of the Mooncat,' Hannah explained, turning to Marie. 'She told us, when we were children, that it could give people special dreams. Well, Leigh dreamed about her last night. He's been trying to tell you. It concerned Alice. Something about Christmas trees, wasn't it, Leigh? And what else did you tell me?'

'A penny and a pound, Nigel kept saying. I can't remember.' Leigh stamped his foot in frustration. 'I know it's important.' He was aware of his grandfather's impatience.

Hannah prompted him. 'What about a penny and a pound? Calm down and then it will come to you. Take a deep breath and count to five.'

'Any news, Simon?' Jack turned to speak to his son who had been in contact with the police for the last few minutes.

'In for a penny, in for a pound. That was it. That's what Nigel kept on saying. Look for Christmas trees and in for a penny, in for a pound.' Leigh began to jump up and down with excitement.

'In for a penny, in for a pound!' Jack exclaimed. 'Don't you remember who used to say that, Hannah? That Zacc Pound. He was always saying it. "That's me," he used to say. "In for a penny. In for a pound." And the Christmas trees – I bet that was him at The Triangle. I'll ring the police. They'll probably know where he is hanging out.'

Marie was looking from one to the other. 'Who's Zacc Pound?' she asked. 'Why should he take Alice?'

'Well if it is him,' Hannah said, 'he is probably wanting to upset us. He used to work here. He was a strange little man with a rather demented mother who needed a lot of attention. They used to live in that old house next to the church. He came looking for work one day, just odd jobs at first and we felt sorry for him. His mother, apparently, was an absolute tyrant and we took him on full-time after a few weeks. He had a wonderful way with plants. They all seemed to flourish. But then Jack had to sack him for being light-fingered. He was a bit of a shady character but I wouldn't have thought he would…' She didn't finish what she had begun to say as Jack came back into the kitchen.

'Did you get through? What did they say?' Simon asked.

'It was the sergeant we spoke to yesterday. I didn't tell him that we'd had a message from beyond. He would think we were barmy and perhaps we are. I told him that somebody had rung to say they'd seen someone resembling Pound at The Triangle cutting down trees. I knew they would sit up and take notice. They seemed to be more interested in theft than in what they obviously think is a schoolgirl tantrum.'

'So, where does this Pound fellow live?' Simon was back on his feet and reaching for his jacket.

Jack shrugged. 'I'm sorry. I haven't a clue. He used to live with his mother in the village but she's been dead for quite a while and the house was re-let. I used to feel sorry for him, but he showed his true colours, didn't he, Hannah? I remember him shouting that we'd be sorry and as for that witch of a mother…' He stopped, noticing the expression of concern on Leigh's face. His voice lowered to its normal pitch as he turned towards Simon. 'The police should be able to track him down. They're bound to have rubbed shoulders with him. A leopard doesn't change its spots. The sergeant advised us to wait here and they will contact us as soon as they locate him.'

Hannah took Ella a drink, and asked Leigh if he would stay with her for a while. They seemed to have a calming influence on each other, and at the moment it was Leigh's turn for reassurances.

Under Hannah's direction, everyone ate toast and had another drink, although it was an effort, and any further conversation seemed pointless. The frustration of knowing something and not being able to act on it was like torture, and the initial excitement of Leigh's revelations began to wane with increasing doubts of the Mooncat's power. When the phone suddenly rang, they all jumped to their feet. Simon was first to the door, and racing down the hall.

'You've found her!' the others heard him shout. 'Oh thank God! Marie! Alice is safe! They're taking her to the station.'

'You're all right now, darling. We'll soon get you home.' Sergeant Dave Townend had finished communicating with the officer on the desk at the local police station, and turned around to speak to the white-faced child, who was struggling with the seat belt in the back seat of the police car. He felt mounting anger against the likes of Zacc Pound, as he regarded her tear-stained face. The swine will really get the book thrown at him if I have anything to do with it, he thought grimly, although his 'defence' was likely to plead diminished responsibility. Obviously Zacc was not the brightest boy on the block. He should get a prison sentence just for frightening this child, even if that was all that he had done. He had to admit that he was surprised when Jack Clayton had pointed a finger of suspicion at Zacc. A thief he might be, but child abduction was a bit out of his league. Anyway, all would be revealed when they got the poor kid back to the station, he thought.

He was waiting for some backup from the station. They didn't want to leave the house unguarded and he had put in a request for a woman officer to be in attendance. If they didn't hurry up, Zacc Pound would be returning from the market and no doubt he would try to make a break for the main road if he caught sight of a police car. With no details of his vehicle, he could soon be miles away. Brains or no brains, he was a slippery customer.

The sound of tyres crunching through leaves in the lane alerted him to someone's arrival.

'It's all right, Serge. It's Brian and Susie,' the young police constable called from the shed, where he had been observing signs of the previously stored trees, and making notes of the state of the cottage.

A few minutes later, the young police woman climbed into the back seat of the car next to Alice, while her working partner parked the second car amongst the trees, out of sight of anyone approaching along the lane.

'Where the hell did that come from?' Alice heard the sergeant exclaim. She knew without looking that he was talking about the white cat. The prickly feeling was back, making the hairs stand up on her arms. 'God! What a beautiful cat. Did you see it? White with big yellow eyes. My missus would love that. She's crazy about cats. Is it Zacc Pound's?' He half turned, directing the question towards Alice.

'No,' she replied. 'He hates cats. It just comes and goes.'

'Sounds like the Cheshire Cat. Do you know the Alice stories?'

Alice nodded. 'I am Alice,' she said but didn't follow it with her usual 'Alice in Wonderland'.

'Well, if it's a stray, I think I'll come back and see if I can catch it. It doesn't look feral, but there's no one else around here for miles.'

They had reached the main road by this time with no sign of a returning Zacc. Alice rubbed at the red marks on her wrists where the rope had dug in.

'Leave it, dear,' the policewoman advised, intent on maintaining all signs of abuse until they reached the station.

Alice nodded, and sank back into the seat. She smiled to herself at the idea of the policeman trying to catch the cat. She was not prepared to discuss it with anyone except Leigh, not even with her grandmother, who was not really her grandmother, she reminded herself. She knew without asking Leigh, that he must have made contact with the Mooncat. And now, in spite of her ordeal, she felt exhilarated by the strange energy that seemed to surround her, making her skin tingle.

Marie and Simon were already at the police station when Sergeant Townend pulled into the yard with his precious passenger, and, minutes later, Alice was safely held in her mother's close embrace. She calmly, but briefly, answered all of their questions, no longer intent on revenge. In a way she felt that she would be betraying a kindred spirit, an adopted person who understood her unhappiness in her new-found status.

The sergeant could scarcely disguise his disappointment when the examination showed nothing more than bruised wrists and lack of sleep. It would be an abduction charge of course. He consoled himself with that thought. Whatever the outcome, it was another notch up the promotional ladder.

'But Alice! Zacc Pound is a thief. We don't owe him anything. We had to sack him. He was stealing the takings from plant sales. Don't you understand?' Jack was angry, not with his granddaughter, but with anyone who threatened his family. Everything seemed to be going wrong just lately. God, I'm tired, he thought. I could do with a large brandy. He wanted to walk away and leave it all to Simon but Hannah wouldn't stand back, and he felt duty-bound to stay by her side.

'But he was kind to me some of the time,' Alice was protesting. 'He's had a bad life. His mother used to shut him in the coal shed and, now she's dead, he has nowhere to go and no money. Would you have given him some money for me?' She wanted to ask whether she was important enough when she was only adopted but she didn't know whether they knew that she knew about it. Leigh might know. She decided to wait until they were on their own and then she could tell him about the white cat as well.

At that moment, Simon came into the kitchen clenching his fists in exasperation. 'I've just been on the phone with the police again. They've bungled it by the sound of it. Zacc Pound must have got wind of them and he's scarpered. They want to know if they can come over and get a description of the van and what he was wearing. I said it wasn't a good idea at the moment. Alice has had enough for one day. Perhaps you could tell me a little bit now, Alice, and then they will be satisfied. Can you remember what the van was like?'

Alice shook her head. 'It might have been red,' she lied.

'What about Zacc? Can you remember what he was wearing?'

Alice had a clear picture of him, but she shook her head. Suddenly, the reluctance to betray a kindred spirit was replaced with fear of the revenge, which the Lord, and apparently his mother demanded from beyond the grave. Perhaps co-operation with the police could cause further anger and who knows what could happen next? She turned to cling to her mother, no longer needing to share her adoption status with anyone. In fact, at this moment, she had lost the desire even to contemplate it. All she wanted was for life to go back to normal.

'I'll ring back and tell them that you can't recall any details other than the colour of the van. Red, you said, didn't you?'

Alice nodded, and the tears began to roll down her cheeks.

'A hot bath and a rest I think,' Hannah said.

Everyone agreed and relaxed into their own thoughts, as Alice was gathered up once more into the security of her family.

4

"Today is a smooth, white seashell. Hold it close and listen to the beauty of the hours."

anon

Having missed Ella's birthday celebrations the day before, Hannah decided to have an ordinary Sunday tea, but with the birthday cake for good measure. The dramatic events, which had consumed so much time, energy and emotion, were pushed into a kind of mutual, temporary, family amnesia. The word adoption did not escape beyond anyone's thoughts, although Marie and Simon longed to reassure Alice, and Alice was longing, albeit with some dread, for an explanation, which would mollify and restore her confidence in family life.

Rachel had declined the invitation to the late birthday tea, with the excuse that they had been invited to Steve's parents and couldn't really change their plans. It was pretty obvious that she was making excuses, but understandably most likely that she had been unable to rest, fretting over her part in this dreadful abduction business and the possible outcome.

Hannah wondered whether there had been any verbal contact between Leigh and Alice, since she had woken up. They had shared little looks and meaningful eye contact before Alice was tucked up in her bed, her physical sense of well-being somewhat restored already by the warmth of the hot, scented bath water.

She had slept until one o'clock, and struggled to eat a small portion of the Sunday lunch; roast chicken, with sprouts, carrots and mashed potato. Hannah, finding herself alone in the preparation, had little enthusiasm to provide any extra trimmings, and later dispassionately scraped a plateful of left-overs into the bin. Ella, it seemed, was the only one with an appetite.

Unbeknown to their grandmother, Leigh and Alice already were in a little world of their own, which encompassed the past, present and future. They had whispered together in the confines of the old back kitchen, during the final preparations of the midday meal, while Marie helped Hannah in the dishing up and Simon and Jack closed up the greenhouses.

Leigh told Alice of the twins' confession, and confirmed that he had made contact with the old lady in black, who, he explained, was called Mrs Knight, and was known to their grandparents in the past. He became enlivened by Alice's description of the white cat, which had appeared in the derelict cottage, and struggled to put his ideas into words, as the significance of this kind of transmigration seemed to dance like a strange bubble of awareness in front of him.

'It rubbed against my leg, but I didn't feel it,' Alice explained. 'And when I tried to stroke it, there was nothing there. It vanished into thin air, like a ghost. It didn't half scare that Zacc.' They both giggled, relaxing back into normal child-like behaviour. 'I'd like to see that fat policeman trying to catch it. He did say it was like the Cheshire Cat, so he can't be too bad. Haven't you heard of the Cheshire Cat?'

Leigh had prompted the question by his puzzled expression.

'It's in *Alice in Wonderland*. Don't tell me you've never heard of *Alice in Wonderland*!'

Leigh shook his head.

'I've got two books. One's pretty hard to read, but the other one is more for your age. Do you want to borrow it? It's about a little girl called Alice – I'm called after her – who falls down a rabbit hole, and meets all kinds of strange people.'

'I'll have the hard one,' Leigh said.

'Anyway,' Alice continued, 'was it this old Mrs Knight who told you where I was?'

'No. At first I saw the Mooncat like I did last time, only this time it changed into Nigel. He said about the Christmas trees and then "In for a penny. In for a pound". I couldn't understand it, and no one would listen to me. Why couldn't he have just said this guy's name?'

'Perhaps it's more exciting that way. I don't know. It's like being tested. Things always seem to get twisted into puzzles in dreams, don't they? People reckon it's just your mind muddled up but we know it's more than that, don't we? Was Lucy there, by the way? You didn't mention her.'

Leigh shook his head. He had been wondering about Lucy. He had the feeling that she had distanced herself from him. Perhaps she would rather be with their parents, wherever they were. He shrugged his shoulders and made a non-committal gesture with his upturned hands. To be quite honest, he didn't miss Lucy, now that he had Alice to share in his exploration of the mysteries of time.

Simon and Marie had decided to keep Alice away from school for the last week of the autumn term, and asked her if she would like to stay with her grandparents at Willow Cottage. Marie worked as a secretary at the same college, where Simon was a lecturer, which normally was convenient in that her working hours corresponded with Alice's school terms and holidays. Alice was a very healthy child, with apparently a good immune system, and rarely complicated their arrangements through sickness. In this instance, although Marie longed to spend days on her own with Alice, explaining and reassuring, her workload was exceptionally heavy, and when her daughter seemed relieved at the prospect of not attending school until the next term, she relaxed. She knew, deep down, that they were shelving this 'adoption business', as it had become known, but she told herself that Alice needed to recover from her ordeal before the quagmire of explanations was explored.

Hannah decided to abandon the daily timetable that she had established with Leigh over the last two months. She knew that both of the children were in much greater need of love than they were of the so-called 'three Rs'. Besides, she reasoned, they were as bright as buttons and Christmas called for creativity rather than academic development.

She, like Marie, was avoiding the subject of adoption. It wasn't her place to give any explanations. She had no wish to tread on any toes. Even before all this trouble, she had noticed signs of resentment if she made any suggestions. There were little looks, and being called Hannah instead of the usual Mum. Of course, she thought as she peeled the potatoes ready for the evening meal, they must consider her ideas to be old-fashioned, although she didn't feel any older. Jack was decidedly out of touch and well set in his ways. There was so much change. But was it progress? She decided that it wasn't, as she put the potatoes in a pan, turning the tap on hard, and splashing water up onto the kitchen window.

As she wiped the splashes away with some kitchen towel, her mind returned to the photograph album, which she had unearthed in the Glory Hole recently, during a search for packets of green and red crepe paper. The Glory Hole, so named because it housed a miscellany of clutter (Aunt Kate's description not hers), was a walk-in type of cupboard in the old back kitchen. As a child, its contents had fascinated her. During those years of wartime and post-war austerity, the simplest objects were treasured; a well used box of paints, an old compendium of board games, Happy Families cards, wrapping paper from presents received before the war, an old telescope – the list went on and on in her memory. Of course, all that was lost when Willow Cottage was sold, but the cupboard soon became the habitat of new treasures when Hannah and Jack were informed years later that the cottage was on the market, and ripe for development, and they had moved in with their young family.

Now, as she rubbed the splashes off the windowsill and put the pan of potatoes on the stove ready to cook at a later hour, a plan of action began to form in her mind. Looking at family photographs was a good way to link up with the past and to liken both hers and

Jack's fragmented childhood with the recent upheavals in the lives of her two grandchildren. It could certainly create talking points, she decided, and it would be fun to rediscover treasures from her own children's past in the dark corners of the Glory Hole.

She had rewrapped the album in the plastic carrier bag but she could still visualise that early pre-war photograph of her parents. It had lain undiscovered, jammed in the back of a drawer in Eastfield Cottage, the home of Elsie and Tom Porter, until she and Jack had gone there years later. She had almost forgotten what her parents looked like at that time and this photograph was her only visual memory now. She often felt that it belonged in a photograph frame in view of everyone, but Jack's strained relationship with his blood family and his consequent adoption by his foster parents complicated the issue, and she simplified everything by having no old photographs on display.

It was clear to see the family likenesses. Rachel was becoming more and more like her grandmother Sylvia Flynn, Hannah's mother, and the genetic link between Martin Flynn and his great-grandson Leigh was undeniable. As she had turned the pages, she had been reminded of a previous time when this photograph album had seen the light of day. It was during that holiday, when Mark and Sarah had brought their first-born Leigh to Willow Cottage. Sarah wanted to explore Mark's roots as she called them. That memory was 'bitter-sweet' for Hannah, another one stored in that dark corner of her mind.

The two children were quite excited to have a change of occupation. They were tiring of making Christmas streamers out of the crepe paper that their grandmother had found in the Glory Hole. The Christmas tree had been erected in its usual place in the gallery, the lights twinkling high above the 'Great Hall', as Jack laughingly described the living room.

Alice was very enthusiastic, having explored the cupboard once on her own. 'There's all sorts of goodies in there!' she exclaimed. 'Board games and tins of dice and tiddlywinks.' She stopped, her face flushing. 'I had a little look once,' she explained. 'Were they yours when you were little, Grandma?'

'No. I didn't have many possessions. During the war, there were only second-hand toys. We played card games quite a lot, and listened to the radio. There was no television of course. I used to spend hours reading, although some of the books were old-fashioned and quite hard to read. They didn't have the beautiful illustrations, not like children's books do today. Most of the "goodies" as you call them, Alice, belonged to my family, after we came to Willow Cottage when they were children.'

'I thought you had always lived here, Grandma.'

'No. I was evacuated here when I was nine, after my mother and my grandparents died in an air raid. At first, I stayed with a couple who worked on the land and lived in a very old cottage. Do you remember me telling you about it, Alice, when you were doing your project?' She turned to Leigh. 'There was no water toilet. Just an earth closet; a wooden box with a hole cut in it, in a kind of shed in the garden, and no bathroom like we have now. A zinc bath was hung up on a hook in the back yard, and wasn't used very often, as all the water had to be heated up either in the copper or in a kettle on the range. In fact, there wasn't even a water supply. The water had to be fetched in buckets from a pump in the farmyard further up the lane. It was the same at school. We had to take it in turns to fetch the water each day from the village pump. Soap was on ration as well. You were only allowed so much a week. Mind you, Elsie and Tom Porter didn't seem very concerned with cleanliness.' She wrinkled up her nose at the memory of the body odour and the stale smells which emanated from the grubby little house.

'It was better when I came here, much as you know it now, except that it was not a garden centre. Mr and Mrs Churchill were my foster parents, and I called them Uncle Harry and Aunt Kate. Auntie Ella did the housework while Aunt Kate was teaching. Then, after Aunt Kate died, Uncle Harry sold Willow Cottage. She didn't explain how Harry's sister Margot Sergeant poisoned her brother's mind with her jealousy. That was a memory trail she did not wish to go down. The children were too young to understand of course, as she had been. She felt guilty these days if she dwelt on her past. She couldn't understand Harry's attitude then, but as the years advanced she had a clearer view of his problems. But the clock had ticked on, and there could be no looking back with regret.

'It must have been hard for you not to live here anymore. Where did you go?' Alice asked.

'I had a teaching job in Hull and lived on my own. Auntie Ella had married and gone to live near Hexham. That's in Northumberland, right up near Scotland. Do you remember, Alice? I took Leigh up there when we fetched Auntie Ella. It's beautiful, isn't it, Leigh? Then I went back to Cragthorpe, where I was first evacuated, just for the weekend, mind you, and your granddad was running the village shop. He had been an evacuee as well, and Mr and Mrs Turner, the village shopkeepers had adopted him.'

'Had his parents been bombed?' Leigh asked.

'No. But they were very poor, and had a big family. Besides, Granddad didn't want to go back to Hull. Lots of children were very unsettled after evacuation. Anyway, let's see what's in the Glory Hole. It's been in need of a tidy-up for years.'

The Glory Hole was large enough to accommodate the three of them, although, after a large dressing-up box was pulled out and things spilled over onto the floor from the shelves, Hannah found that she was forced to step back and give the children space to investigate. They rummaged through the piles of paper, paint boxes, comics, a collection of Christmas annuals, old felt tip pens, coloured crayons, sticky paper, a box of model cars and farm vehicles, various dolls with an assortment of clothes and a general heap of the so-called clutter.

Hannah smiled at the children's excitement. It felt like Christmas morning come early, and she was really enjoying the experience herself. She and Jack were products of a wartime philosophy. Nothing was ever thrown away if it could come in for some kind of rainy day, and this day certainly qualified. Books and art materials seemed as precious now as they had done in her youth.

Eventually, after they had sorted things into neat piles on the shelves, she drew their attention to the photograph album. 'Well, look what's here!' she exclaimed, with contrived excitement. 'It's the old family album. Now I can show you all the people I have been talking about.'

Leigh seemed happy to share Hannah's memories of her parents, and was pleased when Alice said that he looked like Hannah's father, Great Granddad Flynn.

'What about Granddad's real parents?' Alice asked.

'I don't know,' Hannah replied. 'We haven't got a photograph of them, and I never met them. But Mr and Mrs Turner were very kind loving people. Here they are, look.' She turned to the next page.

'I wonder what my mother looked like.' Alice turned her head quickly away as a tear rolled unchecked down her face. 'All my mum knows is that she was too ill to look after me, and she doesn't know what happened to her. I think she has died. She didn't know anything about my father.'

'Oh Alice, darling, don't cry. It's what we are now that matters. Being sad doesn't change anything. Aunt Kate and Uncle Harry were not really my aunt and uncle, and Auntie Ella wasn't my auntie either, but here she is still with us, now called your Auntie Ella, and she is not really your auntie, is she? If I had not been evacuated, she wouldn't have all of you to love her. We never know what is going to be important in our futures, do we? So, only wish for happy things and don't look back.'

She stopped, suddenly noticing their subdued expressions, and reproached herself for expecting wise heads to be on such young shoulders. Yet somehow these two did seem to be receptive, and she sensed the strong bond which linked the three of them, regardless of age.

Leigh returned the conversation to the photograph album. 'Is Uncle Patrick in here?' he asked. 'He's not dead, is he?'

'Oh no! He's very much alive. That's another twist in the family, Alice. When my father came home from the war, he had no one to help him. He had lost a leg and was in a bad way. Then along came Jessica, a nurse who used to live in Jamaica, and they got married and had a son called Patrick. So I ended up with a brother after I had been an only one for all those years.'

'So did you go and live with them?''

'No, I was married to your granddad by that time.'

Hannah's voice level had dropped and the two children stared at her. She felt no inclination to explain how her father had changed beyond all recognition. She had always glossed over his bouts of depression and his time of alcohol dependency, preferring to stick with her childhood explanation that he had lost his memory, and one day would return to her. Now, she smiled at the thought of him as a young antique dealer with a great love of poetry and reading.

'Why haven't we seen Patrick?' Alice asked. 'He must be getting quite old by now.'

Hannah struggled to find the words to explain the racial tensions, which had finally driven Patrick to return his mother to her native country, and then simply said that his mother was homesick and one day he may return to Hull, the city of his birth. 'There are so many dots to join together,' she murmured.

One last happening of that day convinced Hannah that her grandson was the special child, who had communicated with her long before he was born, turning her concept of time upside down. He had stopped talking in the middle of recounting some episode in his father's childhood at Willow Cottage and stared up at the ceiling. Hannah and Alice followed his gaze and seeing nothing untoward, they looked at each other and waited for him to continue.

'Go on then,' Alice said eventually, poking him in the ribs. 'Have you gone into a trance or something?'

'No. I've just had a very creepy feeling. I think I've been in this house before. I think I lived here. I know there used to be a door here.' He pointed to the back wall of the cupboard. 'That used to be a way out into a kind of square before it all got joined together. You know that suddenly came into my head, like a picture. Honestly, Alice, I'm not making it up.'

Hannah nodded. 'You are right. It has always been like this, as far as I can remember, but Uncle Harry did tell me that the front kitchen was an addition and that is why this is called the old back kitchen. Apparently, there is an old lintel in that back wall behind the shelves concealed by a layer or two of wallpaper. I often think that it would be a good short cut into the front kitchen, instead of going round by the hallway.

'Hannah, where are you? We've got throats like the Sahara out here. Have you forgotten our three o'clock cups of tea?' That was Jack's voice.

Hannah sighed. Leigh's revelations about the bricked-up doorway were fascinating, and she was so thirsty for the airy-fairy stuff, as Jack called it, these days. He would have an explanation for it, she thought with some bitterness, as she filled up the kettle and put the teabags into the pot.

5

"There are many events in the womb of time, which will be delivered."

Shakespeare

Emma Clayton returned the phone handset onto the holder, and sank down onto the settee. That was typical of her mother, she thought, full of family news and not a bit interested in what she was doing with her life. Of course this business with Alice was awful, but it would never have happened if they had explained to the girl as soon as she was old enough to understand. She knew that she was feeling spiteful and being unfair. She had never felt able to compete with her brothers, and now, although Mark was dead, his son seemed to occupy his place in her mother's affections. In fact it was like one giant family guilt trip. She wondered how Rachel was feeling; poor Rachel, with that awful husband of hers and her interfering in-laws. Apparently, the twins had spilled the beans. She gave a twisted little grin as she imagined their spiteful pleasure. It was something I would probably have done, she thought, especially if the boys were getting all of the attention. According to her mother, Alice and Leigh were getting on splendidly. She felt another wave of sympathy for Karl and Kirsty, even though she had never warmed to them during her infrequent visits home during the last four years.

There had been no space in the conversation to give her mother any of her news. After the abduction drama, Hannah had moved on to the problems with Auntie Ella.

Apparently, Ella didn't know what day it was half of the time, and probably didn't care. Perhaps she was quite happy without being taken over.

There was no 'How are you?' or 'Good to hear your voice.' All she got was 'Wherever have you been?' and 'We thought you'd got lost.' She'd apologised for missing her mother's birthday. Rachel had rung up to remind her, but it was too late to alter her plans. Good dutiful Rachel, she muttered, she wouldn't forget. There were so many things left unsaid, as usual. How could she announce that she was pregnant and contemplating having an abortion? She knew what her mother's reaction would be. Hannah did not believe in termination, but then she'd never been called upon to make such a decision. She'd wanted children.

Then why did I ring her up, Emma asked herself? Why did I want my mother to be there for me? Why do I feel guilty? She stood up and pushed against the rickety table, which wobbled violently, shaking the mug of coffee. She swore at the sight of the spilt liquid, and then burst into tears.

The phone rang. Emma stared at it, wondering whether to answer. Perhaps it was her mother, regretting her indifference and picking up on her daughter's unhappiness with that famous intuition. Did she want to speak to her mother again? Could she risk blurting out her secret? She let it ring a few times, composing herself, before putting the receiver to her ear. It was only Dom, asking her if she fancied going out for a bite to eat later on. Normally, she would have been glad of the company. Eating alone was no fun at the best of times. But she needed advice and reassurances. Dom was not the father. It was not possible to contact that culprit as she mentally called him. It had been a 'one-night stand', with too much to drink and no trace of him in the morning. She couldn't even remember what he looked like, never mind putting a name to him. She knew that she should have acted the next morning and possibly terminated it then, but she was so naïve about such things. She'd had a dreadful migraine, which had lasted for three days, and somehow life had drifted back to the normal 'nine-to-five' routine.

She dabbed at the spilt coffee with a tea towel. Housework had never been high on her list of priorities. A pile of magazines occupied an armchair, and two more mugs waited to join plates and dishes in the sink. She had been restless for some time, with little job satisfaction, but had become resigned to the dull routine as a means of earning sufficient money to pay the rent on her flat on Anlaby Road, although living over a shop on a busy artery road into the city was not where she wanted to be. She called it her flat, a somewhat boastful description of what was little more than a glorified bed-sit. A dark alleyway linked the small backyards of the shops, each restricted area being separated from its neighbours by a series of old brick walls, where years of decay and lack of sunshine had encouraged the spread of green mould, and, here and there, a rampant growth of ivy. An elder tree, which Emma described as an opportunist, defied all the rules of horticulture by taking root in a crevice in the mortar, and now hung triumphantly waiting for the spring. Flights of rusting metal stairs, which allowed access to the first floor and also served as fire escapes, led up to small landings, each with an unadorned and in some cases unpainted door.

Emma's living space was basically furnished, and in need of decoration. The scullery, with its view to the rear of the building, contained a gas stove, a small wall cupboard, a base unit and a stainless steel sink The floors were covered in green patterned linoleum, the surface worn by years of tread. An old settee, its shabbiness concealed by a cream coloured throw-over, was positioned in front of the gas fire, and an armchair with an obviously different history was pushed up against the wall. A narrow bed was concealed in the far corner behind a length of pegboard on which Emma had secured newspaper cuttings of what she considered to be her best efforts at good journalism. The window looking out over the street was draped with a cream-figured net curtain, its transparency masked by the dirt on the outside of the glass.

Emma regarded the shabbiness of her surroundings, trying to imagine how her mother would react if she came to visit. She knew, if she was honest with herself that she was ashamed of her lifestyle. She had been living a lie ever since she came here, and now, out of the blue, she found herself redundant, not entitled to any compensation, and with morning sickness as an added burden.

How would her parents react to that? No doubt they would welcome her home like the prodigal son. Even that was masculine, she thought, her mind back on the whole business of male dominance. The men at work had not fallen foul of this redundancy scheme. Apparently, they had different job descriptions, whereas the women were lumped together in general skills.

She threw the tea towel into the sink, and sank down into the armchair, pushing the magazines onto the floor. She didn't want to go home as a failure after struggling with a degree course in English for three years and getting surprisingly good results. Her mother was so proud of her and wanted her to stay on for another year to qualify for a teaching diploma, but Emma had no desire to spend her life with children. She saw herself as a top reporter, working for a national publication, but all she had aspired to so far, was the small, local, tittle-tattle kind of reporting, which she found utterly boring. She'd led her family to believe that she travelled around, staying overnight in four-star hotels, and wining and dining notables in order to get top stories. They were all far enough away not to query these fantasies, taking it for granted that after all her studying, she would be in line for a well-paid job. So far no one had been curious enough to see any of the results of her glamorous life style. The terrible drama of Mark's death had overshadowed other family interests, and she had seen little of them all since the funeral.

The only recent brightness on last week's horizon had been her appointment with Sally Blenkin. Her so-called superior Luke Emmin, had gone down with a bout of 'flu', otherwise he would have jumped in with both feet, she thought, a spiteful little smile turning up the corners of her mouth. She'd recognised the name instantly, not only because Sally was a well-known Hull author, but because of her association with her mother Hannah. She remembered studying Sally's face in the old photograph album, admiring her long blond hair and animated expression. She had appeared as a role model to the young girl, even though she had never expected to meet her. Now that Sally had returned after many years in Australia, she had caught the interest of the editor and Emma had been given the story. When Sally discovered the identity of her interviewer, she insisted on paying for a slap-up meal, and giving Emma plenty of information and anecdotes to fill the weekly spot. Her boss was very impressed, but then Luke returned, and Emma, unwittingly, was on route for the door marked 'Way Out'. At least it would be one press cutting, which would interest her mother, she thought, as she made herself a fresh cup of coffee.

'Some women would give their back teeth to have a baby,' Sally said. She had settled down on Emma's settee, after tugging the throw-over into place, and had listened to the hysterical outburst, which was a continuation of the phone call on the previous evening.

'Yes, I know,' Emma agreed, thinking of her sister-in-law Marie, who after three miscarriages was told that she would never conceive again.

'You may have a daughter who will charm the birds off the trees, with a first-rate brain to beat the socks off the men. Somebody like you, Emma.'

Emma grimaced. 'Girls usually take after their fathers. I can't remember what its father looked like. I don't even remember his name.' She stopped short realising that she had acknowledged its existence as a person, not just as a pregnancy. 'Didn't you ever think of marrying, and having a family? I mean, you haven't, have you? You know—got a husband or been pregnant?' She stopped talking again, her face colouring up and then she began to apologise. 'Sorry. I shouldn't ask such personal questions. It's none of my business.' She had been instructed during her initial training, not to probe too deeply into people's private lives, unless information was volunteered. Of course it all hinged on the skill of the interviewer, but this was no time for manipulation.

'Oh don't worry. I've got a hide like an elephant. You have to have where I've been. I've long since given up on the idea of marriage. I did have quite a serious relationship once with a guy called Paul. In fact your mother was going to share a flat with me after I'd thrown him out, but then we got back together again and I lost touch with Hannah for years. I'm not very good with relationships. I've made quite a hash of things really and I have actually been in your situation. You know. The abortion bit. Look, sweetheart, why don't you put your mum in the picture? OK, so she gravitates towards her sons – mothers usually do. They seem to think boys can't survive without being mothered. Mine's exactly the same. But when it comes to the crunch, she'll be there for you.'

'Do you think so? She never comes to see me. She's been to America, and then up to Northumberland. She never seems to have time for me.'

'Have you ever asked her?' Sally gave Emma a knowing look. 'She's perhaps afraid to intrude in your life. You are a bit prickly, you know. Anyway, don't worry about managing. I'll lend you some money if you are short, and come round to my place if you need a change of company or surroundings.' She looked around the flat, and Emma sensed the criticism, seeing the shabbiness and untidiness through her eyes, and sinking deeper into depression.

After Sally left, Emma sat and stared at the blank screen of the television. It was very good of her to offer a helping hand towards the rent, but her mother would go mad at her contemplating accepting financial aid from a comparative stranger. After all, it was a big leap from the friendship of youth to the relationship between two mature women who had each taken a very different path in life.

Was it a boy or a girl? The queasiness was back and with it the realisation of her predicament. Could she end someone's life even if she did not want the responsibility of a child? All of her upbringing suddenly came to the fore; the sanctity of life, the love of a family, the personal responsibility. She stroked her hand over the flatness of her stomach and thought about it, whoever it was.

Christmas, as always in these days of plenty in the late eighties, consisted of over-indulgences, which of course included food; the inevitable large turkey, which struggled to find space in the oven, and which appeared in various guises over the next two days; the fruit bowls piled up with oranges, apples, pears, grapes and bananas; boxes of dates and figs, which seemed to serve purely an ornamental or traditional function; sweet dishes, filled up regularly with glistening, foil-wrapped assorted chocolates, a variety of nuts, some which resisted the hardiest of nutcrackers, and were left in the bottom of the dish for a time of less plenty; tins containing mouth-watering biscuits far removed in their exotic description from the normal morning coffee selection, and packets of crisps and other snacks, which the children loved, but the adults described as eating some kind of chaff. Of course, the sherry trifles were obligatory, accompanying the ham and turkey teas on Christmas Day and Boxing Day.

'Why do we go so mad at Christmas?' Jack commented.

'You say that every year, Dad,' Rachel responded.

'I know, because it happens every year. We were lucky to get a chicken and a few vegetables when I was growing up. Chicken was a real treat, wasn't it, Hannah?'

Hannah smiled and nodded, not prepared to follow that train of thought. Jack was living more and more in the past. There was so much going on in the present. But Jack persisted.

'You would think we were expecting a siege, wouldn't you?' He turned to his fellow men for support.

Simon and Steve nodded their heads in agreement, having over-indulged on Christmas Day; Simon at home with Marie and Alice, and Steve sharing the day with Rachel, Karl and Kirstie at his parents' home.

'Well, none of you men appear to be on a diet,' Rachel commented, looking across at Steve. She was still feeling irritated by Steve's comments about the inevitable ham tea and trifle, traditional at Willow Cottage on Boxing Day. Yesterday, at his parents' Christmas Day tea, they'd sat down to a choice of prawn cocktails, or stuffed mushrooms, followed by a pork and rice dish, the name of which eluded her, and which had defeated her in finding the necessary space in her digestive system. The final challenge was the meringue, filled with fresh cream, and topped with fruits of the forest.

Hannah was trying not to think of Mark and instead directed her concern towards Emma. She had been so pleased to see her when she arrived on Christmas Eve but immediately worried by her obvious loss of weight. 'Are you all right?' she had asked as Emma walked through the door. Instinctively, both of them knew that she was really asking 'Are you pregnant?'

'I'm fine, thanks,' Emma had replied, turning away from the long look, which her mother levelled at her. 'I'll put my case out of the way. Where am I sleeping? In my normal room, or is that taken these days?'

'No. It's just as you left it. Ella's in the boys' room and Leigh is in the kitchen room. We have to keep an eye on Ella. She sometimes wanders, although she slept like a log last night after all the preparations. She often amazes me. If it's to do with food, she's really in her element. Mind you, she's constantly forgetting it's Christmas.'

Hannah had chattered on, trying to keep the atmosphere light, but her suspicions about her daughter would not go away. It was the hollowness under her eyes, which caused such deep shadows, and a certain pallor under the skin, which she recognised from her own past, when she had stared at herself in the mirror, and tried to rub some colour into her cheeks.

But it was more than that, she thought later, as she lay in bed unable to sleep. There seemed to be a deep ingrained instinct, a genetic memory, which linked mothers and daughters. She couldn't remember recognising the condition each time with Marie, her daughter-in-law, before the inevitable miscarriage. Yet she knew that Rachel was pregnant, even before Rachel was certain herself. Emma had never mentioned a boyfriend, had she? She didn't seem to be interested in the opposite sex. Life was such a worry these days. Pregnancy had always been a worry, but now there didn't even seem to be a need of a relationship, and what about all the dangers of unprotected sex? If Emma was pregnant, then what were the circumstances? Perhaps she wasn't. But Hannah knew that she was right. It was a mother's instinct to know.

Would her own mother have recognised her condition at the beginning of her four pregnancies? How she had longed for reassurances. Thoughts of her mother induced that familiar surge of sadness, her mind back once again to that last goodbye, half-turning for a final glimpse of her mother's face, as she began her journey into the future. At the time, it had all seemed like a big adventure, She was with her father and the Blenkin family, who lived next door in Tennyson Street. That reminded her that she and Sally had still not had that promised re-union. It would be a giggle, she guessed. Sally always made her giggle with her silly comments. Mind you, she thought, she didn't mince her words. She returned to memories of the day of their evacuation and how Sally berated her two brothers for each one scuffling their feet in bombsite brick debris along the side of the road. There had been no tears at first. Her grandparents must have still been in bed. She couldn't remember seeing them. In fact, she couldn't even remember what they looked like. All the photographs had been destroyed in that fatal air raid. There were no last hugs. People kept a tight grip on their emotions in those days. She was reminded of her own family's comments. They accused her and Jack of being unemotional, even cold, but being undemonstrative was not a sign of not caring. Cuddling seemed to belong in early childhood. She had been a great one for baby cuddling, wanting to smother them in kisses, and squeeze them to bits, as she used to say.

Her thoughts wandered to the recent news of the Lockerbie air disaster. There had been further coverage yesterday in the national press, describing the reactions of friends and relations. 'What a dreadful time for it to happen,' the reporter had commented, 'just before Christmas.' But it would be dreadful at any time, she reasoned. Mark's death was dreadful last summer.

She rolled over onto her side, and pressed the pillow into her face. Jack was snoring again, and she contemplated going into the spare bed, until she remembered that there wasn't one, with Emma still here. She jabbed him in the ribs, and he snorted halfway through a snore, took two normal breaths, and returned to the rhythmic 'saw mill' scenario.

Hannah sat up, and reached for her dressing gown without turning on the light. She had always been something of an expert at finding her way around in the dark, a habit she had begun in childhood, when she used to close her eyes and pretend to be blind. These days it was quite an asset during power cuts, which were not infrequent in country areas during stormy weather. She was the one who found the torch, or who, sure-footedly, reached the kitchen dresser to seek out the candles.

She counted the steps past both Ella's and Emma's room, silently treading down the stairs and along the hall towards the steep stone steps, which led down to the front kitchen. Her actions froze for a moment, as the door creaked loudly. 'That needs oiling,' she muttered, not for the first time. Leigh had such an acute sense of hearing. They had soon learnt not to make any unguarded statements in his vicinity. Although there was a door at both ends of the little twisting staircase, which led up to the kitchen bedroom, any activity in the kitchen could well cause disturbed sleep. She knew that Leigh still had night terrors and now that Alice had returned home, she wondered about the wisdom of allowing him to sleep away from the main bedrooms. She made herself a cup of tea, and sat down at the kitchen table, her mind wandering over the last few days.

They had gone overboard with presents for the children. She knew that they were trying to compensate for the traumas of the last weeks, although it was hard to compete with Karl's and Kirstie's other grandparents. The twins boasted of a colour television each for their bedrooms, a model farm with a remote-controlled tractor, a three-storey Georgian style doll's house complete with miniature furniture and residents, and electronic gadgets which did amazing things at the press of a button.

Life seemed to be advancing at such a pace that she and Jack couldn't keep up. To be honest, they had no desire to keep up. It was so comfortable to stay with Christmas charades and Pass the Donkey. Everyone else enjoyed themselves, in spite of it being old-fashioned, or traditional as she preferred to call it. Even the twins tried to hide their disappointment at the predominance of books amongst their gifts, and joined in with the games, although from the little looks which they gave Alice from time to time, she guessed that they were still feeling uncomfortable about their part in their cousin's recent unhappiness.

Her thoughts wandered from the twins to Alice. She knew that Marie had spent time with the child discussing her adoption. She had skirted over the illegitimacy angle. Probably Alice would have accepted it without question. Children were so 'street wise' these days. Being illegitimate had been such a stigma in the past. She could remember when she was a child, growing up in Norbrooke during her evacuation, how a little girl called Betty was pointed out to her as having no father. She couldn't see why the girl was bullied. After all she herself didn't have a mother anymore and she had no idea where her father was. It was only in later years that she understood the word 'bastard', and why it was considered to be such an insult.

Alice seemed to have accepted the explanation without question. Marie and Simon were reassured by her lack of curiosity, Hannah was not so sure. With memories of her own mixed loyalties, she guessed that behind those clear blue eyes was a tangle of speculation, which would not fit happily into Alice's wonderland of childish imagination.

'Why didn't you tell me?' Hannah asked. It was morning coffee time and she was sitting opposite Emma at the kitchen table. Jack and Leigh were busy taking down the trimmings in the living room, although the tree would be left up in the gallery until Twelfth Night.

'Well, you knew already didn't you? I could tell by your face.' Emma gave a wry smile. 'Nothing escapes your eagle eye. Have you mentioned it to Dad?'

'I did have my suspicions when I first saw you, I must admit, but why didn't you tell me when I rang you up? Or didn't you know then? Are you planning to get married, or are you going to be modern and not bother?'

'No, nothing like that. Ships that pass in the night, I suppose you would say. I didn't dare tell anybody, although I did tell Sally.' She stopped and her pale face coloured across her cheekbones. 'Sorry, I forgot to tell you that I have met Sally Blenkin.'

Hannah frowned. 'You could have said—she could have said as well. So, what else have you been discussing with Sally Blenkin?'

'Oh Mum, it wasn't like that. I did an article about her for work. My boss was interested in her. He could remember her as a young writer before she went to Australia. I recognised her straight away. She has hardly changed from when she had that photograph taken. You know. The one in your photograph album.'

Hannah nodded. That sounded about right, she thought.

'She was so surprised when she found out who I was. She was really kind to me, and took me out to a swanky place for dinner. I did the best report ever with all the info she gave me. She'd told me to keep in touch and after I'd spoken to you, you seemed to have so many problems that I didn't want to bother you with mine. I just don't know how I'm going to cope.'

Hannah reached for a tissue, anticipating forthcoming tears. She felt like crying herself ten minutes later, after her daughter had unburdened all of her problems; no father for the child, no job and no money. She sighed. The answer, of course, was for Emma to come back home. It wasn't such a long time since it had been quite acceptable for her to be fed and clothed. She'd earned some money during her university years but Hannah and Jack had supported her in the main.

'I did consider an abortion,' Emma said, and Hannah was jolted out of her contemplations, shaking her head in protest.

'You mustn't do that. This is a human life we're talking about, even if you don't know who the father is, and you mustn't take risks with your body. Look at poor Marie. I'm not saying that she had an abortion, but three miscarriages have put paid to her chance of a normal pregnancy. Have you been to the doctor's yet? You ought to have a good check-up. I suppose there are circumstances where termination is on the cards.' Hannah could not voice her concerns about the dangers of casual sex.

'I know, Mum. It's a hard decision and I'm so scared it's going to ruin my life. Somebody may want to adopt it, I suppose, but I still have to get through the next eight months.'

Hannah stood up and went round to the back of Emma's chair,

putting her hands on her shoulders and pressing her face against the side of her daughter's head. 'Don't worry, darling. You've got us. We'll all help.'

They decided to keep the news from Jack for the time being. Now that Emma had the promise of future help, she could try to find another job, not necessarily in journalism; just something, which would support her for a few more months. Of course, it wouldn't be long before everyone noticed her condition, Hannah thought. It wasn't the kind of thing one could hide, but these days it was accepted as part of everyday living; the single mother; the modern young woman.

Hannah's heart hardened back into her practical strengths. They'd all just have to get on with things, she reasoned, reminding herself that after Emma was born, there were four children under the age of eight, and she was working long hours in the shop or as they got older, doing supply teaching to swell the funds. She left Emma to get ready for her proposed trip to the city sales with Rachel, turning her attention to Ella who was intent on making custard for the second time that day!

One hour later, Emma was feeling restored after her confessions and her escape from the tensions which prevailed at Willow Cottage. She asked Rachel if she had noticed the change in their father just lately. Rachel, caught up in her own problems, shrugged and replied that everyone was stressed at the moment.

Emma decided that perhaps this wasn't the time to mention that her father was drinking quite heavily. She couldn't understand why no one else seemed to have noticed it. She had always been close to her father. She sensed his moods, and although he appeared to be coping with Mark's death, she knew that his impatience and cynicism was really a cry for help. She had heard a slight slurring in his speech on a couple of occasions and at first put it down to tiredness, but yesterday she had seen him going into the long greenhouse and reaching under the bench. He had turned to see whether he was being observed before he took a long drink from a bottle of what looked like brandy. Of course, he'd always enjoyed a glass of beer and wine on special occasions, but his secrecy worried her, and she didn't know whether to alert her mother.

Perhaps she should tell Rachel. After all she saw more of them on a regular basis.

'Did you know Dad's becoming a secret drinker?'

Rachel did not take her eyes off the road ahead, and for a moment made no reply. Then she spoke slowly, with a note of bitterness tinged with sadness in her voice. 'Is there any wonder?' she said. 'There's no peace in the house anymore. Leigh is the be all and end all, and Auntie Ella gets worse. You've no idea what it's been like. If I liked alcohol I would become a secret drinker.'

It's her marriage, Emma realised. She's trying to tell me that she is unhappy. Poor Rachel, keeping all of her problems to herself, and there's me, thinking that I'm the only one that's unhappy. Christmas was such a cover-up, a mask to hide behind with all the fun and games. One big game of charades she decided, glancing sideways at her sister and suddenly noticing a slight blueness showing under a layer of foundation cream on her left cheek, as they rounded a bend in the road, and sunlight burst through a gap in the tall hedge. Surely Steve was not knocking her about! God! There was so much her mother needed to know but then perhaps she already knew and she needed to escape as well.

The dark mornings and equally dark evenings of January were soon replaced with the hopes of brighter days in February, when the first snowdrops and aconites began to emerge through the tattered undergrowth, the victim of the winter's torment. It was the same every year of course, but always with some time variance, although talk of global warming triggered by such alarming events as the hurricanes during October of 1987, led people to comment more now about that variance. "Were the daffodils in bud as early as this last year?" "There's plenty of time for snow yet, you'll see." "Never mind getting warmer, I'm perished! Roll on the spring!" All of Jack and Hannah's friends and neighbours maintained the British tradition of discussing the weather. Prophecies of future doom and gloom by the scientists were readily dismissed in favour of old wives' tales and country predictions.

In spite of the winter blues, the school half-term holiday seemed to come with surprising alacrity for most parents. Being involved with the education system, Simon and Marie welcomed the break along with their students, and hearing of Hannah's wish to visit Emma and her friend Sally and the suggestion that perhaps Alice and Leigh would enjoy exploring Hull, Simon volunteered to stay with Jack and Ella at Willow Cottage. Marie reluctantly agreed. She had planned some early spring cleaning, and did not relish long periods of time with Ella or with Jack for that matter, although Simon enjoyed having chats with his father away from the women folk.

Jack had not been too keen on the idea at first. 'You're not all going to fit in Emma's place, are you?' he queried. 'Apparently it's only a bed-sit.' Over the last few days he had returned to his grumpiness, and Hannah heard herself gabbling in protest. She had not enlightened him about Emma's expectations as she called them, or about Sally's involvement in her plans. He was very critical of Sally's way of life. But then he always had been, she decided. Perhaps it was jealousy and his belief that Sally could soon seduce her into irresponsible behaviour. He had never forgotten the plans they'd had to share Sally's flat in London, and considered that it was only his intervention, which had saved Hannah from disaster. Anyway, he didn't know anything about Sally. Men could be so irritating, wanting their women to be there in their traditional roles, but expecting them to turn on the charm and glamour when the occasion arose. She often envied Sally's lifestyle, although, if she was honest, she knew nothing about it. They had a lot of catching-up to do. She had always put her friend into a feminist role, imagining her as a modern-day Emily Pankhurst. Or there was Amy Johnson. She was from Hull; another free spirit. Ever since she had heard Sally's voice on the other end of the phone last September, she had been longing to see her again. So much had happened to prevent the promised reunion, what with Ella's problems, and then the dreadful business with Alice. And of course, Christmas celebrations got in the way of everything.

She suddenly felt guilty at her lack of enthusiasm, but family commitments were pressing in on all sides, and she desperately needed some freedom. 'We're not fastened at the hip,' she remembered saying to Jack. That was not a kind sentiment, especially as Jack was not feeling too bright. Anyway, he wouldn't welcome Emma's news. She was the baby of the family. It had been a difficult birth with debilitating after-effects, and it was Jack who had got up in the night, making bottles, or rocking the crib, until Emma was well into her third month. She knew that he would be devastated by news of her condition, especially as she had no idea who the father was. Jack didn't agree with the promiscuous behaviour, which was becoming more and more commonplace these days. Still, he wasn't perfect. More exercise and less whisky would probably do him good,' she muttered. The bitterness was back and with it the need to escape.

It was a lovely day, unusually mild for late February, and as they crossed the Humber Bridge, Hannah was readily affected by the children's excitement. The sun was shining across the vast surface of water and long sand bars both glistened and glowed in a breathtaking yellow ochre, a colour she loved to use when she dabbled with paints. The reinforced concrete towers rising up in front of her had a mesmerising quality, and she resisted the temptation to allow her eyes to be drawn upwards towards the sky.

She commented on the buildings, which she recognised on the North Bank, and the old pier at New Holland, which jutted out into the river, pointing like a long finger in the direction of Hull.

'That was the way we had to go before the bridge was built,' she explained. 'There were three ferry boats named after castles. People drove their cars onto the deck and even farm animals were taken across sometimes.'

'Was that in the Roman days?' Alice asked, with a little note of mischief in her voice.

Hannah smiled. 'Not quite that long ago. The bridge was built in 1981, the longest suspension bridge in the world. It seems like only last year to me but you would have both been toddlers, so it will seem a long time to you.'

'I don't think time really matters,' Leigh said. 'Do we have to pay now?'

They had come to a halt at the toll bar, and Hannah wound down the window, offering a five-pound note, and waiting for her change. The traffic light changed from red to green and the children waved goodbye to the stern-faced man, who ignored them, his eyes focussing on the truck, which had pulled up behind them.

'I think he must get fed up,' Alice commented. 'He doesn't look very happy.'

'It's a job like any other,' Hannah replied. 'It gives him space to day-dream doesn't it?'

Once away from the bridge, she was back into more familiar territory, and soon found her way to Emma's flat on Anlaby Road, one of a number of major roads, which led to the city centre. 'The fair comes into a street further up this road,' she explained. 'It's the biggest travelling fair in the country but you'll have to wait until early October. I used to live near here when I was a little girl. We'll go and see Tennyson Street some time. When I was a new teacher I had a flat nearer to town. I don't know if it will still be there. Everything changes so much these days. I can't remember the traffic being so noisy, but then very few people could afford to have cars in those days. There were plenty on bikes and of course buses every ten minutes or so.'

Hannah stopped talking and concentrated on looking for somewhere to park. She had located the relevant row of shops, and indicated that she was making a right-hand turn up a narrow street, which appeared to be a dead end. She struggled to park the car in a very tight spot, with little space for access to the boot, and decided to leave their belongings locked away. Perhaps Sally's flat would offer more secure parking, she thought, then reproached herself for already getting into a panic.

The children were not aware of her anxieties and had no idea that this was a stressful situation. It was different and that was exciting. They made their way back to look for the alleyway, which led to Emma's flat. "Look for a chemist, next to a paper shop," Emma had instructed. "The alley in between leads to the back ways, and mine is the second fire escape along with a black door at the top."

Emma must have been keeping watch through the kitchen window, for she opened the door at the top as they made their way up the steep metal steps. She laughed as Hannah stood gasping for air. 'I used to be like that,' she said, 'I run up them now.'

'Not for much longer,' Hannah warned, somewhat alarmed by her own lack of fitness. Her heart was beating so fast that she thought it would jump out of her chest. It was reassuring to notice that both of the children were also catching their breaths.

Even though Emma had made a real effort to spruce up her flat, it did not impress Hannah, and after a quick glance beyond the entrance and through into the tiny kitchen, she maintained eye-to-eye contact with her daughter in an attempt to mask her dismay.

'I know it's all pretty crumby,' Emma said, immediately recognising her mother's critical expression. 'It's all I can manage at the moment, until I can get a better job.'

'Never mind. We'll sort it out. Right you two, hands washed. I've brought some sandwiches, darling. I didn't know how you were fixed, food-wise that is. Let's have the kettle on. You can make the tea.'

Everyone did as they were told, responding to the schoolteacher tones in Hannah's voice. The children did not register any feelings of resentment or question their role in this world of adult supremacy. They were no doubt saving it for a future day. However, Emma had long since grown out of the role, and she banged some mugs down impatiently on to the small square of Formica, which served as a worktop next to the draining board.

Hannah rubbed her hand across her forehead. She'd had a dull ache over her eyes for several days, and driving through city traffic had added to the tension. 'I thought I'd take the kids to see my old hunting grounds. Sally may like to come as well and share some reminiscences, although it all may be changed beyond recognition. Is Walpole Street School still there?' Hannah knew that she was talking too quickly.

Emma's heart softened. She recognised that sign of nervousness. After all, she had inherited the habit from her mother. Rachel had only commented on the family trait recently. 'You're gabbling like Mum,' she'd said. 'What's the matter?'

She had reached the sugar stage. 'Have the kids got a sweet tooth? I don't have to ask you, do I? It is still three, isn't it? I don't know how you keep so slim.'

Hannah smiled, relaxing with the compliment. 'I think it's three all round,' she replied, 'although they would probably prefer a soft drink.'

Alice and Leigh were thoroughly engrossed in watching the traffic and the pedestrians through the front window. They had lifted the net curtain to get a clearer view, exposing a layer of grime, which had built up on the glass since sometime in the distant past a window cleaner had applied a wash-leather. It reminded Hannah of the first rooms she'd had when she began her teaching career. During that period, bombsites were still a common sight in the war-torn city, and she'd had a dismal view of one through the greying net at the window. Still, that was during a period of continued austerity. There was no need these days for a daughter of hers to put up with such depressing surroundings. She'd talk about it sometime with Sally.

An hour later, with no opportunity to discuss Emma's problems, and the children tiring of looking out of the window, they decided to take their overnight luggage to Sally's flat on the other side of the city. Hannah spent more time than usual in freshening up as she called it. She'd treated herself to some expensive foundation cream, and a perfume spray, which had made Jack cough when she had sprayed it on before she left.

'That will do,' she said, giving her hair a final pat. No doubt Sally would be all dressed up – fur coat and no knickers. That was an awful thing to think, she mouthed to the mirror. But it was the sudden memory of her father saying it about Sally's mother, which had popped into her head. She could never understand its meaning, as a little girl, except that it must be rude, because her mother admonished him with a blow from a rolled-up newspaper and sharp words. No. Sally would certainly be sophisticated. She was a well-travelled lady and apparently had never married or had children. No doubt her breasts would still defy gravity and there would be no disfiguring stretch marks.

An hour later, it was a relief to find that her friend looked quite ordinary, as she waited at the top of the stairs. Admittedly, her trouser suit was well cut and figure-hugging, but her hair was tied back, emphasising the gauntness in her facial bone structure. Wrinkles around her mouth indicated a history of heavy smoking, and her eyes were deeply shadowed.

Hannah was annoyed to be out of breath for the second time that day. 'There is a lift to another landing,' Sally explained, 'but don't you love this Victorian staircase? It keeps me fit and I really like being so high up.' She waved them into her living room beyond the small entrance lobby. 'I know the windows are small and the sloping ceilings are a mixed blessing,' she continued, 'but the tenants on the ground floors and first floors can't see beyond that line of trees, which border the parkland, whereas I have a view over the entire municipal park.'

Hannah's eyes were drawn to a pair of binoculars, which rested on the windowsill, and Sally grinned at Hannah's raised eyebrows. 'There's nothing wrong with a bit of voyeurism, especially when one is a novelist. Anyway, put that bag down, and give me a hug, Hannah Flynn. You haven't changed a bit.'

'Just my name. But Flynn sounds good. I could get used to it again.'

'I never found a name which I liked enough to change mine into, although Blenkin is not exactly inspiring. Memorable though. Most people think it's some kind of strange nom de plume. You're looking good, Emma, and these are the famous grand-kids. You must be Alice. How pretty you are, and could you be Leigh? I was expecting someone much older. You sound very wise on the phone.'

Both the children beamed and became instant disciples alongside of their Auntie Emma, who was already under Sally's spell.

After a great deal of conversation, which hinged on both childhood memories and more recent years, Hannah recognised signs of restlessness in her family members. She knew that in spite of the long telephone conversations she and Sally had had since their mutual birthday communication, they would never tire of talking to each other, and really it would be pointless and cruel to expose the rest of the world to this kind of gluttony.

Sally suggested a meal at a local restaurant rather than a take-away, although she assured the two youngsters that the menu was highly suitable for their tastes. Hannah suppressed her so-called 'out of the ark' views on the suitability of beef burgers or chicken concoctions for the healthy development of young people, Sally's attitude liberating her as Jack knew that it would.

Leigh and Alice looked at each other, already sensing a kind of victory, and Emma relaxed in the company of these two older women, both needing to abandon the restraints of the past, and reaching out into a future of new age thinking, whatever it entailed.

They planned to spend the next morning investigating the history of the city. The children were not very impressed with Wilberforce House, except for the figure of William Wilberforce seated at his desk, although they could relate to the transport museum. They wandered along the narrow streets, and posed on the corner of the famous Land of Green Ginger for a photograph, before heading towards the old pier, the starting point for the steam-propelled ferryboats, which carried passengers over the river to New Holland on the south bank, in the days before the bridge was built.

Alice was very impressed by the tall buildings and the busy streets in comparison to Lincoln, but Leigh assured her that it was nothing compared to Chicago.

Hannah was disappointed to find, after some wandering about and speculation, that Walpole Street School had become the latest victim of a demolition team, and a new shopping development put paid to her limited senses of direction.

Emma introduced them to a Chinese restaurant, a haunt of her student days, where apparently one could eat one's fill, returning any number of times to top up one's plate with a variety of tasty snacks. Hannah had to admit that it was a pleasurable experience, and the children's eyes were like saucers as they regarded the myriad of dishes.

A ride on a corporation bus transported them back beyond Emma's flat to Tennyson Street, the next stage on the nostalgia trail, where Hannah and Sally had first become acquainted when they were nine years old. They vaguely knew what to expect, having both returned earlier in their lives, but it was a moving experience nevertheless. The gap in the terrace, where their houses had been situated, seemed solid in its emptiness, Hannah thought. She visualised the line of the roof, and the passageway, which divided the two dwellings at ground level, the three windows on each side and the two front doors, drawing lines and connecting the dots in her memory. She had already instructed Sally not to comment on the layout. She wanted to put her grandchildren's psychic powers to the test. Sally had rolled her eyes in the way that Hannah remembered she had always done at times when she was critical of her friend's points of view. She knew that it was good-humoured criticism, but it embarrassed her, and she hoped that the children would confound her friend's cynicism by some amazing acts of perception.

They crossed the street and began to walk through the bomb-created gap, now a cemented, pot-holed track used as an access to the ten foot, an alley, which ran along the back of the row of terraced houses. Hannah knew that Sally was counting the steps, visualising the size of their parents' living rooms, which led into kitchens beyond. It was not hard to do this, as the remaining houses indicated the dimensions, but it was not only the size. Both of them were retracing their footsteps in and out, up and down, caught up in childhood memories.

Leigh had stopped walking at a point beyond the back boundaries of the houses. Alice turned, her eyes wide with expectation. She joins up Leigh's dots, Hannah thought, with a sudden realisation of their symbiosis. He makes a spiritual connection, and she seems to bring it all down to earth. Sally and Emma were walking ahead. Sally was pointing out the track which ran parallel to the ten foot, explaining that it was once the railway line on which goods trains made their way backwards and forwards to Doncaster. Now, it served as a pedestrian link to another main road into the city. They turned to see where the others were, at the same moment as Leigh gave a cry and fell to the ground.

Hannah instantly knew that somehow he had become part of that terrible event in the past, which had destroyed her mother. She remembered how the brick-built air-raid shelter was sited close to the back door of the house, where Leigh now lay. As she sank to her knees beside him, she reproached herself for exposing him to unknown dangers. She was indulging her own need for spiritual enlightenment, without understanding his capabilities. His emotions were still so raw after the death of his parents and Alice was becoming caught up in it at a time when she needed normality more than anything else.

Leigh opened his eyes and struggled to his feet. 'Oh my God, Sylvia,' he said. 'Oh my God.'

Those words would stay with Hannah forever. She knew, without a shadow of a doubt, that they were the last words spoken to her mother most likely by her grandmother before that fatal bomb, and somehow they had become encapsulated in a time bubble. As her mind travelled back into her childhood, she had a sudden recollection of her grandmother's habit of saying 'Oh my God', especially during times of stress.

Leigh struggled to his feet, and grinned as though nothing untoward had happened, and he and Alice ran back to the car, jumping the pot holes in the rough track. But it was a pilgrimage that Hannah vowed never to make again. The past should stay dead and buried, she thought. Why do I agonise over it?

'Perhaps it is because you never had proper closure after the death of your mother,' Marie suggested the following day when Hannah verbalised her worries. 'Being away from your family, and then there was no funeral or anything. It must have had a bad effect on you.'

Any further plans of physical explorations of the past had lost their appeal. However, Sally's attempts to console and cosset her young guests seemed so maternal and somewhat out of character that Hannah's mind was inexorably drawn back to the past in the image of Sally's mother, with her rough tongue, and hard hands, but no doubt a heart of gold, she mused. She asked Sally about her parents later on, as they sat watching the television. The children were asleep in the spare bedroom, and Emma had returned to her flat.

Sally pressed the off button on the remote control. 'What a load of rubbish!' she exclaimed. 'God knows why we look at it. It's like a drug.' She turned to address her friend. 'My father's dead, of course. He was about eight years older than my mother, and smoked and drank himself into an early grave, if you call pegging out at eighty early. It seemed ancient to me then, but now with sixty looming up on the horizon, mortality begins to make me nervous. My mother is still in Lincolnshire. She doesn't really change. The boys keep an eye on her. Still, they always were her precious sons. Not like me, dashing off to the other end of the universe, according to her. But we get on OK these days. No grandchildren from me of course. My creations are on people's bookshelves. Six grandkids should be enough, and now Gavin's oldest is pregnant, so she's well pleased to be in line for the great-gran label.'

'Is she still living in that farm cottage and helping out at the farm, or has she retired?'

'No. She left four years ago, after my father died. The farmer gave her their old fishing caravan sited near the clay pits at Barton on Humber. Not much cop, but she loves it. You could call in and see her on your way home. It's only about half a mile detour. You must have noticed the signs before you were approaching the bridge. It would make her day. She always said what a great little kid you were.'

'Did she really?' Hannah tried to cast her mind back to Sally's mother, but an image of a large lady in shabby clothes with a cigarette in her mouth, hurling abuse at her family, did not seem to sit happily with any form of endearment.

The next morning, Sally decided that she would also take the opportunity to see her mother. 'I'll share your company for a bit longer and that'll be nice. I'll go ahead and show you the way. The only problem is she'll expect me to stay the night. Can you imagine me in a caravan? She really ought to be in a retirement home, but she won't hear of it.'

'I know. Ella's like that. I've really got to get to grips with her when I go home. It makes you wonder how we're all going to end up.'

'You'll be completely ga-ga.' Sally shrieked with laughter at the idea.

'Oh! Thanks for that vote of confidence. I can't see you growing old very gracefully. You'll be like the poem about the woman who is going to wear purple and a red hat and learn to spit.'

'I don't think so. I'll leave the poetry to you. I'll stick with the novels, thank you.'

Barton on Humber seemed to be a place which time had forgotten. The small shops along the main street had an old-fashioned air, offering personal service, a facility in short supply in its large neighbour over the water. Sally indicated ahead of them that she was turning right into a small car park. Amazingly, there were two empty spaces next to each other, and they sat in the luxury of midday sunshine, with the car doors open, discussing a plan of action.

'It's a shame not to explore the place,' Sally said. 'It's got quite a history. It was once the biggest port on the Humber, but then Hull grew up on the north bank, taking all of the trade with it. Still, if Barton had grown into a city, it would have been more of a target during the war. Do you mind if we visit the museum at Baysgarth Park? It was once the home of a family called the Nelthorpes but now it belongs to the town. I plan to use it as a background in my next novel but I'm going to do a bit of research first.'

It was good to be out in the sunshine after the rather cold, windy days that had marked the first two weeks of February. The children enjoyed the feeling of intimacy in the small rooms of the museum, finding the small exhibits more interesting than the somewhat political scene of Wilberforce House.

'Barton is a Saxon settlement, built on marshy ground and very vulnerable to anyone who invaded England via the River Humber. Rope-making was a flourishing business at one time, and quantities of beer were brewed here.' Everyone stood still to listen to a tall, thin gentleman who suddenly appeared around the corner of an information stand.

'My first bike was made here at the Hopper factory.' Sally continued the sort of guided tour where the tall man had left off. 'Hopper bikes were quite famous in the days when everyone rode a bicycle to work or school. These days, of course, children expect to go by car, which is a shame, don't you think?'

Leigh and Sally stared at her, and then at each other, before turning and looking pointedly through the window at Sally's sleek, black convertible in the car park. Leigh shrugged his shoulders and Alice laughed.

Hannah would have liked time to wander around the two churches, particularly the ancient Saxon church of St Peter's, but she could see that the children were beginning to tire.

'Let's go and see the ducks,' Sally said, her voice sounding harsh with the effort of enthusing. She was dreading seeing her mother again and would have willingly turned tail and hurried back to her peaceful flat in Hull. She had never wanted responsibility and had wished a number of times just lately that she was back in Australia, inaccessible and family free.

'I thought we were going to see your Mummy,' Leigh said. 'She'll think we've got lost.'

'No. I don't suppose she'll have remembered. She gets mixed up with phone calls. She's very old.' Sally tried to make a joke of it, but Hannah could tell from her face that she did not find it funny. Suddenly she realised that she was seeing the real Sally, someone who couldn't face responsibilities and wanted to run away and hide.

They got back into their respective cars and she followed her friend out of the car park, noticing her sudden accelerations and the number of times she had to brake hard. However would she cope with a husband and an extended family? Poor Sally. There was no longer any satisfaction in gloating over her own strengths. She genuinely felt sorrow, and wanted to gather her friend up along with the children, Emma, Ella and the rest.

However, Sally seemed restored to her usual outwardly cheerful self by the time they reached the grassy banks of the famous ancient clay pits, now filled with clear water and surrounded by trees and scrub; part of an extensive nature reserve

'There's been an awful lot of digging out done here, children. All those pantiles on cottage roofs that you see in Lincolnshire will have been made from Barton clay, and now the flooded clay pits make a wonderful home for ducks, geese and swans, and favourite places for fishermen. It's also where my mother lives. Over there, look.'

Hannah decided to take charge, walking ahead to the rather shabby caravan with the inappropriate name of 'Rose Cottage' painted crudely above the door. The roses, if they had ever existed, were long since smothered by weeds, the dead brown remnants of which tangled up against the scratched paintwork on the caravan sides.

She instantly recognised the round face, which was pressed up against the window. It was Mrs Blenkin. Fat and jolly Mrs Blenkin was how she had once described her. As they drew close, the face disappeared, and moments later the door swung open, revealing the now extremely fat Millie Blenkin.

'Where have you found this lot, Sall?' she shouted. 'I ain't got a biscuit in the 'ouse.'

'It's Hannah Flynn. You remember her? Tennyson Street? Sylvia Flynn's daughter?'

'Good Lord, so it is. Well I never thought I'd see you again. Still, I never thought I would see her again either. It's a wonder you haven't gone to Timbuktu by now.' She wagged a disapproving finger in the direction of her daughter. 'Still, that's our Sall. She never could stick at things.'

'I think Sally's amazing, Mrs Blenkin. You ought to be really proud of her. Did you see the write-up she had in the paper? Our Emma wrote it. She's my youngest.' Hannah was gabbling and she looked desperately towards the children, wanting them to do what she was always telling them not to do when adults were talking.

'You've got a lovely house, Mrs Blenkin,' Leigh said, his sensitivity coming to his grandmother's aid. 'Can we feed the ducks?'

'Of course you can, you little darlings. I've got a big bag of special food. Bread's not good for them, you know.'

The children had taken stock of the situation, positioning themselves on each side of Mrs Blenkin, and holding her hands as they walked along the waterside to the fishermen's peg, where the geese watched and waited for that familiar large figure.

Sally made some tea and found some biscuits in the cupboard. 'She always says she hasn't any. Do you see what I mean about getting her into a home?'

'She still seems pretty capable, Sally. She certainly doesn't look starving, does she? And she's far more with it than Ella. How old is she now?'

'Seventy-six. She was twenty when she had me.'

'That's not very old. My mother would have been the same age if she had lived. Don't write her off yet. You'll regret it one day.'

The drive from Barton to Lincoln was quiet, with very little traffic on the roads. The cathedral came into view a long way before they reached the edge of the city, as they journeyed along the straight Roman road, mile after mile. Eventually, both the children fell asleep, leaving Hannah the freedom to contemplate the weekend.

Emma had tried to be cheerful during their stay, joking with the children, and making a great effort to impress Sally, who, obviously, she regarded as some kind of heroine. Hannah gave a little shrug. How the feet of clay showed themselves as one got older, she thought, and wondered about her own clay feet, particularly concerning her recent impatience with Jack.

The children had been so good and she hoped they had enjoyed the change of surroundings. Her mind couldn't settle on Leigh's 'falling-down episode', as she called it in a later conversation with Jack, when she tried to avoid using any medical terminology, which could possibly dilute the spiritual significance.

She tried to visualise her grandson's face, strange and white, but her attention did not move beyond her driving, her left hand changing to a lower gear, ready to negotiate the last major roundabout. It had all become as elusive as a dream. This often happened, she thought, memories kind of zig-zagging away, as though it was too painful and harmful to dwell on them. Was she like Sally? Did she also want to run away?

6

"At times it is folly to hasten. At other times to delay. The wise do everything in its proper time."

Ovid

Hannah listened to the toilet flushing and the tank filling up for the third time. Ella would be awake next and wanting to get up even though it was only two o'clock. The wind was howling outside, proving the weather forecasters wrong again, and the noise of the old sash windows rattling loudly with each gust of cold air, competed with the creaks and groans of the roof timbers. She strained to hear above the noises of the house. Was he still being sick? 'He's going to the doctor's,' she muttered, 'if I have to drag him there.'

Why were men so awkward? 'It's indigestion.' That was the only comment he made when she asked him how he felt. But it had been going on for a long time now. At first she had put it down to the stress of coping with a broken leg only days after the news of Mark's death, but when she cast her mind back, he had been taking indigestion tablets for a long time before that. In spite of Emma's secret doubts, she was aware of his increasing dependency on alcohol. She had readily made excuses, dismissing it as a fleeting indulgence; a substitute for nicotine. Stopping smoking had been so hard for him. Everybody she knew in her generation, seemed to start smoking during those years after the war, aping their elders. She could remember the cinemas being full of smoke; people puffing away, as they watched their screen heroes doing the same thing. There was no talk of the dangers of passive smoking in those days, and cancer was not reaching the epidemic proportions it apparently was today. The occasional glass of brandy or whisky seemed almost medicinal in comparison.

That was the sound of the toilet flushing again. Minutes later Jack came back into the bedroom and sank down onto his side of the bed, pulling the covers over him and sighing.

'Oh Jack! I wish I could help,' Hannah said, pulling herself up and leaning over to try and see his face beyond the sheet.

'I'm all right,' he murmured. 'Something I've eaten, I expect. Go to sleep.'

'How can I sleep? You're worrying me to death. I'm making an appointment for you tomorrow. You can't go on like this. What if you've got an ulcer? They can soon sort it, you know. You just need the right medication. Those indigestion tablets aren't a bit of good.'

Jack grunted and pulled the covers over his ears. 'Go to sleep,' he said again.

Sleep was impossible for Hannah, although Jack began his incessant snoring less than a minute later, Hannah's sympathy turned inevitably to irritation, followed by guilt at her lack of patience. The sound of Ella rummaging around in her bedroom was the last straw.

The next morning, when Jack had gone to open up the five-barred gate, which led into the customers' car park, Hannah rang the local surgery, and made an appointment for him to see Doctor Broughton. She was glad it was the senior doctor. Jack could not relax with the younger ones. She knew that he didn't have much faith in youth these days. He couldn't keep up with modern ways. Sometimes, she was inclined to agree with him. She'd noticed, as a retired teacher, that standards did seem to be falling both in the written and in the spoken word. English grammar did not have the same importance in the school curriculum, she thought, with memories of parsing and of becoming familiar with parts of speech in her school lessons. Young people these days were very vague about prepositions and pronouns, and as for apostrophes, well it might as well all be in Chinese!

She rang the outside bell to summon Jack and his work mate Mike in for coffee.

'I've made an appointment for you, Jack,' she said, with a defiant note in her voice. She put the coffee in front of him as he sat down at the kitchen table. 'It's the last one this morning, so you should have a bit more space for a chat, and it's Doctor Broughton. You like him, don't you? Good old-fashioned doctor, isn't he? Do you know him?' She turned to Mike Cross, who was looking quizzically at Jack. 'He's lived in the village for years and knows our family better than anyone else, I think. At least our anatomies.'

'Have you got a problem, Jack?' Mike Cross asked. ' I've noticed you don't look very good. I was telling my wife that you're not really back on your feet. Things take longer to heal when you are older. You want to be careful.' He turned to Hannah. 'I keep telling him to let me do the heavy jobs. Still, the weather should be picking up soon. Get this month over, and the days will be a bit longer.'

Hannah was aware of Jack's impatience, and irritated by Mike's trite comments. Why did people say the same things about the weather year after year? She guessed that Mike would be repeating his words to his wife that evening, and she would probably nod wisely and say something about the tulips being well on, in time for the Spalding parade. She turned away from Jack's long stare, and emptied some biscuits out of the packet onto the plate. She wanted to say, 'Oh well, please yourself,' but she knew that he needed her strength, and it was not the time for any petty-mindedness.

However, surprisingly, Jack made no objections, and changed out of his working clothes without being prompted, ready for his twelve-fifteen appointment. He did not even argue when she got into the driving seat of the car. However, he declined her offer to accompany him into the doctor's surgery.

She gave his hand a squeeze. He looked so tired, she thought. Those green eyes, which she had always found so attractive, had lost their sparkle. She longed to make him better and vowed to give him all the time in the world.

A lady, waving a stick and struggling to get around the door, was the last patient before Jack. A few minutes later, Doctor Broughton's smiling face peered into the waiting room through the glass partition. He picked up a bundle of medical notes, and signalled Jack to go into his surgery. Hannah thumbed through the pile of magazines stacked up in an untidy pile on the small table in the middle of the waiting room. There was not much choice and she selected a glossy monthly, its cover promising scintillating articles inside. She turned the pages, staring blankly at the latest fashions, only her sense of hearing on the alert.

The clock on the wall seemed to have developed a loud tick, and the tannoy system was emitting inaudible sounds, defeating the object of supplying a distraction. She strained to hear the latest weather forecast although the weather was the furthest thing away from her mind.

That was Jack's voice now. She stretched forward, and replaced the unread magazine on the table, putting her glasses back in her handbag.

Doctor Broughton followed Jack back into the waiting room.

'I'm arranging an endoscopy for Jack,' he explained. 'There's something going on, but I won't prescribe anything yet other than an anti-acid. As soon as they've taken a look, we'll have a bit more of an idea. It'll probably turn out to be inflammation. We all get problems with acid reflux from time to time, and you've had a lot of worries just lately.'

'What's an endoscopy?' Hannah asked.

'Oh sorry! I don't suppose you've come across that before. It's simply having a look down the digestive tract. It doesn't take long.' He patted Hannah on the arm. 'In the meantime, Jack, just take it easy. We're none of us getting any younger. It's about time we all thought of reducing our workload. I'm looking forward to getting my life back. We're planning a cruise next year.'

'I can think of nothing worse,' Jack said, as they made their way to the car.

'What?'

'A cruise. I've never fancied it, have you? Too much water with nothing else. I'd rather go to the Lake District. You get the best of everything there—water, mountains, villages.'

'Shall we go in the summer then? I'm sure Simon and Marie wouldn't mind taking over for a week.'

Hannah knew that her voice was too loud, and too enthusiastic, yet she couldn't seem to calm it down. The visit to the doctor's had increased the stress and already she wanted to turn the clock back, regretting making the appointment. She had been sure that the doctor would diagnose a small ulcer. She really had no idea what that would mean, but she had heard of ulcers. They seemed to be pretty common. Now she recognised an undercurrent in the doctor's concern and an icy chill suddenly gripped her stomach.

When they reached the car, Jack got into the driving seat and steered out of the car park, back onto the village street. 'The most likely thing is an ulcer or a hernia,' he said, as if reading her mind. 'They'll soon know when they stick this camera down my throat. I'm not looking forward to that. Still, as you're always telling me, it can't be any worse than having a baby.'

Hannah laughed, and began to relax, but then she noticed how thin his fingers were as he gripped the steering wheel, and the icy feeling was back.

Hannah's concern for Jack's health was growing with her awareness of his negativity. She knew without a shadow of doubt that he was becoming alcohol dependent, and begged him to consider his health and her happiness. He assured her that he was only having the occasional drink, but she became familiar with his hiding places, discovering empty bottles and hating him for his deception, yet loving him for his vulnerability in the way a mother first admonishes, and then consoles her child, after an act of foolishness has had life-threatening results.

She did not confide in her family, not wishing to distress them, and made numerous excuses for his increasing need for extra sleep. She was trying to protect everyone including Jack, and in the process she neglected herself. Her tears were so silent that the pain of sobbing became a tight tension in her chest, as she lay awake until the early hours listening to his heavy breathing.

Thankfully, Leigh had settled down into a routine, attending the local village school, and appearing to behave like a normal eight-year-old. But Ella, deprived of her young companion for most of the day, was sinking deeper into dementia. As much as she was loath to let her dear old friend drift away on her own, Hannah knew that Jack was her priority, and she could not risk neglecting either of them. Doctor Broughton had promised his support in recommending that a place should be found in a suitable residential home, and it was just a question of which one.

As no one could imagine Ella in an urban environment, enquiries were made within a ten-mile radius of Norbrooke. There were several establishments that seemed to fit the bill – large country houses adapted for residential care – but Hannah was guarded in her judgement. As Jack often said, proudly quoting Shakespeare, 'All that glisters is not gold.' There were so many things to consider and the main stumbling block of course was Ella's increasing dementia. It had not been diagnosed as Alzheimer's disease, which was some kind of blessing in that a number of homes were not equipped to deal with this condition. However, increasing signs of dementia put her firmly into the nursing rather than solely residential category, and that narrowed the field to a choice of three.

Marie and Simon had offered to take over the running of the nursery during the Easter break. Jack was waiting for an appointment to come through and both he and Hannah were reassured by the passing of several weeks, which seemed to indicate that it couldn't be that urgent. Marie had her doubts, expressing her dissatisfaction with the National Health Service to Simon.

Hannah hoped that Alice's company during the break would distract Leigh from his great concern for Ella. Both the small boy and the old woman seemed to disappear into a secret world as though they were equal in age, and time did not matter. Sometimes, she almost felt that she was drawn in as well. It was that strange feeling of being on the edge of understanding, suddenly clear, and then it all thinning away out of one's grasp.

"Mount Lodge" had sounded promising. The matron had assured her that she had no reservations about dementia. 'Don't worry, my dear,' she'd said on the phone. 'We have a highly trained staff who understand the elderly and all of their problems.'

Hannah had left Ella in Marie's capable hands. She seemed to be almost back in her own character that day and even Leigh had deserted her, wandering off with Alice to look for birds' nests in the garden and checking the progress of the tadpoles in the pond. Such good behaviour prompted Hannah to wonder if all of this nursing home business was necessary. It reminded her of the times when someone in the family was sick, but who made an apparent full recovery when confronted with the doctor. It had happened to her once, she remembered; the dreadful earache that had vanished into thin air.

No. It had to be done, she told herself as she headed down the road towards Mount Lodge. It was less than three miles away and its closeness would be very convenient. They must have passed it hundreds of times on their way to the city, and yet never noticed it. Apparently, it was set back in some trees down a narrow lane.

She went past it and reached the roundabout, knowing that she had missed it. After three aborted attempts, she turned into what seemed like little more than a footpath. The surface of this track was potholed, and the tyres on her car splashed through collected water from the early morning rain. It was not a good first impression and even before she saw the actual place, Hannah had set her mind against it. The dark trees, which crowded close in to the building, appeared to drip their melancholy down the rendered, stained walls. Large quantities of paint had peeled off the window frames, and dreary, now off-white net curtains prevented any view of the inside of the rooms and their occupants.

Hannah parked the car and set off with some reluctance, but curious nevertheless, towards what appeared to be the main entrance. The gravelled path was already ankle-high in weeds. Small seeded nettles, notoriously fierce, brushed against her ankles, piercing her tights, and young thistles promised similar pain in their approaching maturity. She pressed the yellowing plastic doorbell, noticing the peeling red paint on the door, which exposed a previous coat of green.

Well so far 'nil points' she thought, with memories of the Eurovision Song Contest, which had recently been satirised on the television. A young woman in a green uniform opened the door, allowing the strong smell of urine to escape. Hannah wanted to turn around there and then and make her escape from this dreadful environment, but common courtesy made her follow the care assistant across the reception hall to Matron's office. That lady's strong voice penetrated the fabric of the door as she engaged in an apparent phone call.

'Would you mind waiting? She won't be long. She's on the phone.'

The assistant nodded her head in the direction of the chair placed against the wall, and then towards the door. She's shouting as though I am deaf, Hannah thought, wondering whether her own mature looks registered old age in the mind of the carer, or was it a habit this young woman had acquired through work experience. Of course, it could be that she was naturally a loud person. Matron's voice was equally raucous, rising in a crescendo of expletives, before the sound of the telephone receiver being slammed down on the stand indicated the end of the call.

Hannah waited for a few moments before leaving her chair and tapping nervously on the door, anticipating apologies for the verbal outburst. However, the matron's smiling face induced a strange feeling of guilt within her instead, as though she should be apologising for the intrusion. This often seemed to happen. She had long concluded that women of this ilk belonged to a special breed, and it was pointless for her to do anything other than concur on whatever issue arose from this interview. She knew it was a coward's way out, but the sooner she could escape from the company of this woman the better she would feel.

However, her planned indifference was no defence against the obvious horrors of the nursing home lounge. Slumped in shabby armchairs, a group of elderly ladies, as she later explained to Jack, seemed to be in a twilight zone. A distinctive Irish voice begged for help. 'Jesus!' she cried. 'Get me out of here. Are you there, nurse?

Nurse! Oh God! Have they all died? I'll have to do it myself. I'm falling. Oh, I need to go. Help! I need to go.'

Matron strode on, her voice seemingly raised against the inconvenience of the interruption. She flung open a door at the far end of the lounge. 'This is the dining room,' she said. 'They get a good midday meal at twelve, and tea at four-thirty. A cup of cocoa settles them for the night. Most of them are on some kind of sleeping tablet or tranquilliser as part of their medication. I expect your aunt requires them. There is no other answer to dementia. Like that poor soul in the lounge. She never stops. She's due for her injection.'

Ella would be lucky to have a room, in view of the present high demand, Matron pointed out, as her heels clicked along a narrow corridor flanked by unadorned, cream-painted walls. She indicated an open door on the left, somewhat ominously highlighted, Hannah thought, by a large fire extinguisher attached to a bracket on one side. They squeezed in to the small room past a collection of boxes and carrier bags. Apparently the previous occupant had died earlier in the week and relatives were still clearing her possessions, but Hannah could foresee that even after restoration to a state of tidiness, the shabbiness and no doubt the odour that rose from the worn carpet would remain.

Back outside the door, an old lady shuffled towards them. She was dressed for sleep, with a long nightgown, and knitted bed jacket, which hung loosely around the sharp bones of her shoulders and arms. There seemed to be little recognition of anything in her pale blue eyes, yet she appeared to be able to see sufficiently to negotiate the narrowness of the corridor.

'Gladys! What are you doing out here? You know it's not allowed. Nurse will be here soon. Come along. Back you go.'

The matron's voice echoed along the walls and up to the ceiling, harsh and discordant. 'She can't get far. She thinks she is going on a holiday. She ought to be locked in for her own safety, but that's abuse these days. So, what can we do?' She grinned, exposing large front teeth, which reminded Hannah of a horse, and she almost expected a loud whinny to follow.

They made their way back into the lounge. The Irish lady was now in a slumped position like her companions, all protests and apparently bodily needs suppressed by her medication.

'It was dreadful,' Hannah told Marie. 'She couldn't possibly go there.'

Marie frowned. She'd had a hard time with Ella, who had reverted back to her eccentric behaviour almost as soon as Hannah's car had disappeared through the main gate. 'What about the others then?' she asked. 'Did you say there were two more with vacancies?'

'Well one actually. The matron at Belle Vue rang me this morning to cancel my appointment this afternoon. Apparently she had double booked. In any case that place is a fair way off. It would be a forty-mile round trip every time we went to visit. I'd really decided that there was only a choice of two in the first place. You ought to have seen Mount Lodge, Marie. It was dreadful. Truly awful. I can't get the memory of a poor old Irish woman out of my mind. That could be Ella. We'll have to wait and see what tomorrow brings. I've got an appointment at two o'clock at Daisy Cottage.'

Initially, Hannah had been drawn to the name and then told herself that she was being a romantic idiot. She'd rung up the Social Services that morning for some reassurances after the disillusionment of the previous day. It seemed to her that the officer brushed aside her complaints about the standard of Mount Lodge. Was it indifference, she wondered, or had the woman heard it all so many times that she was not listening any more?

'Well, you'll like Daisy Cottage,' she was saying. 'It's been tastefully modernised and is in a lovely setting.'

But what about the residents, Hannah wanted to ask? Do they like it?

Apparently, the matron and owner of Daisy Cottage was in fact called Daisy. The Social Services lady didn't know whether this was a strange coincidence, abruptly closing the conversation with a reminder that places were getting scarce.

A few days previously, Hannah had warmed to the matron's voice while she scribbled down the directions and the allotted time of her appointment. As with the previous place, it was not recommended that Ella should accompany her on this first visit. That was a relief for Hannah, although Marie's heart sank at the thought of another hour or so battling with the old lady's sudden whims.

It had all sounded reassuring then, but so had Mount Lodge, Hannah thought, as she drove along the main road in the direction of Daisy Cottage. She was remembering an article, which she had read that morning in the daily newspaper. It was commenting on a recent television programme; one she had thankfully missed, which had highlighted age abuse. It was strange how one was suddenly bombarded with information. It was the same in Jack's case. Since his initial doctor's visit there seemed to have been a spate of reports on digestive problems, and everyone who knew Jack apparently also knew of someone with the same symptoms.

The wind was buffeting against the side of the car. It was not good weather for Easter, although Hannah reminded herself about the proverbial ill wind and how somebody would benefit. Perhaps it would be her family at Willow Cottage Nursery. Bad weather was not good for business, but it did afford more spare time, and money certainly was not the be-all and end-all of her life at the moment.

Daisy Cottage Nursing Home was about a quarter of a mile off the Gainsborough road, a mile and a half from the nearest village. Hannah looked out for the row of poplar trees, and the old barn, landmarks that Daisy Buckerfield had described. 'A hundred yards further on you will see a sign post on the right. It is a narrow road so take care, but there are passing places,' she'd advised.

This information had not unduly worried Hannah. There were many winding, narrow roads in Lincolnshire. There was no mistaking the row of poplar trees. They stood out like sentinels against the skyline, their purpose to break the force of the wind. Today, they struggled, shivering like zany lollipops, Hannah decided, their fresh leaves twisting to expose their silvery-green backs as shafts of sunlight penetrated the dark clouds.

The sharp right-hand turning, and the sign pointing to Daisy Cottage were clear to see. The passing places were indicated at regular intervals, but, as it happened, they were unnecessary. There was not another vehicle in sight. Unlike the track, which had led to Mount Lodge, this road was well maintained, and the hedgerows promising dense spring growth were a composite of hawthorn, black thorn and wild rose. Winter was still there in the darkness of the branches. There was a marked contrast with the fresh green of the meadows, home for the first lambs of the year, which had lost the initial tenderness of youth, but still stayed close to their mothers, sheltering from the driving gusts of wind.

She could see a sign further along the road, and slowed down. It pointed to a driveway on the right. A board announced Daisy Cottage Nursing Home in big green letters and each corner was embellished with groups of large daisies painted in white and yellow against a dark blue background. Hannah mentally labelled it as 'Mickey Mouse' and contemplated instead the splendid wrought-iron gates, remnants perhaps of a glorious past. The grounds were certainly typical of an important country house. The lawns were a perfect foil for the stone building, and the surrounding parkland was reminiscent of Capability Brown. Trees and shrubs hugged the contours of the gardens and narrow paths wandered through carpets of daffodils and blue speedwell. The gravel crunched under the car tyres as she slowly approached the front entrance to the cottage. Wow! Some cottage, she thought. It reminded her of a large house in Norbrooke, which had been called The Cottage, purely to distinguish it from the even larger main house. By tradition, The Cottage became the home of the grandparents when the next generation took over the responsibility of the estate. Not for them, of course, the small retirement bungalow. The domestic staff usually accompanied them to their new abode, to enable their elderly employers to continue to live in luxury. Hannah guessed that there must have been a similar arrangement here, and no doubt there was a larger house close by, although she didn't recall ever hearing any details of one. Jack would probably know. She would bring him here sometime to see Ella when he was better. He would love these grounds although the gaudy board at the gate would not appeal.

Daisy Buckerfield was exactly as Hannah had imagined her to be. She matched her voice, plump, round-faced and good-natured, if her ready smile and twinkling eyes were anything to go by. Her small office smelt fresh and clean, the desk shining from a regular application of polish. The walls were decorated with delicately patterned wallpaper, and pale blue curtains looked fresh against the small squared windows. Stained and varnished floorboards completed the picture, and Hannah, perched on the edge of the plump, velvet upholstery of the carved-back chair, feeling that she should have paid an entrance fee for the privilege.

After checking the details of Ella's present condition, referring to the doctor's report and the recommendations of the Social Services, funding was discussed and any excesses above the government allowances were indicated. Hannah was impressed by the matron's business-like approach, such a contrast to the slipshod ways at Mount Lodge, but yet she did not feel intimidated or pressured in any way.

'Right,' Daisy said. 'Now we've got all of that out of the way we can have a stroll around. Many of the residents are having an afternoon nap. They like to go up to their rooms after lunch and can rest on their beds if they wish. Chairs are not always comfortable, are they?'

'It all smells so fresh,' Hannah commented as they approached the lounge.

'I'm glad you think so. I do worry. Of course we can't avoid the occasional accidents and one can get used to one's own environment, without realising that it may not please other people. Of course, spending a little extra on the best cleaning products does pay dividends.'

She opened the door into the lounge. Three elderly ladies and one gentleman occupied a cluster of chairs near the large bay window, which allowed a splendid view over the parkland. Daisy waved to them and they waved back before returning their attention to the television set in the corner of the room.

'We won't disturb them. They are the most able of our residents. Many of them are quite poorly and need a lot of care, but they are very courageous. I think they belong to a tough generation. Coping with the hardship of two world wars with the depression slotted in between must have made a lasting impression.'

Hannah nodded. She hadn't really thought about the past quite like that. Ella was born in 1904. She'd gone through a lot of hardship in her life, and she deserved to have some luxury now. Even if she didn't understand what was going on, at least she was going to be comfortable and well fed.

'There are a few bedrooms on the ground floor. None are available at the moment. But it's no problem being higher up. They all have bells and there are two lifts as well as stairs. This is one of our larger rooms with an attached bathroom. It's Mary's. You saw her down in the lounge. She has mobility problems, but otherwise she is pretty independent.'

Hannah looked in, admiring the spaciousness and feeling of luxury. Photographs and personal belongings added a touch of intimacy, giving the room an atmosphere of homeliness. She could just imagine Ella here, with all of her little bits and pieces, as she called them.

Daisy closed the door behind them. 'Now, I'll show you the only spare room we have,' she said. 'It's not very big but at least Ella won't have to share like some do in the large bedrooms. It doesn't always work, particularly if you get two bossy ladies together.' She laughed as she indicated the lift at the end of the corridor. Hannah was nervous in lifts, especially this kind with its criss-crossed metal door, which slid to before the main outside door automatically closed. The space inside was limiting and she could feel the heat from Daisy's plump body, and smell the excesses of her deodorant. Apparently, they were climbing to the second floor, at the very top of the building. The lift gave a jerk as it reached its destination and the lock clicked to indicate that it was safe to open the door. Hannah noticed that it did not match the lower arrangement. Not that it mattered, she thought, impatient with her phobia, yet aware of the perspiration on her upper lip. She would use the stairs next time. But would there be a next time, she wondered?

Her concern began to increase. The whole atmosphere had changed on this floor. The narrow corridor, which allowed access along the length of the attic, was illuminated by a series of small skylights, the glass by its grimy appearance probably difficult to clean. The rooms were positioned on either side of this corridor, reminding Hannah of a typical hotel lay-out. The paintwork around the doors was chipped and the carpet had certainly seen better days. Daisy, noticing her client's hesitation and her quick intake of breath, was quick to apologise. 'This floor is in need of some refurbishment as I'm sure you have noticed. It is a high priority but funds are tight, and we don't want to drop our general care standards. You know, we feel that food and cleanliness are more necessary than surroundings, but of course it is close to the top of our list.'

They had reached a door numbered twenty-nine and she stopped speaking, turning the key in the lock. As the small room came into view, it reminded Hannah of the bedroom in Eastfield Cottage, where she had first been evacuated as a child, an image of which still appeared from time to time in her worst nightmares. A narrow bed was positioned behind the door and a small pine dressing table and matching wardrobe stood next to each other on the opposite wall, limiting the space in between. A naked bulb hung on a flex from the ceiling and the green striped curtains were like narrow pigtails along either side of the dormer window.

Could she inflict this on Ella? She was not used to luxury, but she loved the sunshine. This would seem like a prison to her. The anxiety was back, and with it the sense of guilt.

'You can bring some of her possessions,' Daisy Buckerfield was saying. 'That would brighten it up. Obviously we'll provide the basics, and it shouldn't be long before we get another vacancy.'

She means before someone dies, Hannah thought unreasonably. She went to the window. This room looked out over the back of the cottage. It seemed that construction work was in progress, and piles of building materials competed with dustbins and a cement mixer for space.

'That's the old stable block,' Daisy explained. 'I am having it converted into one- and two-bedroomed units for people who need a little more security but are still reasonably independent. The rent can include nursing care if required. They should be popular.'

So there was money to spare, Hannah thought, and no doubt large profits to be made.

'I'll let you know,' she said, as they shook hands at the door of the office.

She could scarcely concentrate on driving along the narrow road, as she left Daisy Cottage behind her. She kept trying to visualise Ella in that tiny room, staring down at building works, or listening for the sounds of steps on the corridor. She would be lost.

The Daisy woman – she couldn't remember her name now – was she Mrs or Miss? – oh well, she had said that Ella would soon forget the present day, and that most of the residents lived in the past. So where in her past would Ella think she was? That thought certainly was no consolation. But what else could they do? She tapped her fingers on the steering wheel as she waited for pedestrians to clear the crossing.

'Don't leave it too long,' the Matron had advised. 'There is a shortage of rooms at the moment, especially for dementia cases.'

Is that how we end up, Hannah thought, a 'case'?

'You really must reach a decision, Mother,' Simon advised later. 'Ella needs protection and so does everyone else.' He glanced meaningfully across at his wife, who was still suffering from Ella's attempts to wash the kitchen floor with a very wet mop. 'It's not only in the house,' he continued, 'she could wander off onto the road and cause a traffic accident. We can't watch her all the time, can we? I know we all love her, and it's going to be hard, especially for you, but maybe it won't be hard for her. You're beating yourself up about this, Mum, but sometimes there are no answers, you know. Sometimes we have to accept things. Perhaps she'll be quite contented in a world of her own, who knows? The matron sounds very reasonable from what you've said. That first place has given you a bad impression. I'm sure that you of all people could make that little room cosy with some of her treasures and some pretty bedding and curtains. After all, Ella's never had a huge bedroom, has she? It's not been stately living, has it?'

Hannah glared at him. 'You've none of you had a bad life,' she snapped. 'I know you didn't have many luxuries but…'

'Oh Mum!' Simon interrupted. 'I'm not criticising Ella's room, or your past. I'm just trying to get you to put things into perspective.'

'We'll see. What would you like for supper? There isn't much choice but beggars can't be choosers.'

Marie frowned at Simon, and shook her head. 'Come on, Alice,' she said. 'Let's peel some spuds.'

After a great deal of deliberation, the family decided that Daisy Cottage was the best option for the time being. As Jack said, 'Nothing need be set in stone, and really at the end of the day it's Ella's physical well-being that matters. Happiness is another kettle of fish.'

The completion of the necessary paper work and financial arrangements gave everyone a breathing space and eased the transition of Ella and her possessions from Norbrooke to Daisy Cottage, diluting the trauma into daily anxieties rather than one big pain. Ella sailed happily through the week, sometimes being sweetness itself, and increasing Hannah's feelings of guilt and misgivings, but then a day later creating havoc in the kitchen, her actions threatening the welfare of the other occupants of Willow Cottage.

Leigh had the knack of calming her down, but he needed to be a child and relax in the school holiday. Hannah knew that the burden was too great for his tender age and conversely for Jack's advancing years. She appreciated Simon and Marie's help in the garden, and Alice was company for Leigh, but everyone needed feeding and, although it was a combined effort, she felt that the ultimate responsibility was hers. Being at the centre of family life had always seemed a natural function and vital to her sense of security, but now she felt drained and had an overwhelming desire to escape to the isolation of her bedroom.

Simon's remarks about Ella's comparatively humble status in life still rankled in Hannah's thoughts. She knew that he was only trying to help, but deep down his words had struck a chord. It was true that Ella had always been put to the bottom of the pile, so to speak. She had never asked for much in her life and consequently had not received much. It had always been an 'Oh good old Auntie Ella, she won't mind' kind of philosophy, Hannah thought. Well, good old Auntie Ella was going to have the best now, with no expenses spared.

A new mattress was ordered for the single bed, and two complete sets of sheets, pillowcases, duvet covers and frilly valances with matching curtains were parcelled up ready to take to the nursing home.

Marie secretly wondered about the practicalities of personal bedding arrangements. She knew from her grandmother's stay in a nursing home that daily accidents entailed the frequent stripping of beds, and she guessed that Ella's pretty sheets would end up in someone else's room before the month was out. But Ella would appreciate the comfort of a good mattress, in spite of the hardness of the obligatory waterproof covers.

Ella had spent her final Easter Sunday and the holiday Monday surrounded by the only 'family' she now had. She wandered around, enjoying her involvement in the preparation of food, oblivious to the planned changes in her future. Her possessions were packed into the shabby suitcases, which had accompanied her from Hexham the previous year. A photograph of her late husband Jim had been newly framed and was destined to occupy a prominent place on her bedroom wall.

She eyed her suitcases standing ready in the hall, and rocked with excitement. 'I can't wait to get to Skeggy,' she said over and over again to anyone who was in earshot. These words both upset and amused Hannah. Ella had gone to Skegness for her annual holiday, every year after the end of the war, and had met Jim there. They were such happy years for her at Willow Cottage with Aunt Kate and Uncle Harry. How quickly time had moved on, Hannah thought, but then Ella was moving it back again as easily as turning back the pages of a book. Would she miss the sea and the sand? Perhaps not. It was the change of company she'd always enjoyed, and eating meals that she had not cooked. She'd always enthused over the lovely flowerbeds along the front. No. Now she came to think about it, sand and sea had never come into the equation.

'Well,' Hannah said philosophically to Jack, 'time will tell. We've done our best.'

Jack watched the car pulling out onto the village road, his face settling back into weariness now that it was no longer necessary, for the next hour at any rate, to play the role of head of the family.

Hannah was amazed at the way Ella settled into her new surroundings. It seemed to be almost a relief for her aunt to be in a confined space, as though she needed to reduce her boundaries in tune with her diminishing capabilities.

Daisy Buckerfield, with her great wisdom and compassion, instructed the care workers to show Ella some aspect of the catering arrangements occasionally, or allow her to put fresh fruit in the dish in the middle of the dining table. She did not consider that the response to child-like whims was in any way patronising. It could only be construed as a form of abuse when it was accompanied by derision and lack of courtesy, Daisy explained. 'Any sign of abuse in my establishment,' she said, 'and it's instant dismissal.'

After several visits to the nursing home, Hannah began to look forward to sharing a cup of tea with Daisy Buckerfield, either before or after spending time with Ella. During one of their chats, Daisy confessed to being fifty-eight in two days time, and they talked about their youth, delighting in sharing memories of post-war life. All the old familiar anecdotes, which had not surfaced for a long time, were given an airing away from the raised eyebrows, sighs or violin-playing actions of each family.

An outside observer would recognise the need of both of them for a companion, no longer linked by demands of the flesh, but by a code of sisterhood. Although they were regarding the approaching age of sixty with some dread, they longed to be frivolous; to let their hair down; to kick up their heels. Daisy had one son, whose partner, with an established career had no desire to procreate. 'Consequently,' she said, 'they have left their childhood a long way behind them, and expect me to be an older version of themselves. What they'll do when I reach my second childhood, I dread to think.'

Hannah told her of Sally's fears about her responsibility for her mother, and was surprised when Daisy sympathised with her friend. 'It's obvious that she worries a great deal about her mother in spite of her seemingly callous attitude. You know it's very true about blood being thicker than water.' She paused, realising that she had touched on a raw nerve. 'I'm not implying that you don't care deeply about Ella, but I'm sure your mother would have been special. What I am trying to say is don't be too hard on your friend, and I am digging a big hole for myself. Time to shut up, I think!'

'Emma's had a scan,' Hannah said, changing the subject. 'She would like to come home. She still hasn't got a job and she's not coping very well, But I don't know how Jack would handle it.'

'I've just had a brilliant idea! You know, I could do with some help. I bet she's pretty good with paperwork, and she could always live here. One of the new units is ready for letting. Her money is as good as anyone else's.' Daisy's voice was rising with excitement.

'But she's got less than five months to go,' Hannah protested. 'You don't really want to share in the late stages of pregnancy, do you?'

'Why not? My son's not giving me the chance to get broody by proxy, so Emma will be doing me a favour.'

'I'll give her a ring tonight. It would be great to have her so close and without putting extra pressure on Jack. I could always tell him that she is working for social services, which would be true in a way, and sounds quite impressive. Not that your place is not impressive. Oh! You know what I mean. It's my turn to dig a hole now.'

7

Father Time… "hurrying us through blissful days, how light his tread. Or dragging our feet in emptiness, with future dread of more to follow. Watching clock, tick-tock, unending motion. In sips and swallows, bitter-sweet, this is his daily potion."

Jacqueline Kemp

Jack listened to Hannah's hurried explanation concerning Emma's latest plans. He always recognised his wife's nervousness by the speed with which she spoke, and knew now that she was evading the truth. She headed for the bathroom, giving him no time to comment.

Do they think that men are stupid, he asked himself? He'd seen the signs of pregnancy so many times in his life, and had noticed Emma's wan face and her apparent stomach upsets during the Christmas break. He had guessed that Hannah's sudden decision to take the children to Hull was a kind of 'red herring', and he had reservations about Sally Blenkin. In his opinion, her way of life, with her feminist issues, threatened the status quo.

Still, he reasoned, he was not being honest either. He knew that he was drinking too much. The addiction had crept up on him over the last few years. He couldn't think why. But then Mark's death had knocked him sideways and everything seemed to have changed since then. Obviously, they couldn't leave Leigh in America, and he was a good child at the moment, but what would he be like in ten years time? And now this business with Emma. No one had mentioned a man in tow. 'What a mess these young people get their lives into,' he said, his thoughts spilling over into speech. How he longed for a return to his own youth these days. We rebelled, didn't we, he thought, and still wanted to, but all the pleasures of the flesh somehow became diminished with the advancing years. Young people cope with lack of sleep, and over-indulgencies, but suddenly a bad habit becomes an obsession, a crutch to get one through the days. He reproached himself again for his weakness, but nevertheless made his way to the greenhouse and his bottle of whisky.

The hospital appointment had arrived in the post that morning. He was instructed to attend at the Endoscopy Unit the following Tuesday. He was not looking forward to an endoscopy, having been enlightened about the procedure by well-meaning acquaintances, who'd had the same thing or had learnt the graphic details in conversations with friends or relations. He smiled, without humour, his eyes dull with anxiety, as he thought of Hannah's answer to all discomforts. 'It can't be as bad as having a baby. You men don't know the half.' She'd always maintained that the human race would have long since become extinct if men had the babies, and yet she was the one who'd wanted four children. He would have been quite happy with one.

Hannah gave Jack's hand a squeeze, reassured by the returning pressure of his fingers. The surge of emotion that travelled through her body reminded her of when they were in their early twenties. In those days, reunions and partings were a roller-coaster of physical highs and lows.

They were directed by the receptionist to a group of chairs positioned out of sight of the main waiting area. An elderly couple occupied two of the seats. The woman nodded in acknowledgement, but her companion, a thin, bald-headed man, stared at the floor, his hands tightly clasped on his lap.

Hannah sighed. 'These places are so depressing,' she whispered to Jack. 'You'd think they could brighten them up a bit.'

'What, and spend more money? Then they would get it in the neck for wasting the taxpayers' hard-earned cash, when apparently there aren't enough beds or nurses to go around.'

Jack's comments or perhaps the harshness of his voice, seemed to alarm the bald-headed man who jumped to his feet, and began to walk across the beige-coloured floor tiles. The woman made tutting noises and reached across to tug at his sleeve. 'He's going deaf,' she said. 'I don't know. Old age doesn't do us any favours, does it?'

Hannah smiled out of politeness. She wanted to point out that she herself was only fifty-six, but she didn't want to seem discourteous. Instead, she merely nodded, giving Jack a little nudge with her arm.

The man was still standing, looking bemused, when moments later a nurse appeared around the corner with a wad of notes in her hand.

'Alfred Ludd,' she announced, looking from one man to the other.

'That's him. That's Alf.' The woman pointed at her husband as though he was some kind of an exhibit, Hannah thought, with wry amusement.

The nurse grinned affably. 'Come along, dear,' she said. 'The doctor's ready to see you, and you are Jack Clayton.' It was a statement of fact rather than a question, followed by a request to follow her for the weighing, and the checks on the heart rate, blood pressure and oxygen levels, which preceded the investigation, and were recorded on the next sheet of notes.

Hannah followed Jack into a curtained area enclosing a bed, and helped him into a blue cotton wrap that looked well used in its crumpled state. Jack's main concern was his lack of dignity, and he sat on the edge of the bed, his hands pressing into the mattress, as though he was preparing for take-off. The sounds coming from an adjacent room were far from reassuring. Hannah allowed her thoughts to wander to Ella. Daisy had rung that morning to wish Jack well, and the conversation had moved on to Ella's increasing problems and the latest developments in Emma's pregnancy. She sighed and Jack told her to go and get herself a coffee. She said that she would do no such thing, and returned to 'juggling the family balls', as Marie would say.

After quite a lengthy wait, Jack was called into the adjoining room. Hannah heard the door bang to behind him, and crossed her fingers. Her ears strained for the slightest noise, but the silence was broken only by the voice of the woman, who had briefly made their acquaintance in the waiting room. Apparently, they were now in the next curtained area. 'Come on, Alf,' Hannah heard her say. 'Anyone would think you were dying. Good God! It's not as if you've had the knife! Not like what I did.'

Hannah heard him say something about being half choked, and his lady retaliating sarcastically with, 'Anybody would think they'd cut your bleeding throat. You'll drive me to that one of these days.'

'Here you are, dear.' A nurse's voice intervened. 'A nice cup of tea. It was two sugars, wasn't it?'

'Three,' Alf said.

'Two's plenty for him, duck. I don't suppose I could have one, could I? He's doing my head in.'

Hannah stored the conversation up in her memory, ready to recount it to Jack on the way home. However, it was to remain an untold story.

A few minutes later, Jack's face appeared around the curtain. Hannah stood up and reached for his shirt and jacket.

'Well, that didn't take long, did it, sweetheart? You were very brave. I couldn't hear a sound.' Hannah lowered her voice to a whisper. 'You did better than him next door.'

She stopped her nervous chatter, suddenly noticing a look of defeat on Jack's face.

'What's the matter?' She helped him on with his shirt.

'Irregular cells,' he said. 'He wants to speak to us both after I'm dressed and had a cup of tea.'

'Irregular cells? What does that mean?'

'Apparently something there they don't like the look of.'

'So, is it an ulcer then?' Hannah guided his arm into his jacket sleeve.

'They don't commit themselves, do they? I expect I'll have to have more tests.'

They were directed into another room, which had a melancholy air, Hannah thought, as though it was especially designed for sadness. The nurse unsmilingly offered them a cup of tea, wedging the door open to allow in more air and light, but even so the atmosphere hung heavily and darkly around them.

The sound of footsteps heralded the arrival of the doctor. He perched on the edge of a side table and glanced down at the medical notes in his hand before beginning to speak.

The word 'cancer' stood out from the technical details as though it was written in capital letters and suspended in the space above his head. The shock of hearing it caused a sharp pain to travel across Hannah's heart. She watched his lips moving, and his expressions altering as he emphasised certain words or glanced down to look at his notes. Her gaze was steadfast, her muscles immobilised as he painted the deadly scenario.

She heard the words, 'major operation', 'risk of death on the operating table', 'chemotherapy', 'no chance of a cure', 'maybe a short respite', 'side effects', 'sickness, inability to eat', 'back after four years,' Hannah had stopped listening. Her agony had reached saturation point. Jack's voice brought her attention back to the dark melancholy room and its three occupants.

'What if I do nothing?'

'Perhaps six months. One year at the most,' came the answer.

A sob caught at Hannah's throat. The doctor turned his gaze towards her as though surprised by her intrusion, she thought. She had the bizarre feeling that she must apologise. 'Sorry, it's the pain of it,' she mumbled.

'Oh there's no pain,' he assured her. 'You just can't eat.'

She stared at him, wanting to scream, but instead she allowed the anger to infuse into her body, taking away the strength in her limbs, and reducing her voice to a whispered, 'Oh I see.'

Could he be playing such an everyday role that he had become desensitised in the process? Surely it was not indifference, she reasoned? But then perhaps it was the only way he could cope. The only way he could obey the rules of the medical profession, whose members were obliged to tell the truth even if that truth was mind-crippling. Apparently it was all about the danger of being taken to court for misrepresentation. These thoughts buzzed around in her head, as they walked along the corridor.

'Way out,' Jack said, pointing to the sign, and guiding Hannah left at the next junction. Those were the last words he spoke until they arrived back home, and Hannah did not break the spell of his silence. It was as though their minds had been blown away, both afraid of the debilitating effects of negativity.

Jack stared ahead, driving like an automaton, Hannah thought, his knuckles white against the blackness of the steering wheel. Soon, the throbbing of the engine and the motion of the car induced in Hannah an overwhelming urge to sleep, and she awoke with a start as the car swung in through the gates of Willow Cottage.

The sound of tyres crunching in the gravel brought Simon and Marie out of the house to greet them, but they too were reduced to silence, as the stony expression on each face inhibited curiosity. The only question asked in the sanctuary of the kitchen was the inevitable one for all occasions – 'Do you want a cup of tea?'

'I must go to the bathroom first,' Jack said. He did not look at Hannah, but she knew that she was expected to be the harbinger of his bad news – his despair. She waited until the kitchen door closed behind him before mouthing the word 'cancer'.

Marie's hand began to shake, as she poured the tea into Hannah's cup, and she exclaimed over the resultant spillage on the clean white cloth. The rather mundane necessity of mopping it up became a brief distraction, giving both of the women a narrow breathing space in which to compose themselves. But for Simon, gripping the back of the kitchen chair, and staring unseeingly along the drive to the willow trees, there was no escape; his mind was in turmoil, and unusually in tune with that of his father.

The change in Jack's attitude was both inspiring and disconcerting. He had had a long, private chat with Doctor Broughton, in which they had discussed all the manifestations of cancer of the oesophagus. Jack refused to talk about the future with his family. All of his energies now were directed to the present. He abandoned alcohol, and focussed his mind, already sharpened by the abstinence, on the path which he had chosen to take; a non-invasive form of treatment, without the dangers and the horrors of a major operation, and the chemotherapy with its inevitable aftermath of sickness and a shattered life.

As a nature lover, and a gardener, he had always taken an interest in herbalism, maintaining that nature provided a cure for everything if mankind was wise enough to recognise it. Accounts of rain-forest dwellers, who extracted their medicine from the trees and plants that grew in great profusion around them, were often discussed by the family in the lee of television programmes or newspaper reports. It now became part of a serious study. Books were borrowed from the library, and Simon used his developing computer skills to source the latest information on the World Wide Web. A space was made in the kitchen cupboards for pots, packets and bottles of vitamin and mineral substances.

An holistic clinic in London was recommended by a friend, and a series of weekly appointments was set up. At first, Jack insisted on driving the car to Newark to pick up the London train. Apparently it was all part of the positive attitude, which he must maintain in order for his body to heal. Hannah travelled with him, and, in a strange way at first, enjoyed this weekly journey. There was such intimacy between them. It was not like being joined at the hip, she thought, reminded of the times when she had used that modern expression and of her professed cravings for severance. She attempted to exonerate herself from that guilt by blaming it on the after-affects of the menopause, but she knew that it was more complex. Now, it was as though their very souls had merged into a single entity. She would later describe it as pure, unconditional love.

The holistic practitioner tried various methods in his dedicated mission to do what many of the medical profession described as a complete waste of time in the halting of cancer. Hypnosis, deep meditation and visualisation, controlled breathing exercises, and 'hands-on' healing regularly featured in the two-hourly session. An alkaline diet was discussed, which prohibited acidic foods such as red meat and encouraged a high vegetable intake, and a total abstinence from alcohol.

At first, Jack thrived on this intense therapy, and Hannah was lifted by his positive attitude into a bizarre state of euphoria, loving him so intensely that the rest of the world seemed outside of their unity. She worked automatically through everyday chores, emotionally indifferent to her family's needs.

However, it began to become apparent that although the treatment was maintaining the rest of Jack's body in a surprisingly good level of health, the tumour was advancing and constricting the passage of food. They both knew this, although Jack did not offer to discuss it, and Hannah needed to come to terms with the reality, feeling that she was now clinging by her fingertips on the edge of Jack's optimism.

'Dr Broughton is like the rock of Gibraltar,' she told Simon and Marie, who came every weekend to help Mike in the garden. 'He is amazed at Jack's weight maintenance, but has suggested that the hospital could facilitate the swallowing action by a common medical procedure.'

'It's just to give you time for the natural healing to work,' she explained to Jack. 'But, you know, it's not too late for some chemotherapy and the operation is still an option.'

He reluctantly agreed to the placing of a stent, which would open up the digestive tract, but made no comment about Hannah's other proposals, other than to say that he had no intentions of becoming a permanent invalid, and that the body was capable of healing itself.

He changed the subject to commenting on the weather forecast, and Hannah turned away, blinking against the tears, which threatened to overflow her eyes, and hurting with the pain of tension in her chest.

Paying the holistic healer's fees was becoming a nightmare in itself. On the sixth visit, Hannah sat in the waiting room reading a magazine, and occasionally glancing up to study a newcomer, either smiling in recognition, or looking away in the initial contact. In the early days, she had enjoyed sharing small talk, but today her mind was preoccupied with family finances and she did not welcome any intrusions. At first, it did not seem to matter how much anything cost. How do you put a price on life, they'd all thought? But so much of their money was tied up in the business and it depended on how much they could release. Simon had come up with the idea of selling his house and the three of them moving in. He could raise a mortgage and, at the end of his college year in June, could run the nursery full-time.

Hannah had not passed this idea on to Jack. She knew what his reaction would be and she would feel the same. It reminded her of an old lady called Bessie at the nursing home, who sat wrapped around in a large shawl, rocking comfort into her old bones and murmuring over and over, 'Cast aside. I've been cast aside.' Apparently, according to Emma, who often spent time with the residents when she wasn't doing secretarial work for Daisy, the old lady used to run a garden ornament business, which was now in the control of her son. Her daughter-in-law, who, it seemed, Bessie disliked, was in charge of the financial side, and had made it quite clear that her mother-in-law was getting in the way. How would Jack feel at this stage? Would he feel cast aside?

Hannah stared at the large red-faced gentleman who had just entered the waiting room. He looked wealthy, but certainly not healthy, and how wise was he to put his faith in alternative medicine, she wondered, her mind jumping back to the old familiar adage? He sank down into the deep leather sofa, and reached across for the copy of *The Times*. She glanced at her watch. There was a good half-hour left yet. She got up and walked into the entrance hall of what was once a very smart London house. She could see life going on beyond the front door; people hurrying by on their way to keep appointments, or anticipating spending money in a large store. It had all seemed so exciting the first time that they had travelled by taxi from King's Cross railway station to the clinic, passing theatres which she associated with the television, like the London Palladium, and seeing advertisements for local attractions on the large bill boards. It was a very long time since she had been to London, and the noise of the traffic, and the constant motion was in direct contrast to the stillness of the Lincolnshire countryside.

Now, as she wandered along the street, glancing up at the top windows, in the tall elegant facades, she idly wondered if they were Georgian or mid-Victorian. Did time really matter? Did anything matter?

The fitting of the device had given Jack a new lease of life, in that meal-times were less stressful, and he could share in the daily family routine without embarrassment for everybody. Four months passed by on a new level of expectations, although as the family really knew, nothing could ever be the same again. Hannah experienced days of deep depression, when life seemed to be on hold, as though they were treading water.

The family, with their own personal agendas, no longer seemed part of the big picture in Hannah's mind. They were now well and truly part of their own big pictures, putting down their roots. She likened them to baby spider plants, dangling for a long time from the parent plant, growing into maturity and eventually touching down into the waiting soil.

Daisy Cottage had become Emma's rooting place. Daisy Buckerfield revelled in the role of a kind of surrogate grandmother-to-be. Her great affection for Emma was very apparent, and as the days of the pregnancy progressed, she indulged her every whim. The residents, who were still able to relate to pregnancy and with strong memories of their own experiences, became great-grandparents in waiting. Hannah was contented for her daughter to grow at her own pace. Health was a major issue now. Ambition could wait.

Jack was spending less and less time in the garden. He enjoyed pottering in the greenhouse, especially during the summer evenings, when the sun had lost its strength. Simon and Marie, together with Alice, had moved in at the end of the summer term, and there was much discussion between them and Hannah about future arrangements. They could not include Jack in these discussions. They knew that it would be asking him to accept failure. He refused to acknowledge defeat even though, in spite of the various treatments, the terminal nature of his illness was becoming more and more apparent.

As Hannah said one day, when she was confiding with Daisy during her weekly visit to see Ella, 'We are all treading on egg shells. Poor Jack. How can we discuss his death with him, when he has such a determination to survive?'

Daisy had tried to comfort her. 'I am amazed on a daily basis,' she said. 'The human body, in all of its parts, has such a will to live. Look at your Ella for example. OK, so she has retreated into a world of her own, but it seems to be a very good world; half in and half out of reality. A happy compromise in my opinion. We all need to compromise. There are no guarantees. Have you ever thought, God forbid it, that your life could end tomorrow? That you could go before Jack. That's a sobering thought, isn't it? But like I said, there are no guarantees. Of course you need to prepare to move on, but in the meantime, take the best out of life. One day, I may share my moving-on kind of days with you. At the moment I'm too caught up with the present.'

Although Hannah had temporarily abdicated from her role as the matriarch, in as much as she did not offer any practical help, she was aware, of course, that everyone's lives had their complications.

Apart from Simon and Marie's feelings of insecurity, and Emma's all-consuming fears and thrills of pregnancy, she had noticed that Rachel was depressed, and promised herself that she would put aside some time for her elder daughter She guessed that the worry over Alice was preying on her mind, and perhaps she was broody. After all, the twins were at school and Emma was getting all the limelight.

Rachel, indeed, was very depressed. Since the twins' involvement with the abduction, she felt a constant need to apologise, avoiding eye contact with Marie and taking little part in family discussions. It would seem to a stranger that she lacked affection for her parents, yet she desperately wanted to gather them up and smother them with kisses. She had been devastated by the news of her father's illness, locking away the agony in an all-consuming silence.

The feeling of possible rejection, and lack of self-worth had spilled over from her relationship with Steve. From the beginning, she had been a victim rather than a partner, and had been afraid to break off the engagement, as his parents launched themselves into all the wedding arrangements, discussing every expense, it seemed, with a kind of gloating pride. She had protested at first that it was not their place to pay. Her father would be embarrassed, and, in any case, she preferred to have a quiet wedding, with her sister and her little niece Alice as bridesmaids. Her wishes and those of her parents had been completely over-ruled. When she looked back on those times, she despised herself for her cowardice. Now that she no longer loved Steve, she was becoming preoccupied both in soul-searching, and making accusations, neither of which could be recommended for allaying depression.

They think the sun shines out of his every orifice, she thought bitterly, gaining a little satisfaction from this modern-day kind of philosophy. She wouldn't have dared to say that to his face. Her right hand wandered to her left wrist, still aching from the tight grip of his fingers that morning, when she had attempted to pick up the phone to ring her brother. It had not been a huge issue. In fact she couldn't remember now what the argument had been about, but it was in front of Karl and Kirstie, and something had snapped inside her head.

It wasn't the first time he had hurt her. She had run out of fingers to count the quarrels that had culminated in both physical as well as mental pain. But yet she'd described it as the last nail in the coffin of their marriage. That particular expression had upset her as soon as it had come into her head, and now it would not go away. How could she leave him and where would she go? Certainly, she couldn't go to Willow Cottage, when her mother was preparing for widowhood, and Simon and Marie were shouldering so much responsibility.

In any case, she could not bear the idea of leaving her children. She guessed that they would immediately be taken over by her in-laws. They doted on their only grandchildren, and constantly interfered with her attempts to give them a good perspective on life. It was obvious that Steve had learnt arrogance at his mother's knee, she thought. If she walked out now, he would fight her all the way for custody. She had no proof of his cruelty. It would be his word against hers. He lived in a world of male arrogance and she felt threatened not only by him, but by his friends and family, all bloated by a life of affluence.

She sank down on to the settee, and closed her eyes. Perhaps after Dad's died, she thought, and burst into tears.

Emma emptied out the baby clothes from the large drawer at the bottom of her wardrobe, and spread them out on the bed. Whatever the sex, she had decided that her baby would be dressed in white. She hated the modern trend to put newborn babies in bright colours. Already, she felt very protective towards her child, revelling in the complete possession, with no one else making any claims, and not having the inconvenience of a man about the place. Daisy understood perfectly, she said, although she didn't explain why, and Emma didn't like to ask.

She carefully folded a little matinee jacket, and pressed it to her face, smelling the new wool, and enjoying the softness against her skin. At that moment, her baby kicked and stretched, pressing its heels up under her ribs and causing her to arch her back in an effort to accommodate the movement. Although she had no proof, she was convinced that it was a girl. She also knew that its hair would be thick and dark. She had dreamed of this child so many times. Her mother understood. Dreaming was something they all understood in their family, she reflected. Some people never dreamed or even day-dreamed. How dull their lives must be.

A knock on the door brought her mind back from the future. It was Jane Dry, the new care-worker, on her way home, after working a late shift at Daisy Cottage. Emma had invited her to call in to borrow a book, about which she had enthused during a coffee break.

'How's it gone today? Have you had a good shift?' Emma noticed how Jane's mouth turned up at the corners, and how her eyes twinkled with good humour.

'Yes, I'm getting to know the routine. There are some right characters in here, aren't there? We've been having a good laugh.'

'Be careful what you say. Daisy won't have anyone made fun of.'

'Oh I know that. I wouldn't dream of it, but you have to laugh at life, don't you? Otherwise, you'd spend all your time crying.'

For a moment, the happiness left her eyes, and Emma saw the face of a woman who had said goodbye to her youth, her face tumbling into signs of fatigue, as the laughter lines became less apparent.

'Old George is a character, isn't he? He hides his secret weapon under the bedclothes.' Jane laughed at Emma's expression. 'His long thin arm,' she explained, her face screwing up in a kind of elfish mischief. 'It comes out as though it's possessed, ready to grab the nearest leg, or the plumpest bum. You want to steer well clear of him. Poor old chap! He must long to return to the days of his lustful youth!'

Emma shuddered at the thought, and picked up the book, which she had placed in readiness for its collection. 'I'm sure you'll enjoy this,' she said. 'It's about social life during the First World War, and was written by an old friend of mine. Please take care of it, won't you? She's going to come over when my baby is born. Did I tell you I'm calling my little girl Poppy? I dreamed about the name last night. I've asked Sally to be a godmother, so you may get to meet her if she stays here overnight.'

'That sounds great. I can't wait to meet her or Poppy. That's a lovely name. It reminds me of the summer time, when all the bees are looking for honey, and everything smells delicious.'

For a few seconds, Emma noticed a return of the signs of fatigue on her face, this time with shades of sadness, and she held back from asking whether she had any children, a question which had been on the tip of her tongue.

'Thanks for the book. It looks just down my street. Sally Blenkin. That's a good name.' Jane opened the book and read the brief synopsis on the inside of the sleeve. 'These historical novels need plenty of research, I guess. It would be beyond me, but if ever she needs to know about the life of a home help she can come to me. I could tell her a tale or two about the people I used to visit. One old girl we had to look after slept with all her possessions in a big double bed. Pots, pans, ornaments, in fact everything but the kitchen sink! Two of us had to go at the same time, as she tried to stab one home help. She fed the wild birds, which she enticed through the window. She showed me a dead bird in her handbag. She wouldn't part with it. There were bird droppings everywhere. Poor old soul! She insisted that she was cousin to the Queen. Perhaps she was one of that lot. She spoke very posh. I was told that she had a very high-up job when she was younger. You'd never think it if you saw the state of her flat. There was rotting food, and junk everywhere. Still, who knows?' Jane shrugged her shoulders.

Emma watched her walking to the car park, and had the powerful feeling that Jane Dry was going to play an important part in all of their lives. It was apparent that she certainly called a spade a spade, she thought. The residents would love her kind of honesty, based very much on compassion. There was such warmth in her personality and her shortness in stature did not appear to handicap her in any way. 'Five foot and a peanut,' she'd said, as Emma had filled in her details for the records. Her green uniform had needed to be shortened by a good couple of inches. The colour set her apart from the trained nursing staff but, as far as the residents were concerned, she was 'Nurse' along with everyone else, including Emma.

'The next thing will be Emma's baby,' Marie said. 'God knows how she's going to cope without a partner. It's so irresponsible, especially these days.' She clattered the cups and plates into the sink with little regard for their fragility. She had expressed these doubts and opinions a number of times during the last few weeks, and Simon grunted irritably.

'That's her problem,' he retorted. 'We all have our cross to bear.'

He was feeling very tired after a disturbed night of listening to Jack tossing and turning in the next room. He wished he could do more than merely keep the business ticking over and put it all on to a more permanent footing, but that would be an acceptance of his father's approaching death.

It was ironical, he thought, that it takes such extreme circumstances to draw people together. He had always felt that his father did not really approve of him. He'd worked so hard at school, getting high grades in the subjects he required for a degree in horticultural studies, and he had rarely given his parents grounds for complaint. He and Mark had always shared the same interests as small children, favouring Jack physically, but they had grown apart as Mark looked for his green pastures away from his roots.

Perhaps that was what his father admired, he thought, as he pulled on his Wellington boots in readiness for the mud caused by the summer storm of the previous day. Perhaps he regretted the path he had chosen, and longed for adventure. He had certainly gone into decline since Mark's death.

Couldn't Marie see that he must grab this opportunity of securing his father's love while there was still time? Couldn't she stop criticising the rest of the family? This was about his flesh and blood. Nothing could change it.

8

'I've never done it before,' Hannah said to Marie. They were sitting
in the front kitchen having late elevenses. Jack had decided to stay
in bed after a very disturbed night.

'Never done what?'

'Visited a fortune teller.'

'That's the last thing I would expect you to do. I would have
thought you have enough weird things happening without getting
outside help.' Marie stirred her coffee and looked slightly
uncomfortable, sensing that she had overstepped the mark. Although
she had developed a strong relationship with her mother-in-law over
the years, she still felt over-awed by the 'school marmish' image
that Hannah occasionally portrayed.

'It's not for me. Well not really. I just wish that I could help Jack.
I feel so desperate most of the time. I don't seem to be able to tune
in any more. Apparently she doesn't claim to be a fortune teller. I
don't know what she calls herself, but I suppose she doesn't want
to have the 'palm crossed with silver' kind of image. She lives at
Tilham. I'm sure I've mentioned her before. She always had

142

premonitions when she was a child, a bit like Leigh and Alice, I suppose.'

Marie frowned. In her opinion, a vivid imagination was something to be discouraged. It could lead to night terrors, and psychological disturbances. Her daughter's close association with Leigh since they had all moved in to Willow Cottage for the summer holidays was driving the child further and further into a world of mysticism, and it worried Marie intensely. In spite of her gentle nature, she had always preferred life without the so-called rose-tinted spectacles. Black was black and white was white in her eyes.

'I'm going tomorrow afternoon,' Hannah was saying. 'I should only be gone for an hour. Do you mind keeping an eye on Jack?'

Rebecca Lickis certainly did not resemble the archetypal fortune-teller in any way. Her blonde hair was swept back in a bun, secured at the nape of her neck by an elegant jewelled clip. Her features were strong, her eyes a piercing blue, and she was wearing a navy pin-stripe trouser suit, which would have been more in keeping in some kind of commercial premises than in the small semi-detached house on the edge of the village.

Hannah accepted the cup of strong coffee and the thin biscuit, which rested on a fine china plate. She felt quite nervous, like a small child fearing clumsiness, and wished she had never come.

'Which is it to be? I can do Tarot, or Angel cards. I have coloured ribbons, a crystal ball, or perhaps you prefer to rely on spiritual contact without the tools. I don't mind. In the end it all adds up to the same thing. I can tell that you can tune in. Some people need all the trappings. It fits in with their kind of reality, you know.' She left no space for Hannah to reply, and continued, 'So we'll just get on with it, shall we?'

She closed her eyes, and Hannah was aware of a strange stillness, which now filled the room. She watched as Rebecca Lickis' face slowly took on a translucent quality, which appeared to soften the hard lines of her nose and mouth. She was aware of a different energy, as though the air was vibrating. It was way beyond the strangeness of dreaming, for this was reality and could not be explained away.

'I have a lady,' Rebecca suddenly said. She opened her eyes and looked at Hannah. 'It's Sylvia. This is your mother with us, isn't it?'

Hannah experienced a huge surge of emotion, almost overpowering her senses. The tears welled up in her eyes and her heart thudded.

'I do not need to describe this lady, only to say that she passed on very early in your life. It seems like no time at all to her. Time is not what it seems. But she is telling me that Jack's time has come. You understand "Jack"?' Hannah nodded, not trusting herself to speak. 'Every life has its time on this earthly plain. I call it a God-given spark, which bursts into a flame, and lights up a corner of the universe. And then it is blown out, leaving nothing behind of its earthly life but memories. But as I have proved to you, and you must already know, each spiritual energy moves on into a future, which we do not understand. We can only see through chinks. Only know, my dear, that it is not your time to go yet. All lives must overlap to a greater or a lesser degree. You still have light to shed. Your mother is watching over you and I see strong links with Ireland.'

'My father was Irish.'

'The links are yet to come for you, although everything is in place and waiting to happen. You will have a new path to tread. I am being told that you have a healer in the family. It is too soon yet for his flame to burn brightly. Time will tell, but you would be wise to seek out some healing. You are precious too, you know. I see a strong link with the earth. Are you a keen gardener?'

Hannah nodded, and then said, 'Yes. We have a big area of land.' She was loath to give out any information, although she knew that enough evidence had been given as proof already.

'Everything will continue as it should. The planet does not stop turning in the heavens, no matter what. There is a great deal of love coming to you from the other side. Be happy.'

Hannah sensed the falling level of the energies in the room. Rebecca Lickis sank back into her chair, her features once more fixed in their own kind of severity. She smoothed back a wisp of hair, which had escaped from the confines of her hair clip.

Hannah shuffled nervously in the chair, not knowing whether she should stand up and bring the appointment to a close. 'Thank you very much,' she murmured. 'How much do I owe you?'

'I do not charge, but you may leave a donation if you wish.' The lady inclined her head in the direction of the sideboard, and then stared fixedly out of the window. Hannah could see that a lace runner covered the centre of the sideboard and here and there banknotes of different denominations had been tucked underneath. The values were apparent by the edges left exposed, and not wishing to appear ungrateful, or impoverished, she opened her purse and took out a twenty-pound note, whilst Rebecca Lickis continued to stare out of the window. It was not easy for Hannah to extricate herself from the depths of the upholstered armchair. She reached across to the sideboard and pushed the note under the runner, feeling guilty of some kind of subterfuge; perhaps cheating the government out of its fair share of taxes.

Rebecca Lickis stood up and opened the door. 'Make sure you are grounded before you drive your car,' she said.

Grounded? Did that mean coming back down to earth, Hannah wondered? She certainly did feel very light-headed. But then she did not normally drink strong coffee. It could be too much caffeine, she reasoned. But she knew that it was nothing to do with caffeine. She deliberately dragged her feet in the gravel path, and then sank down heavily into the car seat. Her legs now felt leaden, the state of euphoria thinning, and as she sat there waiting for her energy to return and enable her to drive the car home, she began to reproach herself. She had spent twenty pounds on wanting proof of something she already knew. Marie was right. She did not need a fortune teller. A lot of it could have been merely guess-work, but then Rebecca Lickis got the names right and the Irish connection. How could I be so cynical at a time like this, she asked herself?

'Did she go into a trance?' Marie asked. She'd waited for Hannah to speak while she brewed a pot of tea, and now impatiently broke the silence.

'Sort of. Her face seemed to change and the atmosphere was electric. I can't really describe it, but I have felt it like that before. She said there was an Irish connection. That would be my father, but it wasn't just in the past. Apparently there's an Irish connection happening now. She talked a lot about time and said there was a healer in the family. Masculine, so it must be Leigh, but apparently he's not ready yet.'

'It could be Karl. We don't really take much notice of him, do we? Those twins are always so together that they don't seem to need anyone else but I don't think they're very happy.'

Marie was pleased that Alice had not been mentioned, although the business about the Irish connection in the future could be linked to Mollie Petch, Alice's birth mother. Why was this family so intent on stirring things up, she asked herself? Why couldn't they just get on with living?

'I missed you,' Jack said. 'How was Ella?'

'Fine.' Hannah looked away from the intensity of his scrutiny. 'Anyway, I'm back now, so your wish is my command, oh master.' She was pleased to see him grin, although the deep lines which were forming on either side of his mouth, and the dullness in his eyes brought her mind back to the surreal world of Rebecca Lickis and her predictions. She vowed never to leave him again. His time was running out. Every minute was precious.

The phone rang at a quarter past six on the following Sunday morning. It was Daisy in a complete panic. 'Emma's gone into labour,' she shrieked. 'How do we know when to go to the hospital? I've forgotten all I ever knew!'

'Time the contractions and ring up the maternity ward. They'll want to know what stage she is at, and then they'll advise you. Don't panic, Daisy. Have you got anybody on the night shift who has had a baby?'

Hannah listened to Daisy's mutterings on the other end of the line.

'Jane Dry is here. She says she's helped to deliver babies. She seems to be an expert on everything. Anyway, she's taken over, and Emma's quite calm, so don't worry. I'll keep you informed.'

Hannah sank back under the covers. Her breath began to quicken with a kind of delayed shock, although she had been expecting the news any day. Emma had been having twinges all the week, and had been told at the clinic that the baby's head was engaged in the right position ready for birth. No matter how many times it had all happened before in the family, it was still a momentous occasion, she thought. Each time was unique; the beginnings of a new life, an unknown quantity. Emma was convinced that it was a girl and had no desire for confirmation. It would be very disappointing for her if it was a boy, although when the delivery was well on the way, all you wanted was to get it over with, no matter the sex. Hannah smiled at the memory. She'd always known that she would have two of each but she had never prophesised in which order. In fact she had been secretly convinced that her first one would be a girl. But it was Mark. That memory made her frown. What a great hole was left in her life without him, and how would she cope without Jack? She hoped that Emma's baby was a girl. She didn't want another male to fill the spaces.

She opened Jack's bedroom door slowly. He was using the spare bedroom now that his sleep was so disturbed. He was awake and half-sitting up.

'Is Emma on the way?' he asked.

Hannah nodded. 'She's fine. Apparently Jane Dry has delivered babies. She's quite a dark horse that one, but a godsend at the moment. Poor Daisy is in a panic!'

'And you're not! Don't worry about me. I know you are dying to be involved.'

His use of the word 'dying' snagged in Hannah's brain. There were so many references to death in everyday language and just lately she seemed to hear them every day: 'I wish I was dead', 'I could die for a smoke', 'my mam will kill me'. Three examples she had heard yesterday in customers' conversations.

'You're wrong as usual.' She patted his leg through the blanket. 'I'm leaving it to the experts. Daisy is so excited. She thinks the world of Emma. I wouldn't steal her glory for anything. Mind you, if anything went wrong...but it's not going to. You and I are going to have a quiet breakfast, and a listen to the radio.'

The telephone rang again at just after nine. Marie answered it, as Hannah hung over the banister waiting for the latest news. However, it was nothing to do with babies.

'Gloria,' Marie mouthed. 'Do you know someone called Gloria?'

Hannah wrapped her dressing gown around herself and went down the stairs. Gloria? The only Gloria she could remember was Jack's sister. They had lost touch with her years ago. Jack had always been estranged from his family, right from his childhood. As his health had deteriorated, she had debated whether to try and make contact with his brothers and sister. She knew that his father had died in Hull prison, but had no idea where his mother could be, or whether in fact, she was still alive. The only one she had actually been acquainted with was Gloria. She was evacuated at the same time as Jack, and ended up staying in a house at the other end of the village. Jack had not returned home, but he told Hannah once, in the early years of their marriage, that his sister never settled, preferring to be in Hull, in spite of the bombs.

She took the phone from Marie, and tentatively said, 'Hello. Who am I speaking to?'

It was Gloria Clayton, or as she was now known, Gloria Baxter. Apparently her eldest daughter had gone for an interview for a job at the newly established publishers in Anlaby. 'I recognised the name immediately,' she said. 'Sally Blenkin. Not a name to forget easily, especially after that big article in the paper. I noticed at the time that it was written by Emma Clayton, and guessed it must be something to do with our Jack, although there are plenty of Claytons around. I remembered that Sally was a friend of yours. They used to live near us in Lidden Street. Anyway, I told our Sophie to ask her if she knew where Jack was hanging out these days and she told me that he was very ill and gave me your number. I know we've gone our separate ways, but at the end of the day, he is my brother.'

She chattered on, recalling the days of their evacuation, when Jack was billeted with the shopkeeper and his wife, and she was sent into a kind of slave labour situation, looking after three young children. 'I hated it,' she said. 'I couldn't wait to get home. But our Jack fell on his feet. I don't blame him for staying put. God knows where he would have ended up if he'd come home. Lidden Street got another bomb, you know, but we all survived. It's all gone now, and good riddance to bad rubbish.'

She left sufficient space in the conversation for Hannah to explain the current situation, and to make a note of her phone number, with a promise to contact her as soon as it was convenient.

Hannah climbed the stairs slowly, not knowing how to broach the subject. Again, this would be an acknowledgement of the seriousness of Jack's condition. It would challenge his positive attitude towards his illness.

'That was your sister on the phone, Jack,' she called out before she reached the bedroom door.

'Who? Gloria? What the hell does she want, and how does she know where to find me?'

'Oh, don't be like that. She seemed to care a lot about you when you were a kid. Actually, it was Sally who gave her our phone number. Apparently Sally is setting up a publishing business. I do remember her saying something about it, and Gloria's daughter, Sophie, applied for a job. Gloria recognised the name from your Lidden Street days. Do you remember? The Blenkins lived next door but one to you, before their house was damaged and they moved in next to us in Tennyson Street.'

'You don't have to remind me. Her mother was the street gossip, and always complaining. All we heard was, "Go and play at the other end of the street. You're a bloody nuisance!" Is she still on the go?'

'Oh Jack! You never listen to me. I told you we went to see her. She lives at Barton clay pits in a caravan. She's not bad. A bit common. But then we hardly come into the silver spoon bracket, do we?'

Jack grunted.

'Anyway, I told her that Emma is in the throes of childbirth. I think she genuinely wants to see you.' Hannah decided not to mention that she had promised to return the call in the near future. She picked up Jack's breakfast tray. 'Would you like another drink, or how about some more porridge? You enjoyed that by the look of your empty bowl. I think I'll make myself some.' She knew that she was gabbling again, avoiding the truth at all costs.

'I think you should be with Emma, It is her first baby. I remember you saying that most women want their mother with them. Don't you remember how you longed for your mother to be there when you had Mark?'

Jack's voice followed her down the staircase, and she stopped, turning to listen, balancing the tray awkwardly against the banister. In actual fact, she was longing to be with her youngest child, and although she was trying to be unselfish and give Daisy an important role to play, it was really what Emma wanted that mattered. Would she be thinking that her parents didn't care, especially when this child was illegitimate? But then she had promised herself never to leave Jack again. If only she knew how much time they had left together.

She put the tray down on the draining board, and went to the phone. Daisy answered and assured her that, according to Jane, it could be hours yet. They were timing the contractions, and the hospital sister said that it was better to stay at home, rather than to hang around at the hospital. 'They seem to be so short-staffed,' she said. 'I know the feeling. Two of the carers have gone off sick, and poor old Bessie is on her way out.'

'I'm coming over,' Hannah said. 'Jack's looking reasonable this morning and I do need to be with Emma. It's not fair to leave it to you. You've got enough to do. See you later, then.' She replaced the receiver before Daisy could argue.

She turned through the gates and into the grounds of Daisy Cottage, noticing the signs of an early autumn in the russet tones of the leaves both in the shrubs and the tall trees which flanked the driveway. It would soon be her birthday again, she mused. How quickly the time was moving on, and yet it seemed years since Jack was given his diagnosis; like another lifetime in fact. The sunshine was not masked by cloud today, and her fingers felt pleasantly warm on the steering wheel. It was good to be alive, and what a gorgeous day on which to be born; 25th August, in the sign of Virgo. It was her birth sign as well. That thought drew her awareness closer to the unborn child.

Emma threw her arms around her mother and burst into tears. 'I'm getting so scared,' she said. 'I just don't know what to expect. You know, in the end, all the books in the world can't explain feelings, can they? They can go through the sequence of events, but I suppose it's different for everybody, and one person can be braver than the next. I'm going like a jelly!'

'I know. I was totally ignorant when I had Mark. An old lady told me it was like being constipated. It is a bit more than that. But you'll cope and once it's all over, the memory of it soon disappears into the past. You will be so busy that you won't have time to dwell on it. Anyway, there's the gas and air and other options.'

In spite of the passing years, Hannah could still remember the intoxicating effects of the gas and air, and the feeling of floating away on a cloud, rising above the pain of the contractions. It was probably the closest she had ever been to 'a trip' as the young ones called it during the 'flower power' years.

'Is Dad all right?' Emma was asking. 'Docs Marie mind you coming? Oh Mum! It's so good to have you all to myself. Ooh gosh!' Her features contorted in pain and she clutched her stomach. 'That was a really big one.' She looked at her watch. 'They're getting closer,' she gasped.

'I hope it's today. You know what they say about Sunday's child – "bonny, blithe, good and gay".'

'I always thought it would be good to be born on a Monday. You know, "fair of face". I emerged on a Wednesday didn't I? … "full of woe".' Emma's face twisted in pain.

A knocking on the door took Hannah's mind away briefly from the pain she was feeling for her daughter. It was Jane Dry, her face wreathed in smiles, and exuding an almost palpable air of confidence.

'I'm off duty now,' she explained. 'So I'm all yours for the rest of the day. Are you timing the contractions? Sorry, Mrs Clayton. Here's me teaching my grandmother to suck eggs. You must be an expert after having four!'

'No. I've forgotten all I ever knew about giving birth. They reckon it's nature's way of perpetuating the species, a kind of amnesia. We all say "never again" but then it doesn't take long to get broody. How many children do you have, Mrs Dry?'

'Oh call me Jane. I've never been married, and I've just helped other people with babies.'

Hannah noticed the flushed cheeks and the quick reaching for her handbag to put her car keys safely away. Beyond that cloak of cheerfulness was a host of secret hopes and regrets, she sensed.

Poppy Clayton was born at approximately four-thirty that day and weighed seven pounds two ounces. Immediately she became the little darling of the ward, with her thick dark hair and deep blue eyes. The nurses called her a little poppet, when Emma told them of her choice of name. She was indeed Emma's dream child, now well established in the material world, and already an important member of the Clayton family.

It had been quite an experience for Hannah. Giving birth oneself did not enable one to witness the actual birth process. With the twins, there had been their father present and she had waited in the wings only experiencing anxiety. But this time, as she held her daughter's hand, the mixture of fear, excitement, incredulity and love created a huge cocktail of emotions, and she wanted to laugh and cry and scream all at the same time.

'Thanks, Mum,' Emma whispered. 'I couldn't have done it without you. Get back to Dad now. Give him a big kiss from me and from Poppy. I can't wait to show her off.' She sank back into the pillow and closed her eyes. Hannah recognised the signs of exhaustion and leaned over to give her daughter a kiss before tiptoeing out into the corridor.

Jane was waiting for her in the reception area. She jumped up and gave Hannah a hug, which seemed as natural as any close family embrace. Normally, Hannah would have backed away from contact with a comparative stranger like Jane Dry, but the warmth of her embrace negated her inhibitions.

'You look as though you need a strong something or other,' Jane remarked, as they made their way to the car park.

'It will have to be tea. One glass of wine flaws me at the best of times. I would end up in a ditch, even if I could stagger to the car.'

'You could always leave your car at Daisy Cottage. I don't mind driving you home.'

Hannah thanked her for all of her help, but assured her that she must get back to Jack and that she may need the car in a hurry. 'I'll be in touch later. I expect Emma will be home soon. It's not like with my first. That was in a maternity home. You couldn't get out of bed for a few days then. Although the rest of the kids were home confinements, and I was back into the harness straight away. Still, it didn't seem to do me any harm.'

They continued the rest of the short journey in a silence broken only by the occasional comment about traffic conditions, each caught up in thoughts past and present.

Jane could not get the greengrocer out of her mind. He appeared one day at the nursing home with an impressive vanload of fresh fruit and vegetables, and the promise of a regular weekly service and an endeavour to suit all requirements.

He had introduced himself as Clive Spryfoot, and had ignored the smothered giggles that came from a couple of carers on their way to prepare a bath for one of the residents.

Jane had observed the greengrocer from the kitchen, around the partially closed door. She couldn't hear what he was saying, but her fellow workers irritated her with their bad manners. She'd caught these two discussing their sex lives above the head of Gerty, a quiet old lady in her nineties, and had been half in mind to tell Daisy at the time, but, as a comparative newcomer, she did not want to overstep the line. However, Daisy had now witnessed their lack of control and no doubt, Jane thought, she would come down on them like a ton of bricks.

It was arranged that Mr Spryfoot would deliver on Tuesdays and Fridays, in order to keep up a fresh supply of perishable items. Daisy insisted on her residents, as she called them, having the best. She was very impressed by the cleanliness and order of his van. Obviously he did not neglect his personal appearance either, albeit his working clothes consisted of well weathered, but recently laundered jeans, and the kind of tee shirts which announced inspirational messages. On this particular day, his chest encouraged the world to 'Keep Smiling'.

Jane's eye took in all the details of his appearance as she peeped through the gap. She noticed that he was tall, thin and handsome, possibly in his mid-forties, with a good head of dark-brown wavy hair and a ready grin.

Now, as she and Hannah approached the lane, which led to the nursing home, she was planning how she could offer to do an extra shift on the following Tuesday, and take charge of the fruit and vegetable order.

Jack cradled Poppy in his arms with such tenderness that Hannah, Rachel and Emma exchanged glances registering surprise. Usually, he steered clear of babies. In fact he was very nervous of being left in the company of small children at the best of times.

'She's your latest descendant. Poppy Clayton. Doesn't that sound good?' Emma smiled in an apologetic way in Rachel's direction, sensing that she may feel that her twins with their different surname were excluded from the Clayton clan. Rachel looked away.

'Corn poppies used to be your mother's favourite flowers. Do you remember, Hannah? You promised to paint me a picture of them one day.' Jack turned back to Emma. 'When I fell in love with her, she told me it was one of her dreams.'

'Well, I'll do it. There are plenty of poppies around. We'll go up the lane for a walk this afternoon. The rain seems to have stopped at long last. The fresh air will do us good.'

Jack's eyes brightened, and Hannah briefly saw in them an echo of their youth, when life was full of dreams.

Jack was loath to return Poppy to the arms of her mother. 'She's fine with me,' he protested.

'I can see that, Dad. You've obviously made quite a hit with her, but she does need changing, and her next feed is due. I don't think you can oblige. I'll bring her back later.' Emma leant forward and they both fumbled in the newness of the situation, nervous of the vulnerability of the tiny form.

The rain began again, and the promised walk was abandoned, the poppy painting remaining in the realms of fantasy. Instead, Jack retired to his bed, and slept as soundly as his tiny granddaughter.

Hannah ran to answer the phone, its shrill bleeping ripping through the silence. It was Sally. Apparently she had been away and had only just picked up on Hannah's message. 'I can't wait to see Poppy!' she yelled. 'You must be so excited.' She dropped her voice to a whisper, in response to Hannah's subdued tones. 'How's Jack? Have I rung at a bad time?'

'No. Everything's fine. He's having a nap at the moment, and Emma and Rachel are here. I'll let you know when we have the christening. Emma told me that you have agreed to be Poppy's godmother.'

Sally chattered on, and Hannah nodded and made the occasional comment, only half-listening, her apathetic responses suddenly prompting suggestions and questions from her friend. Was the local doctor any good? Shouldn't Jack see the specialist again? Why didn't they discuss the future? After she replaced the phone, a huge wave of depression flooded over Hannah and she went into the kitchen to make herself a cup of coffee. Leigh was sitting in the armchair, engrossed in a school library book. He looked up and smiled, and the sweetness of his expression lifted her spirits.

'Don't look so sad, Grandma. Everybody loves you,' he said. 'Don't forget what you told me about all the dominoes fitting together. You are the double six.'

Later that evening, when the children were in bed, and the rest of the family were watching a film on the television, Hannah sat at the kitchen table and wrote a letter to Sally. She knew that it was hard to express herself on the phone, and there was so much she wanted to say.

My Dear Sally,

I found it so hard to talk to you today. You must have noticed and I don't want you to think that I don't want to be in contact. I am trying so hard to keep my emotions under control, that I feel like an automaton – 'Yes thank you – thanks a lot – isn't the weather awful? – see you soon,' and so on. My stock answer at the moment is, 'Oh you know, plodding along.' My whole being has been so stretched and released, and stretched over the last month or so that I really feel like a piece of worn-out elastic, managing to hold together, but not allowing for any great movements in any direction. Like you say, I should contemplate something else. There's plenty to think about, but I dread any feeling of inadequacy, which may accompany it, as I am becoming physically tired. Jack is sleeping badly now and although we are not sharing the same bed, I can hear him coughing and choking, and know that he is sitting up unable to sleep. I feel guilty that I am desperate to sleep, and I wake up with pains in my legs, and backache, and totter to the bathroom. It is like no escape from someone else's destiny. That sounds awful, doesn't it? But I need to survive. I let my mind wander through our lives, and think of all the sacrifices I have made, and then I think of the male/female thing and how it all seems to be loaded, and I begin to feel better. Then I see his courage and how he is trying to cope with the pain, which must be constantly in his head, and I want to cry so much that I have to escape and get a hard lump in my chest from suppressing the tears. The rain seems to be never-ending, and we are not getting out for any walks, which would do us both good. The house feels like a tomb and the old shop clock, which belonged to Jack's adoptive father, ticks louder and louder. We have a new alarm clock, because the other one got dropped, and it ticks like galloping horses, and I want to throw it across the room. Then I can't think about the past, because it is too painful to recall those happy days before that first hospital appointment, and I can't think of the future. But then, can anyone? Daisy reminded me that there are no guarantees. So why should I feel special? You see how I am trying to reason with it all. Guilt at being critical of Jack. Guilt at trying to see beyond the twists and turns. Guilt at doubting the treatment, which comes in all directions. Guilt at not believing in miracles. All I can do really is accept Jack's faith, or bolster up the power of it by believing in it, but that is easier said than done.

The other day, he started tidying up a drawer where he keeps guarantees and things and I felt that there lies between us an unspoken acceptance, or is he just being tidy and needing something to do? Sally, it's all such agony, to know the future and at the same time deny the future. But then I suppose it is just as agonising not to know until it is too late, like sudden death, when one is caught up in unexpected bereavement.

Sometimes, I am totally emotionless, cold as stone and I think I must be inhuman. Other times I am so strong and loving that nothing can hurt me. And then I seem to be a bit of both, pathetic, selfish, hateful, crying. What a mess!

So Sally, you will understand when I can't tell you anything on the phone. I'm not being indifferent or lacking in curiosity, or being pushed around as you suggested. I have moved in all directions of my own free will, but the doctors do answer my questions, and I have done my best to find the right answers for Jack. I rarely let him be on his own when he needs company.

Thanks for being a good friend. We cannot plan anything at the moment. I cannot think beyond today,

Love from Hannah

She signed her name with a flourish and sat back, exhausted by the physical effort of writing. Then she read it, immediately critical of the scribbled words, putting in a comma or a dash here and there, and dotting the 'i's. She reached the end, wanting to screw it up and put it on the fire, but that would be another kind of denial, she told herself. Sally would understand. Under all of that 'larger than life' image she was a very sensitive person. That is why our friendship has survived, she thought. We really are kindred spirits.

At last, there was a change in the weather. It was the promised Indian summer, just in time for Hannah's birthday on the 9th of September. Jack had been to the hospital again and was once more able to enjoy his food, albeit cut up fine. Plenty of soups and broths were the order of the day, and he began to look less haggard than he had done during earlier weeks.

It was decided that the sea air would do both of them good. Simon still had two weeks of his summer vacation left and Jane Dry volunteered her services during her holiday to take over the cooking and leave Marie free to help in the organisation of the business. She assured Hannah that she had nowhere to go, and a change of surroundings would be as good as a holiday.

They chose the Norfolk coast, booking in at a little self-catering country cottage, a short distance from Sheringham, but within easy reach of most facilities. In any case, it was not crowded, being the late summer season, and most families had returned home ready for the beginning of the next school term. Hannah had driven the car, the longest journey she had made since her trip to Northumberland last year. It felt good to be so adventurous, and Jack responded to her courage, taking over her role as navigator with his sense of humour firmly in place.

The cottage was delightful and suited their taste admirably. The accommodation was geared to 'the older couple', with traditional standards, and chintz everywhere. Hannah loved the bright colours, such a contrast to the creams and beiges of modern hotels. The small back garden tumbled around in its untidiness, weeds and late perennials fighting for space. A wooden seat, half hidden in this tiny jungle invited Jack to join it or so he said. The sun shone from dawn to dusk, and they both knew that this was their last chance before the winter cast its long shadows.

They talked of their youth, no longer inhibited by the threatening months of despair. Indeed, those brief days of their shared evacuation experiences seemed like a fairy story. They laughed at the memory of Jack getting his spellings wrong, and progressing from standing on his chair to the desktop as a punishment, swaying backwards and forwards in his confusion to get a word right.

'You always knew the spellings. We all used to call you Miss Clever Britches,' Jack reminded her. 'You were the teacher's pet and didn't the Parkers hate you?'

'You became the hero after you were locked in the cupboard. Do you remember that silly poem you said after everybody laughed at your Gloria. I'll never forget her saying, "Drake is in his hammock and a thousand mile away." She had such a broad accent. Mind you, we must have had a Hull accent. It's unmistakable. I start picking it up immediately if I go to Hull. I noticed when Sally rang up, that she is losing the Australian twang and returning to the East Yorkshire lingo.'

She noticed the tightening of his lips when she mentioned Sally, and wondered why he had such an antipathy towards her. Perhaps it was merely a reminder of his lowly beginnings, she thought, suddenly feeling guilty that she had talked about his sister Gloria. That was another issue that had to be faced some time soon. She directed his thoughts back to their childhood. 'Do you remember the itching seeds in the hips that we picked in the war effort? I bet you tormented the girls after I had gone.'

Jack smiled at the memory. 'I really missed you when you left the Porters. You've never really talked about it. I wonder what caused the fire.'

'Oh goodness knows. Anyway, that's all water under the bridge.' Hannah got up from the seat. 'I think it's about time for a bowl of soup, and then we could have a little ride to Sheringham.'

The last time she had thought of the Porters was on the night of

Alice's abduction. That experience had conjured up bitter thoughts of Tom's actions. At the time she had been tempted to tell Jack about the night of the fire, and how Elsie had pushed Tom into the flames, where he had lain unconscious after hitting his head on the stone floor. The burning straw, which fell from the loft above him, had taken away any chance of his recovery, and that scene had haunted Hannah for many months, triggering night terrors. But she had promised not to divulge the secrets of that night. Elsie had made it clear to her that she would be sent to prison as an arsonist and ultimately responsible for Tom's death, if anybody found out that she was the one who had lit a candle in the barn that night. Even now, years later, long after Elsie's death, she was still afraid of exposure.

They found a little café in Sheringham, halfway down the side of the cliff. A pathway wound down to it and the activities on the beach below kept them entertained. It became a favourite coffee stop and a sanctuary, away from the heat of the sun or the fresh breezes that chilled Jack. They found themselves constantly seeking the safety of the past, moving on from childhood, and reminding each other of those early years of their marriage, when they had kept the shop at Cragthorpe. Jack had never ceased to be grateful to his adoptive parents who had left him the business after their two sons were killed in the war.

'Why didn't you aspire to great heights, like Mrs Thatcher? She grew up in a grocer's shop in Grantham. You ought to be prime minister by now,' Hannah joked.

'What with you and the kids in tow! I don't think so. Anyway, give me the peace and quiet of the countryside any day to the rat race of London.'

Hannah nodded in agreement. They had long since given up on the expensive Harley Street clinic.

The proprietor, a stout, fresh-faced lady who mothered everybody, quickly assessed the situation, and sat and chatted during the quiet times when only Hannah and Jack were customers. 'Stay as long as you like,' she advised Hannah as she paid the bill at the till. 'That man of yours needs all the time he can get.'

Hannah knew that this lady had somehow shared in the traumas of ill-health, and understood the value of time. There was no need of an explanation. She reached forward and squeezed her hand. 'Thank you. You're very kind,' she murmured.

Indeed, time was now of the essence. Everyone wanted the greatest exposure to family life. Every sunny Sunday of that late summer was an excuse for a tea party, which often included Jane, and sometimes Daisy on the invitation list. One particular Sunday was given over to a discussion of plans for the christening of Poppy Clayton.

It seemed that two godmothers and one godfather was the order of the day. It had been decided weeks ago that Sally was to be one of the godmothers. Hannah had already approached Daisy on the matter of the second one, at Emma's request, but that lady had declined, suggesting that Jane would be a more likely candidate. 'I already feel like a grandmother,' she explained, 'and Jane is much younger. She was such an angel on the day of the birth, when I was a bundle of nerves, and everybody loves her. She reminds me of Ella – auntie to everybody.'

Hannah agreed with her. Apparently, during the week of their holiday, she had become Aunt Jane to the children, and life had progressed smoothly and happily through the days of their absence.

She was quite overcome with emotion on this particular Sunday when Emma asked her if she would honour them with her acceptance of the role. 'You are all so good to me,' she sobbed. 'I really don't know what I've done to deserve it.'

The question of a suitable godfather was later discussed over the phone. Hannah could only suggest Simon or Steve but Emma felt that they had enough responsibilities with their own families. 'What about Jane's Clive?' she asked. 'Did Daisy tell you they are talking of tying the knot?'

'Really!'

'I know. Whirlwind doesn't come into it. It was certainly love at first sight. Actually, Jane took me into her confidence. I promised not to tell, but I know you won't spread it around. Apparently she once had a relationship and was pregnant. The bloke didn't want to know about the baby and just walked out on her. She was desperate, and had an abortion, which somehow went wrong and left her with problems. Poor Jane! I could easily have gone down that road, couldn't I? And I would never have known Poppy Clayton. I count my blessings that her father must have been good-looking, and to be fair to him I doubt he has any idea that he has a beautiful daughter. Anyway, I'm sure that Jane would like Clive to be one of the extended family. He's so nice when you get to know him. What do you think?'

'I'll discuss it with your dad. He's besotted with your child. And don't worry. My lips are sealed about Jane's secret. Poor woman! She must feel that life is giving her a second chance, now that her Mr Right has come along.'

Emma laughed. 'That's what she calls him. I think she gets a bit embarrassed over his name, and must wonder if she will cope with being Jane Spryfoot.'

'Well, it's a name that sticks in the memory. I suppose she could always be modern and keep her own name, like the celebrities. I really don't see why women should have to take on another name if they don't like it. Why can't a man take on a woman's name? Or I suppose she could be double-barrelled.'

'What? Dry-Spryfoot! I don't think so,' Emma giggled.

'Everybody loved your hat!' Hannah exclaimed. 'You were the second star of the show.'

Daisy laughed at the other end of the phone. 'It all went splendidly, didn't it? By the way, Jane and Clive are engaged. They didn't want to steal the limelight by announcing it at the christening. I've told them they can rent one of the units if they like. It's pointless them staying empty. I might as well get some rent from them. People seem to be staying in their own homes more and more with the increased social services care in the community, although how long that will last is anybody's guess.'

Hannah replaced the receiver on to its stand and sank back into the chair. It had been a great occasion in spite of Jack's frailty. She hoped that the photograph of him and Poppy would not be cruel in its honesty. Of course Poppy had stolen all the hearts with her delicious muslin gown, and her poppy hair band. They sang a reduced version of 'All things bright and beautiful' and the local organist thanked Hannah for her consideration. Apparently, accompanying all of the verses complete with chorus was quite a trial for her these days, and in any case the vicar needed time to press home the responsibilities that accompanied the role of godparents.

Sally, as usual had dressed for the occasion, and Hannah, as usual, felt dowdy and country market in her company. But it was good to see her again, and she enlivened the family with talk of her new publishing business. 'How about you putting pen to paper, Hannah?' she had asked. 'You were always spouting poetry. I bet you could produce something worthwhile. I'm sure your Emma has got a book in her, and what about you, Rachel? We've all got a story to tell.'

Rachel had smiled and grunted. She certainly did have a story to tell, she'd thought grimly. It was so good to be here with her family without Steve. He was away on company business, and she didn't care if she never saw him again. The twins were so different away from him and his family. They were growing out of infancy, still very close to each other, but discovering new relationships, which gave them more confidence. Today they seemed relaxed with their cousins, she noticed, and she longed to confide in her parents and be on the receiving end of their wisdom.

Ella had joined the party after the church service. A taxi with wheelchair accessibility was organised, and Daisy had arranged for a carer to sit with her. Leigh was delighted to see his favourite 'great aunt' sitting in her special place on the paving slabs, which ran along the side of the cottage, and all of the children took turns to tempt her with snacks or glasses of fizzy pop. Dear old Auntie Ella, Hannah thought, back to the place she loved, but it was highly unlikely that she had any idea what they were celebrating. What would Aunt

Kate and Uncle Harry have made of the occasion? In their era, would the celebration of an illegitimate child's baptism have been kept in a very low key if indeed celebrated at all?

It was to be the last family celebration that Hannah enjoyed with Jack at her side. However, her focus of attention turned away from Jack's illness quite dramatically one Monday afternoon in late October. Jack was asleep in the armchair at the side of the range in the front kitchen, and she was enjoying the relaxation away from the business, permitted by their policy of closing the nursery to the public on a Monday. Admittedly, there was always much to do, but since Simon's return to his duties as a lecturer at the college, they had taken on extra staff, who worked under the guidance of Mike Cross.

She opened her eyes, and pulled herself up in the chair at the sound of a car engine. She recognised the small red hatchback. It was Rachel's little runabout. Steve had bought it for her birthday, and the rest of the family were surprised by his generosity. His previous insistence on being in charge of transporting his wife and children during his free time had, in their opinion, smacked of male chauvinism. Rachel had been a confident driver before she married him. No one, including his wife, understood his change of heart.

However, Rachel was about to explain in a tearful outburst, which quickly followed her unexpected arrival at Willow Cottage. Hannah looked anxiously at Jack, who was easing himself into an upright position, and screwing up his eyes against the bright afternoon sunshine.

'I can't take any more, Mum. It's getting worse and worse. I daren't say anything, because he threatens me and the children, and just lately it's not just been threats. If only his parents knew what their precious son was really like. Anyway, it's the final straw. He's having an affair with one of the staff where he works. She rang up, and he took it on the bedroom extension. I had already picked up the phone in the hall. I felt guilty at eavesdropping but I was so angry, and we had a blazing row. Anyway, I've had enough.' Rachel's voice had sunk to a whisper.

Hannah did not offer any words of comfort. Her immediate concern was for Jack. His eyes were so full of anger and grief, raging against his daughter's pain and his inability to help. 'You must stay here with the children,' he shouted. 'There's plenty of space. He won't be in a hurry to have the children. And his fancy woman won't either. Don't you let him bully you. If he comes here, I'll give him a piece of my mind.' He sank back against the pillow, gasping for breath.

'This is no time to bother us with your problems,' Hannah snapped. 'Surely it could have waited if it has been going on for a long time. Couldn't you have rung up?'

'What do you mean, she should have waited? What, waited until I'm out of the way? Is that what you mean? Why don't you say it?' Jack was sitting bolt upright again, his gaunt features twisting with emotion.

Hannah stared at him, unable to speak. This was the first time that Jack had acknowledged the terminal nature of his illness.

'Don't you think it is on my mind all the time?' he continued. 'I daren't admit defeat, but my mind is on death as soon as I wake up. Will this be my last day? How long have I got? Of course I worry about the business and how you will manage. I know you want Simon to take over, but then I will stop believing in miracles. I mean it, Rachel. Come back home and bring the children with you. If he lays a finger on you he'll have me to reckon with.'

Hannah reached out to clasp his hand. How she wished it had never come to this. They had been living this great pretence so well, or so it had seemed. Perhaps the turning point had arrived. But then what was the point of facing up to the truth, when all that did was to take away every hope?

'Please, Jack. I didn't mean that Rachel shouldn't have said anything to upset you. It's just that so much is going on at the moment. It doesn't seem long since Alice's disappearance, and then all the trauma of Emma's pregnancy. I really need a break from family. We both do. Anyway, you've got another hospital appointment coming up. Look how good you felt after the last treatment.'

'Oh, get me a glass of whiskey, and don't tell me it's bad for me. I don't give a damn!'

✳

Alice awoke from a strange dream. She recalled how she had been wandering down long passages, brushing against people who all seemed to be going in the opposite direction. She tried to recall them. Most of them were old, but occasionally a small child passed by. She seemed to remember that she spoke to one of them, but everything was slipping away from her mind. Then the memory of her grandfather vividly coloured her thoughts. A door had swung open at the end of the tunnel, revealing a small room. He was waiting there, sitting on a chair, and dressed in his Sunday-best suit; the one he had worn at Poppy's christening. 'Are you coming, Granddad?' Had she said that? The words were caught up in her memory. Somehow she knew that he was waiting. He looked so well and now she remembered that she had promised to tell Grandma that he was happy and back to his normal self. She couldn't wait until the weekend when they would be at Willow Cottage, and felt the need to confide in her mother.

Marie told her that it was only a dream and she was not to bother her grandmother. It would only upset her. But Alice knew that it was a special dream. Her skin prickled each time she thought about it, and as soon as they reached Willow Cottage on the following Saturday, she confided in Leigh.

'Do you think he's going to get better? He did look OK. Do you think I should tell Grandma? Mum says it's only a dream, but it does seem like one of those special ones. I get all prickly, like I did when I saw that white cat.'

'Perhaps Nigel will know, or perhaps I can get in touch with Lucy. Goodness knows where she's gone. We'll stroke the Mooncat tonight after tea. I bet Mrs Knight will know.'

They both stared hard at their grandfather, when he joined the family for tea, and noticed that he had some soup but little else.

'Would you like a cake, Granddad?' Alice asked. 'I made them especially for you.'

'I'll have one later, sweetheart,' Jack replied. He stood up, and left the table. Hannah accompanied him, and the other adults exchanged anxious glances.

'Granddad's going to get better,' Alice said.

Marie told her to be quiet and get on with her tea.

9

"I turn to speak, to tell you that I care.
I long to hold your hand, but you're not there.
Daily erosion, the ebb and flow of tide,
Widening the space to when you hadn't died.
But did we really live through all those years?
Do I mourn substance, or my own dark fears?
No past, no future, nothing what it seems.
Just another fairy story, wrapped in dreams."

Lois Fenn

The hospital appointment was cancelled. Jack was too ill to travel. They both knew the truth. They both knew that in spite of the diets and holistic healing, the truth had remained constant from the beginning.

Life is like a maze, Hannah thought, so many paths to take, but yet there was always a target with a bull's eye, with all the arrows drawn inexorably towards it. That's what destiny is, she reasoned. But did she believe in destiny? She'd argued with herself about this for years. Exits and entrances, as Jaques points out in Shakespeare's *As You Like It*. Were they already arranged? She remembered Aunt Kate quoting that very passage when she gloomily predicted her own death. 'Sans everything,' she had said.

Now here was her dear Jack, his features so ravaged by this dreadful illness. She was desperately tired; physically and emotionally drained. Yet, conversely, her mind was actively engaged in remonstrations against her own frailty.

Her thoughts turned to her granddaughter Alice. When the child had excitedly recounted her dream a few weekends ago, Hannah knew that it was given through spirit. It was, as Mrs Knight would say, 'a special dream'. Not the prediction of a miraculous cure, as Alice believed, but proof that Jack would be restored, as he waited to pass into his next dimension. Rebecca Lickis knew the truth. 'Each flame is extinguished when it is time to go,' she'd said but then she had confirmed Hannah's belief in the continuation of the spirit.

Jack's breathing had become harsh and laboured. Hannah tried to prop him up against the pillow, but his body had become heavy in its absolute weariness. His eyelids drooped, trapping in the signs of pain as he sank into a state of unconsciousness.

Daisy came in with a cup of tea. She put it on the small bedside table and stood for a few moments taking in the signs of death. She turned away, and went over to the window, opening it wide. Hannah watched her, and, in that moment, Jack's spirit left the earth plain.

During the week that followed, Hannah's mind still focused on the living Jack, as she sought the right words, shaping them into a tribute in celebration of his life. She did not know what he wanted at the end of his days. He had never broached the subject. She did know that he had a simple belief in the sanctity of life. She supposed, if the truth be known, he was not in tune with the concept of monotheism. He worshipped nature, without the dogma of paganism. Every living thing had its place. Even the slugs, which attacked his plants, were regarded without animosity. She knew that he would have been happy with a simple ceremony, perhaps taking place under the willow trees, but she needed the quiet dignity of a church service with the organ music, hymns and prayers.

It was a family affair, each one supporting the other. Rachel had temporarily moved back to Willow Cottage with the twins, strengthened by her father's courage. Hannah had contacted Gloria, Jack's sister, apologising for not inviting her before. She was a gracious lady, Hannah thought, and possibly a future ally. She regretted Jack's decision not to see her. Old wounds take a lot of healing, she decided.

She moved automatically through the waking hours. It seemed to her that life had become separated into one day at a time, with each day swallowing up the one before. The past was too painful to contemplate, and the future was a blank space.

'I feel as though I am lowered into each day,' she told Daisy, during an early morning telephone call. 'It's like dangling from a rope, unable to touch yesterday or tomorrow, and fearing the gaping chasm of the day.' She knew that she was being dramatic, yet she had the overwhelming impulse to play a role, as she had done when she was a child, in the midst of fantasy.

'I know, sweetheart,' Daisy sympathised. 'People tell you to think of the good times, and how lucky we are to have memories, but it is not as easy as that.'

Hannah nodded. She had tried to go back beyond the pain, but her brain behaved like a spinning top, skidding away from the past, as though it was unwilling to risk contact with the nightmare of the last few months.

'It's a blessed release.' That was another cliché that seemed to be trotted out, she thought. But for whom? It was not a blessed release for the person who was desperate to live. He wants a blessed reprieve to continue living, not a blessed release to leave this world and go to a great unknown, whatever the promises. It could only temporarily relieve the pain for those left behind. She rubbed her eyes against the grittiness of sleep. 'I must go, Daisy,' she said. 'Thanks for listening.'

She went into the kitchen and made herself a strong cup of coffee. Daisy's sympathy had not comforted her. He was so young. He hadn't even reached retirement age. Where were the promised twilight years? At one time they had planned to travel, but she had always known that those were pipe dreams. So why was she pretending now that life would have been one long merry-go-round?

No doubt the days would have drifted by with the yearly holidays blown out of all proportion by anticipation. But had Jack been content with his everyday life? Had she trapped him into family life? The guilt was back, buzzing like the angry bee caught up in the space behind the net curtain and the window. She watched its futile efforts to escape, not offering to help. The idea of staying in this small room forever was so appealing, like being caught up in a frozen moment. But surrounding her fancies was a hard practicality, and suddenly her craving for self-indulgence was replaced with a steely resolve to confront all the demons of bereavement. She stood up and opened the casement window, offering the bee the chance to escape. Almost immediately, her energy level rose, and the outlines of a daily timetable replaced the blank space on the screen of her mind.

The family, as if waiting for a signal, exchanged glances, while she busied herself with cooking the breakfast. They had struggled in a kind of denial of grief, as though such unity would give their mother the strength to continue. There was much reorganisation to be done, but each of them was afraid to break the spell of bereavement, feeling guilty with the desire to remove the black trappings.

Very slowly, minute by minute, the days swung into normality. It was easier now to get up, to function and to sleep. Simon and Marie put their own house on the market, and began to reorganise their working routine. The end of the 'autumn term' was in sight, and with it the Christmas holidays. Rachel was finding it relatively easy to live without Steve. He had moved in with his new partner, allowing Rachel and the twins to return to the house. Jack had been right. He wanted his freedom, and so did his parents who soon stepped aside from any responsibilities, apparently tiring of the role of grandparents, intent instead on retiring to a villa in Spain. Divorce proceedings swung into place, and his fear of exposure on the grounds of cruelty guaranteed a good settlement.

Karl and Kirstie relaxed into this new-found security, away from the breakdown of their parents' marriage, and their sulky and spiteful resentment against life was soon replaced with the normal exuberance of six-year-old children. Their deep brown eyes now reflected playful mischief. Alice, with her natural generosity of spirit, forgave them for any past misdemeanours, and Leigh took Karl off on 'boys only' adventures, when they all met up each Sunday.

Although that first Christmas without Jack was very hard, Hannah focussed on the children, and felt that she was in a new life. 'When Jack died, I died,' she told Daisy. 'I used to call myself "she" when I was a little girl and fantasised, as though I was in a story. Did you ever have a set of Russian dolls, which fitted one inside the other? That's how I used to see each "she", one inside another. Now, I think of the old Hannah as "she", put safely out of sight.'

10

"The past is but the beginning and all that is and has been is but the twilight of the dawn. What is time? The shadow on the dial, the striking of the clock, the running of the sand, day and night, summer and winter, months, years centuries? These are but arbitrary and outward signs. The measure of time, not time itself. Time is the life of the soul."

Henry Wadsworth Longfellow

Time moved on, until eight years had slipped by. Sometimes, it seemed to Hannah that it hung in the air like the stillness of a long summer day, yet conversely it could move like a winter gale – one Friday running into the next Friday at a giddy pace.

The children seemed to move in the same way, surfing on great crests of life, with spurts of physical and mental development. One year Alice was outstripping Leigh in stature, but Leigh was gathering such mental agility that he amazed everybody, and the following year he seemed to gain several inches, now physically looking down on the rest of the family.

There were the normal ups and downs; bouts of infections, school events, annual holidays to the seaside. Everyone, it seemed, was intent on growing into the next chapter of their lives.

With Jack's death, the whole family had changed course. Marie, at first, found it very difficult to leave her home and come to Willow Cottage, which, in spite of a full legal sale and handover, still, in her opinion, belonged to Hannah. It was fine for Simon, she thought. He was master of all that he surveyed, and had the best of both worlds; a mother and a wife. Alice had always favoured Willow Cottage, and her relationship with Leigh had strengthened into more than cousin status. This worried Marie, although she knew that there was no blood connection; a fact which did not comfort her in her constant feelings of insecurity after Alice's reactions to her adoption status all those years ago.

Simon had grown, both physically and morally. It seemed that he had literally stepped into his father's shoes, embracing the outdoor life, and developing a deep love of the countryside. It had always been there of course, embedded into his psyche from the moment of his birth, but the process of growing up had diluted the intensity of his feelings, encouraging a desire to be part of the so called 'Brave New World'. He still sought out new technology, but only what related to the organisation of his business. As far as he was concerned, 'everything in the garden' was wonderful.

Hannah, now approaching sixty-five years of age, and sometimes, as she ruefully confessed to Daisy, 'feeling every inch of it', carved up her time into sustainable units. She still did her stint at the till each morning from nine o'clock until half past eleven, giving Marie time to organise the 'school run' into Lincoln, and the household chores. She prepared lunch for everyone between twelve and one, and then escaped to follow one of her new-found interests.

'Jack would be well impressed with my art work,' she told Daisy, on one of her weekly visits to Daisy Cottage. 'One of these days I will paint the promised Poppy picture, you'll see. I'm still on washes and mixing, but next week we are going to paint bananas and grapes!'

An interest in charity work, triggered by her concern for anyone who fell prey to the dreadful scourge of terminal cancer, led to contacts with like-minded people who enriched her life, taking her away from any self-pitying thoughts, which had blighted her life in those early years of widowhood.

The evenings were spent in catching up with the children's schooling. Teachers never lose interest in education, no matter how long it is since they actually practised in the profession, and Hannah was no exception. Both Alice and Leigh were great achievers, with a wide interest. Alice had a passion for English and History, much to the delight of Hannah, but it was the sciences that fascinated Leigh, and he had an ambition to study some aspect of medicine. Alice had pleased her parents and her grandmother with an impressive array of 'O' levels, and Marie had listed them on the various greetings cards, which she sent to her two sisters and their families in Ireland. At sixteen, Leigh was in the throes of his General Certificate of Education Course, and Hannah spent many hours in helping with his course work and revision. She had known for years that her grandson had a photographic memory. He could describe the layout of a page on which his work was recorded, instructing his grandmother to ignore the crossing-out or turn over to the next page. It was so useful to have such a powerful memory, and she was reminded of her old friend Mrs Knight, who had demonstrated her skills by memorising a pack of marked cards just to keep her mind sharp.

Most Sundays, after the garden centre closed, were devoted to family life. Rachel would arrive in the afternoon with the fourteen-year-old twins. Hannah worried about her elder daughter, but Rachel assured her that she was quite happy in her single status. 'Once bitten, twice shy,' she joked, but with a melancholic expression in her eyes. She was so different from her sister Emma, but she always had been, Hannah reasoned. Emma, with her 'little treasure from heaven', as she called Poppy, was happily coping with motherhood and her job as Daisy's secretary. Aunt Jane and Uncle Clive continued to be 'angels of mercy'. Jane Dry, or Jane Spryfoot as she had become seven years earlier, was as Daisy had predicted, aunt to all the children, and they loved her as much as Auntie Ella had been loved before she died. That dear lady had passed away only a few months after Jack's death, and somehow, sad as it was at the time, the normal passing in old age was reassuring in its peacefulness. They all knew that Ella's life had been made as comfortable as possible and that she had drifted slowly into the next stage. Leigh was very quiet during the week following her death, with a few disturbed nights. Hannah worried about old wounds, but he soon became involved with the affairs of childhood again.

Sally had settled down to a more stable lifestyle compared to the wanderings of her youth, although her enthusiasm was not becoming dimmed by the advancing years. Her publishing business was now making a healthy profit after a shaky start, and she continued to urge Emma to return to her writing skills. It was not that she discounted the responsibilities of parenthood. Indeed, she took her godmother role very seriously, and made frequent visits over the Humber Bridge, calling at Barton to see her mother, who, at the age of eighty-four, defied all of her family's gloomy prophecies, and was still able to feed her beloved ducks and geese every day. It was only a short journey on to Lincoln, resulting in a pleasant weekend all round. She and Hannah had long talks and, as always, Hannah was made restless by her friend's ambitions. She knew without being told, that she was living her life through others, but found her financial security reassuring, with some money invested in the business, and paying hers and Leigh's share in bed and board. She enjoyed her charity pursuits, recently adding *The Talking Newspaper* to her monthly engagements. Her academic aspirations did not extend beyond a monthly trip to the library to change her books, and even then she often renewed them by phone, or took them back unread.

'Don't let Sally make you so restless,' Daisy advised. 'She's different to you. She would have been an Emily Pankhurst sort of woman if she had been born at the beginning of the century.'

'I know. That's what Jack used to say. But she does make me think, and I don't seem to do much of that these days. Somehow or other, I feel as though I am treading water and I am of little consequence.'

Having two close friends like Daisy and Sally was a great blessing, Hannah thought, as she replaced the phone after her daily chat with Daisy Buckerfield. They were so different in every way. Daisy was round and comfortable, with a steady reliable nature. Sally was the direct opposite. Her wiry body indicated flashes of energy and rapid mood changes. She either inspired or exasperated, and Hannah bounced away from Sally's moments of irrationality into the safety of her other friend's placidity.

Nevertheless, she was feeling restless, and it wasn't only Sally's influence as Daisy had implied. She knew that she was not being true to herself. This aimless wandering through the days, weeks and months was soul-destroying. How to kill time in three easy lessons, she thought. Get up, plod through the day, go to bed, and ditto. All it does is maintain the status quo with no important dots to join together anymore; no big picture. Would Jack have told her to come back down to earth and go and do something useful? Or would he have reminded her of how to dream?

'OK,' she said out loud. 'I get the message. I'm not going to forget how to dream.'

She went over to the cupboard in the corner of the kitchen, and opened the door. 'It's time you had a say in the matter,' she said, as she took out the Mooncat and put him on the windowsill.

Over the next few days, everyone commented on the reappearance of the white cat, which sat on the kitchen windowsill staring along the drive towards the willow trees. Poppy was very curious at first, listening to Alice's explanation of his powers, and then patting him on the head and making a wish, as though he was a lucky charm. Emma treated it in the same light, her childhood memories of the significance of special Mooncat dreams, being related to a kind of *Aladdin and his Magic Lamp*, or the fairy tale of the *Soldier and the Tinder-box*.

However, Marie regarded it with a certain hostility, linking it with those years when her daughter had shown an unhealthy interest in the occult, as she called it. It had begun with the arrival of Leigh, and continued for a while after the upset of Alice's disappearance and the dreams of that strange old woman and her cats. After her father-in-law's death, and their move to Willow Cottage, she had worried over Leigh's increasing influence on her daughter, and Hannah's obsession with clairvoyance was not, in her opinion, a good example to set for the youngsters. She remembered how relieved she had felt when Hannah put the Mooncat away for safe-keeping.

'I feel hemmed in sometimes by this family,' she confided to Jane one day. 'I know they all think of me as part of the family. It's like you being called Aunt Jane, although you are not flesh and blood. Well, I feel the same sometimes. A kind of outsider, yet swallowed up by all their likes and dislikes, and not allowed to be me anymore.'

Although she had never really got on with Steve, he was an in-law, or out-law as Simon jokingly called her, with a different surname. However, since the divorce, Rachel had changed her name back from Palmer to Clayton and assumed the title of Ms. And of course, Emma was still of single status. Marie had times of dreadful feelings of isolation. She knew that all that trauma over Alice's abduction, and the consequent questions regarding the adoption had helped to foster these feelings, and now, as she regarded the white cat sitting on the kitchen windowsill again, after his long banishment to a place of safety in the cupboard, she had an overwhelming urge to rebel against the whole Clayton clan.

Jane had sympathised, with that usual generosity of spirit that had made her such a close friend to all of the family since Jack and Ella's deaths.

'Don't worry about these kids' fancies,' she advised. 'We all have them when we are young. I expect they have grown out of it by now. They seem to have their heads in books most of the time. A damn sight better than being glued to the tele or these newfangled games.'

Marie nodded, but continued to worry about the powers of the Mooncat, as it stared out of the kitchen window.

'So this is the Magic Mooncat. I've heard a lot about you.' Daisy patted the pot cat on the head, smiling and shaking her head in what could only be described as indulgently, Hannah thought irritably.

'Well, I have never called it magic,' she retorted. 'That was Sally's name for it when we were in our twenties. I know you don't believe in such things, and you all probably think that I am in the early stages of dementia, but I just feel that I need to focus on something and it's not Sally's doing either, before you jump to any conclusions. She's as cynical as you are.'

'Sorry, darling. I wouldn't dream of being judgmental. I just worry about everybody. You know me. One sniff means a cold.'

'Well, I'm not one of your old dears, and the next ten years are going to count. I feel more positive just having the Mooncat on the windowsill so even if it is only psychological, which it isn't of course – it is doing me good.'

Hannah stood up suddenly and collected the coffee cups and plates, rattling them together, and dropped them into the washing-up bowl, causing the water to splash up over the edge of the sink.

Daisy stared anxiously after her, her eyes trained in observing signs of pain or fatigue, noting the sag of the shoulders under the laciness of the cardigan. She'd hoped that her friend was reaching the end of the grieving period. Not that it ever really went away, she mused. It had been over twenty years since her grandfather had died, and her best defence, in her opinion, had been not to talk about it. But Hannah was different. She'd tried to fill her life with as many activities as she could cram in. Daisy knew this, and also knew that, in spite of her apparent grasp of life, she was never truly happy. Personally, she felt that too much soul-searching was not a good thing, but as Hannah said, even the sight of the cat comforted her. Different strokes for different folks, she thought, and reached for the tea towel, which was drying on the rail in front of the kitchen range.

However, with the best of intentions, she would not have condoned Hannah's plans to consult Rebecca Lickis. She did not think it was healthy to pry into the future, if indeed that was possible. Hannah had no intentions of confiding in anyone. She had had a vivid dream in which Jack played a major role, and their old friend Mrs Knight gave them tea and seed cake.

She had no idea whether Rebecca Lickis still lived in the neighbourhood, and whether she still offered her services as a clairvoyant. Her name did not appear in the local telephone directory. What did I expect, she thought wryly, an entry in Yellow Pages under fortune telling? She wracked her brains to remember how she had contacted her years before, and took it as very significant when she woke up the following morning with the clear memory of recording the telephone number in her diary. She had always been in the habit of keeping a kind of diary of family and world events during the years at Willow Cottage, but since Jack had died, she had given up on this habit, her final entry after Jack's death simply stating that time had stopped.

It was easy to find the diary hidden away in the Glory Hole. There were five in total; foolscap hardback, lined books, each one encompassing several years of her life. She had made entries when she had thought about it, sometimes with large gaps, when she had wracked her brain to remember the events of the previous weeks, or sometimes the recordings were on a daily basis during a major episode of life at Willow Cottage. She soon found them, neatly bound together with twine, stacked up on the top shelf, and lifted them down. She struggled to untie the knot, muttering with impatience, and finally extricated the last one labelled 1986 – 1989. She resisted the temptation to read the entries. It seemed to her to be someone else's life. It all relates to 'she' she thought. Instead, she turned to the back page, with instant recall of the scribbled telephone details.

'So, here goes,' she muttered.

She was somewhat relieved, after all of her initial anxiety, to hear the unmistakable, rather cultured tones of Rebecca's voice.

There was quite a long pause during which the clairvoyant consulted her diary. 'All being well,' she said at last, 'I can fit you in on Thursday at three o'clock. Please confirm this about an hour before, as I have no wish to know any details about you and cannot communicate. Do you understand? It may not be convenient for me.'

Hannah replaced the receiver, feeling slightly uneasy. Such lack of surety on the lady's part set seeds of doubt about her abilities. But, having made up her mind to go, she dismissed them, trying to recall instead the previous encounter with Rebecca Lickis. The Irish connection puzzled her. She had referred to it as something in the future. Yet there had been no indication of any developments during the last eight years.

If it had not been for the voice, Hannah would have had problems in recognising Rebecca Lickis. Her hair, now jet black, tumbled on to her shoulders in a cascade of curls, and the low-cut sweater, worn above a tight-fitting skirt, revealed an abundance of cleavage. However, Hannah noticed that her lips still pressed against each other in a severity of expression, and her icy blue eyes lacked warmth. She remembered those eyes above everything else. Now, they focussed beyond her and Hannah half-turned to see whether she was being followed. The medium turned and led the way into the familiar surroundings of the small living room.

'You are just in time,' she said, waving towards an armchair. 'I have a tight schedule next week on tour as I expect you will have heard.'

Hannah nodded, not wishing to disappoint the lady with her ignorance.

'I think you mentioned that you have been before. I don't remember people or their consultations. My fee is the same as last year, twenty-five pounds per session. If you would like to settle that now, and I must make it clear that I can't guarantee that I will make any connections. It really is out of my hands. You do get a tape recording so you can play it when you get home.'

Hannah nodded, and reached in her handbag for her purse. This is dreadful, she thought. What on earth am I doing here? However, she was reassured as Rebecca Lickis sank back into her chair and the energy in the room began to change, making Hannah's skin prickle.

'I have a gentleman here.' Rebecca's voice was low and Hannah leant forward straining to hear her next words.

'He's been trying to communicate with you in your dreams. Dark hair, green eyes.' She began to cough. 'It's hard to swallow – there's something here.' She pressed her fingers into her chest. 'This is Jack, isn't it?'

Hannah knew that was true. She felt what she could only describe as a drawing sensation and a huge surge of emotion. Tears welled in her eyes. 'Yes,' she whispered. She could do nothing more than stare at this strange lady, feeling frozen into the green upholstered chair, and hardly daring to breath.

'Husband,' Rebecca said. 'I don't have to describe him any further, do I? All you need to know is that he is restored and moving on. But he wants you to move on. He doesn't think you are happy. You do have an Irish connection. Do you understand?'

'You told me that before, but nothing has happened. What kind of Irish connection?'

'Something will happen. Trust me. Trust Jack. He tells me there are dots to join up in your life. The big picture. A jigsaw puzzle. Does that ring a bell? Something about Eastfield and poppies. Does this make sense to you?'

'Yes. I promised to paint him a poppy picture when we were at Eastfield Cottage. I'm going to art classes.'

'He knows this and can't wait much longer. There is much to do and you have much to do as well. You have not fulfilled your destiny. Turn the corners. Look for new horizons. Your family are all moving on. They all have their lives to live, and you must let them live them, but my dear, you have such a story to unfold, with many pages still to turn. Take the bookmark out of your book of life, and start to read. The plot is there, but we must unravel it. But I'm told that you do think a lot about life. Blood and water. Water and blood. There is a difference. A huge difference. As they say, blood will always out. But then, water has a strange way of becoming blood. It's like the water into wine story, St John, Chapter 2. Do you recall it? I always think it was symbolic of lineage somehow, and humility becoming strength. The strength is coming, my dear. Much water must pass under the bridge in the scheme of things. The threads will all join up like *cobwebs in time*.

She took a deep breath and focussed her eyes on Hannah.

'OK, dear,' she said briskly, and leaned across to press the stop control on the tape recorder. 'Now don't drive off immediately. Get yourself grounded. Think about what you are going to have to eat, or what shopping is needed. Don't think about this "reading". Wait until you get home and then listen to the recording.'

She wrote her name and the date on the label and handed the cassette to Hannah.

'Good luck with Ireland,' she said.

'Good luck with your tour.' Hannah grinned, relaxed now in the seemingly normal atmosphere.

Rebecca grimaced. 'Actually, I'm dreading it. It's a big step for me. I really don't know what to expect.'

Hannah nearly said, 'If you don't who does,' but she only thought it instead, still somewhat inhibited by those intense blue eyes.

Although she had decided in the first place not to confide in anyone else, she could not resist telling Daisy on her next visit to the nursing home. She knew as soon as she started that Daisy would not change her ideas of fortune tellers, as she called them.

'But how would she know about Jack?' Hannah bristled with indignation. 'She came straight out with it, and I could feel his closeness.'

'These people pick up on body language and Jack is a common name. What would you have thought if she had guessed another name first and then said Jack? They are good at waffling on.'

'But she came straight out with Sylvia on my first visit. That was my mother's name and you couldn't say that that's common. Anyway, how do you know? Have you consulted someone then?'

'I have actually. I've never really explained about my circumstances. I don't like to dwell on the past. I do understand how lost you feel at times. You have coped so well with the last eight years, but obviously you are still grieving. I did what you have just done, and the whole process made me very unhappy.'

'What happened then?'

'Well, the lady was an absolute charlatan. She filled my head with bogus hopes, and I spent many sleepless nights and pain-filled days as a result of it.'

'Rebecca only gave me words of encouragement. She didn't frighten me. But she must be in touch with another energy or how could she know about Jack's illness?'

'Like I said, guesswork and watching your reactions. Some people can read minds. Perhaps that is what she does.'

'Well, wouldn't that be amazing?'

'Yes, but it doesn't prove that life continues after death. Let Jack go, Hannah. Believe me, it's the best way.'

'You never have told me about your life, except that you have a son. Why did you consult a so-called fortune teller?'

'Well, it's a bit of a long story, but we have got time on our hands. I'll start here at Daisy Cottage and work back a little way. I don't run this place to make huge profits, in spite of what some people might think. I'm very lucky that I inherited the building and the land from my grandparents. It used to be called The Cottage to distinguish it from the "Hall", which was far larger, and a nightmare to maintain. My father inherited it, and we moved in just before the war started. My grandparents retired to The Cottage. Sadly, my mother died from breast cancer during that first year of the war. My father went into the army and was posted down south, and I moved in with my grandparents.' Daisy paused and stared out of the window.

'So the house was left empty then?' Hannah said, prompting her friend to continue.

'No. It was used as a hospital, mainly for burns patients. There were so many young men who suffered dreadful injuries, particularly pilots. I suppose my father was a casualty of the war. He got involved with gambling and was soon heavily in debt. The final blow was the fire. I'm sure you must have heard about it. The Hall was completely gutted. Half the fire engines in the county were called.'

'Now you come to mention it, I do remember something about a fire. Was it arson?'

'No. I think it was old wiring and general decay. Luckily, all the things of value were moved into The Cottage, when the army took over, and I still have most of them. In any case, the whole place had needed modernising and my father had no capital. His answer was to get blind drunk, and run his car into a tree.'

'What? And killed himself? Oh Daisy! No wonder you don't want to talk about the past. We've both been so affected by the war, haven't we? In a strange way, we seem to have lived parallel lives. So, did you have a good marriage then?' In spite of feeling sympathetic, Hannah's curiosity was roused.

'No. He was a real charmer, but a wolf in sheep's clothing. After my grandparents died, he began to show his true colours, and had numerous affairs. He was attracted to the glitz and glamour. I was too plain and down to earth for him, a real country girl, in spite of being a wealthy woman. He'd sold family heirlooms, paintings and jewellery before I found out what he was up to. Anyway, he came to a sticky end. Not deliberate like my father's. It was an accident. Not a nice death, but then is death ever nice?' She stood up. 'So you see, I believed all that happily-ever after rubbish from a fortune teller, before I married him, and let my heart rule my head.'

'But you still do, Daisy. You are the most good-hearted person I know!'

'And all the better for knowing you, dear Hannah.'

Everyone else in the family seemed unaware of Hannah's latest preoccupation with the paranormal. Daisy was sworn to secrecy over the Rebecca Lickis episode, and the cat on the windowsill soon seemed to merge into the background of everyday life. However, Marie still regarded it with animosity, and her fears were justified when she overheard a conversation that was taking place between Leigh and Alice from the other side of the half-opened kitchen door.

'It's working. Lucy's back,' she heard Leigh say.

'When? Last night?'

'Yes. I woke suddenly, and the darkness was full of vibrations as though it was rippling like water.'

'Has she grown up then or is she still a little girl?'

'She seems to be more serious, but it's not that I actually see her with my eyes. It's a different kind of seeing. Do you know what I mean? I suppose you could say I know that it is her.'

Marie strained to hear his subdued voice and a reply from her daughter but there was only silence, and she could visualise them staring at each other in that intimate way which always made her feel uneasy.

Leigh's voice broke the silence. 'She said that the tide of time was on the turn. I don't understand really how time can be tidal. What do you think?'

'Well, I suppose it's a kind of a simile. Tide goes with time. You know what they say about time and tide not waiting. Perhaps she is telling you that something important is going to happen and it's time for change. You know how they seem to speak in riddles. It's the same in dreams. I remember reading an article about life changing every seven years. I'm not sure whether that's in one's own life or generally. Anyway, what else did she have to say?'

'Nothing.' Leigh's voice suddenly sounded harsh and dismissive, and Marie, listening in the hall, decided to make her presence known. They both reacted as she pushed the door wide open, stepping away from each other, Alice moving towards the kitchen sink, and Leigh pulling a chair out ready to sit at the table to have his breakfast. He smoothed the tablecloth in what could be construed as a gesture of embarrassment, whilst Alice stared reproachfully at her mother.

Marie drew back the curtains, letting in the early morning light, which revealed the blueness of the painted cupboards and the bright oranges in the patterned tablecloth.

'It looks like being another good day,' she observed in a rather shrill voice. 'Anything special happening at school this week?'

'No, not particularly. Still, you never know,' Leigh replied.

Marie turned to see him sitting there with a little smile hovering about his mouth. Both he and Alice were staring at the Mooncat, which had now come into view on the windowsill. It was not in its customary position, looking inwards now, rather than away towards the willow trees. Marie felt goose pimples rising on her arms and had a sudden impulse to knock it off its ledge and break it into pieces.

The announcement, which came the following weekend, did not particularly excite Leigh and Alice, and it did not appear to be connected in any way with the predictions of Rebecca Lickis. But it was going to make a radical change in the lives of Karl and Kirstie. Apparently, Rachel had made the acquaintance of the new parish vicar and their interest in each other had become more than just a casual relationship. To say that everyone was astonished was an understatement.

The whole family were gathered for Simon's birthday – Rachel had waited to announce her engagement until the rendering of 'Happy Birthday' had climaxed in the customary clapping and cheering, and Simon had thanked everybody after blowing out the candles on his cake.

The silence, which followed this revelation, was embarrassing. Then everyone began to talk at the same time, which was equally disconcerting. Rachel's face coloured up and for a moment Hannah thought that she was going to burst into tears. She got up from her chair by the fireside and hurried across to give her daughter a big hug.

'Congratulations, sweetheart,' she murmured into Rachel's shoulder. 'You must bring him over to meet us. What's his name by the way?'

'It's not Mr Collins, is it?' Alice called. 'I'm only joking. We're doing *Pride and Prejudice* in our 'A' level course. Do you know the story?'

'Do you think we're a modern-day Bennet family?' Emma laughed. 'There's a scarcity of Darcys and we are all getting a bit long in the tooth, except for you, Alice, of course. You've yet to amaze us with your conquests.'

Marie glared at her and looked across at Simon. She recognised the vacant look in his eye, which appeared when the women overwhelmed him with their 'girl talk' as he called it. He was certainly no wealthy heartthrob like the fictional Mr Darcy, she thought, but she would not change him for the world.

'Apparently he is called Justin – The Reverend Justin Day. I know, it's like something out of a romantic novel – and he has been a confirmed bachelor up to meeting Rachel. I think he is butter in her hands.' Emma's eyes sparkled with impish humour, as she recounted the latest family news to Daisy over a mid-morning cup of coffee.

'It ought to have been Time. You know – his name. Justin Time. That was a favourite joke of one of my uncles when I was in my teens. "Just read a good book," he used to say. "*Born in the Vestry by Justin Time.*"'

Emma's face was blank for a moment, and then she grinned broadly. 'I get it,' she exclaimed. The marriage just came before the birth. I bet most young people would shrug over that now. It seems to be the fashion to have the children as bridesmaids. I know. You don't have to look at me like that, but I have no intention of getting hitched up with anybody. Poppy and I are quite happy as we are.'

It was the first opportunity they had had to chat since this particular Monday had commenced. There had been two deaths over the weekend, with all the necessary paperwork which that involved, and an aftermath of contacting relations. It was part of the job that everyone dreaded, but which had to be faced a number of times a year when working with vulnerable elderly people.

Now, as they relaxed for the first time, Emma was trying to lighten the situation. She repeated Alice's comments about Mr Collins in *Pride and Prejudice*.

'That must have been difficult for poor Rachel if she remembers how stuffy Mr Collins is in the story,' Daisy commented.

'I don't know. She looked a bit blank, bless her. It must have taken a lot of courage to tell us all, although she probably couldn't trust the twins not to say something anyway. You know they're not exactly the souls of discretion.'

'I'm surprised though. I thought she would never commit herself to a relationship again. But she certainly picks the glitzy ones.'

Emma laughed. 'Well, she's come out of one marriage with a good settlement. Two healthy kids and plenty of money. But I wouldn't say being married to a vicar was glitzy, not these days. It's a far cry from the lady of the rectory kind of image, and, from what I can gather, he is heading rapidly out of the male menopause and into the grumpy old man category. Still, she possibly needs some security, and it may get the kids through the teen years a little more smoothly. Good luck to her. That's what I say.'

Daisy smiled and reached for a chocolate biscuit. She had the look in her eye which Hannah had once described as like the wise old owl who lived in an oak. The more he heard, the less he spoke.

11

"Time is a brisk wind, for each hour it brings something new, but who can understand and measure its sharp breath, its mystery and its design?"

Paracelcus

In spite of a continual stream of family dramas during the rest of the summer months, which ranged from a stomach bug doing the rounds to a collision involving Simon's car with a tractor, life went on without the predicted life-changing events. However, Hannah did not have to wait much longer for the dots to begin to join into a new picture. She'd spent an enjoyable weekend in the company of Sally, when they celebrated their shared sixty-sixth birthday on 9th September. In a way, it seemed even more momentous than their sixtieth anniversary, a day which had been depressing for Hannah in its loneliness without Jack at her side.

After the slow rhythm of the summer break, the children initially were excited to return to school, and that excitement peaked on the following Wednesday when Alice appeared at the school gates waving a sheet of paper in the direction of her mother, who was sitting in her car parked on the opposite side of the street. As she dodged an oncoming vehicle, accompanied by Marie's yell of 'Be careful, child,' she grinned broadly. Her exuberance sent vibrations through the body of the car as she slammed the door, and heaved her school bag over into the back seat.

'For goodness sake, Alice, you're seventeen, not seven! How many times do I have to tell you not to run across the road without looking?' Marie stared anxiously into the driving mirror, and slowly pulled out away from the kerb.

'Sorry, Mother. I won't do it again.'

Marie grunted. She knew that her daughter was not taking her seriously, hence the title 'Mother' rather than 'Mum'. It was on the edge of insubordination, she explained to Simon one day, and she did not like it. He had laughed off her worries, but there was always the threat of water not being as thick as blood, she thought. One of these days there was a danger of Alice reminding her that she was not 'Mum'.

'So, what's the paper about?'

'I can't explain. You can read it when we get home.'

They continued the journey in silence, and Marie waited for her daughter to retrieve her bag from the back seat and slam the door before she herself drove the car across to the double garage on the other side of the gravelled forecourt.

As she went in through the front door, she heard Alice's voice raised in excitement, enthusing about a proposed visit to a film set. It's at Dorling Hall on the way to Derby. They're doing *Pride and Prejudice* and we are going to be extras.'

'Slow down! Who's we?' Marie heard her mother-in-law ask.

She went into the living room where Hannah was sitting by a bright coal fire. The heat of the room in contrast to the coolness of the autumn day, made a small shiver travel up her spine, and the animation caught in both the face of her daughter and of her grandmother clicked onto her memory like a snapshot. She felt a sudden surge of jealousy, resenting the closeness of their relationship.

The paper, which Alice had waved so excitedly in the air, explained that a long weekend had been planned during the half-term break when students studying English Literature would have the opportunity to experience the organisation of a television drama, and possibly be used as extras in a crowd scene. As the drama was based on Jane Austen's *Pride and Prejudice*, the head teacher and the governors had decided that it would add a new dimension to the students' study of the book, which was part of their curriculum.

'It's a bit pricey,' Marie said. 'Do you think it will be worth it?'

She knew as soon as she said it, that it was uncalled for. Alice never asked for much. She was not the kind of girl to demand the latest fashionable clothes and seemed quite content to get on with her studies rather than to crave the excitement of the nightclub scene.

But it was too late to undo the damage. Already, Hannah was promising to pay. 'It can be an early Christmas present, darling, I never know what to buy you young things, and we'll go out on a shopping trip beforehand and buy you something trendy for the evenings. You really can't spend all of your time in jeans.'

Alice stared in desperation at her mother and grandmother. 'I'll think about it,' she muttered and gathering up her possessions, she turned and headed off in the direction of her bedroom.

It was left to Simon to resolve the issue. He approached the subject with his usual tact. As far as he was concerned, nothing was too good for Alice. During the long night of her abduction, he had promised whoever was listening at the end of his prayers, that he would do his very best to make his daughter happy if she was returned safely. He explained to his mother that they would rather pay for the few days, although he was sure that Alice would appreciate some spending money. 'She plans to go shopping with her best friend from school. We're a bit behind with the sort of things these kids like, aren't we?'

Hannah smiled, understanding his ploy of embracing the 'wrinkly ideas' himself, and feeling touched by his consideration.

Alice could hardly contain her excitement as the time passed and the planned long weekend drew closer and closer.

'I can't wait until next weekend,' she said to Leigh, on the previous Saturday, They were relaxing on the large cushions that furnished the gallery. It had always been a favourite place for relaxation, high above the rest of the 'Great Hall' as the living room was laughingly named, with a view of the inglenook at the far end, where a log fire blazed in the hearth, casting flickering shadows onto the white plastered walls. 'I know it sounds crazy, but I feel as though I am part of a game. You know – not real – as though it is happening to someone else. Do you remember how we used to pretend we were the travellers on that old board game? The original characters were lost, and we played with fancy buttons instead. Mine was gold with a serrated edge, and what did you have? Oh, I remember. Yours was black and brown, with little holes pierced in it. I was Princess Matilda, and you were Sir Lancelot.'

'And if you landed on square nine, you had to go on a long, twisting route through a strange land where there were all kinds of adventures, before you got back on the straight and narrow. I remember it well although it's ages since we played it. It'll still be in the Glory Hole. You know Grandma. She never throws anything away, although your mum might have done. I keep forgetting this is not Grandma's house anymore, although I don't think the house knows that. We ought to have a look for it and have a game with Poppy.'

'I don't know. It would probably seem tame to her, and the twins. Computer games are more spectacular. We seemed to live in Grandma's and Granddad's time, didn't we? Although I suppose that was only here. My mum and dad were always a bit more with it.' Alice sighed. 'I used to think this was an enchanted cottage. Everything's getting spoilt really.'

'Don't stop thinking it, Alice.' Leigh's voice became harsh with emotion. 'Maybe the past has moved into dark corners where we don't go anymore, but there is always the chance that we could land on square nine and who knows where it would take us, Princess Matilda?'

Alice shivered and turned away from the intense expression in his eyes. 'Well, this won't buy the baby a new dress,' she said, making a creditable imitation of her grandmother, and if she had known it, of her great-grandmother. To an outside observer, her words would have confounded the 'blood thicker than water' theory. Yet, Alice's feelings of anticipation about the future were unwittingly linked to her genetic chemistry.

❄

The arrival at Dorling Hall was indeed like landing on square nine, Alice told Leigh when he answered the phone later that evening. A long straight driveway stretched ahead, flanked by parkland where the grass was being grazed by sheep and deer. Here and there, large mature trees furnished shelter to the occupants of this serene landscape. The building in the distance seemed to be retreating as though it did not wish to be disturbed, Alice thought, reminding her of the long approach on the A15 road to Lincoln, where the cathedral set high on the hill appeared to be equally unreachable. There was a heavy kind of silence in the coach. It had been quite a long journey, and all the chatter had died down as the young people relaxed into their own thoughts.

As they drew closer to the house, the landscape became more formal. Clipped box and conifers replaced the natural spread of the parkland specimens, and stimulated a fresh surge of excitement amongst the students.

'Look at that! It's like a big bird!'

'And there's a pig!'

'Wow! There's all sorts of animals, like a zoo. It must be a full-time job for someone keeping them all clipped in shape.'

The topiary garden seemed to set the scene for the enchantment that was to come. The coach followed the driveway around to the rear of the building and the girls craned their necks to see the strange carvings along the tops of the mullioned windows, and the gargoyles with open mouths disguising the waterspouts draining the water from the roof.

As the coach pulled up in line with a large door, the English teacher, a Mrs Fellows, clapped her hands. 'Right, girls,' she said. 'We have been instructed to use the back entrance at all times. The tradesmen's entrance, I suppose they call it. The front entrance is only used on special occasions for important people like royalty. Even the stars of this production do not get the red carpet treatment, but you must respect their superiority all the same. It is always the rule that people employed as "extras" ' – the teacher waggled two fingers in the air to indicate the apostrophes – 'do not speak to the stars unless they are invited to do so. You do not hang around hoping to get an autograph. I'm sure there will be publicity leaflets, and other handouts. The whole object of this educational "window" ' – the girls waited for the waggling fingers '– is to give you the opportunity to have some first-hand experience of drama direction, and to participate in costume and atmosphere. Your rooms are in the east wing, an area that has been designated for student accommodation. There is a refectory, and meals are at specified times. Please respect the organisation. If you are not there on time, you will go hungry. You will be expected to settle down by eleven o'clock each night. Do I make myself clear?'

Most of the girls nodded and mouthed, 'Yes'. A few gave an exaggerated, 'Yes, Mrs Fellows,' in the tone of voice one would expect from primary school children, and the teacher glared, recognising the underlying insolence.

Alice turned to stare at the offending pupils, although she knew without looking who they were. It was always those four who spoilt things, she thought. If only she had a magic wand to turn them off. She visualised a light switch, which one could click down to make them disappear, and giggled to herself.

Later, after a two-hour long session of working through a quantity of print-outs, which were designed to follow up on the planned activities, and a substantial meal of tomato soup, salmon, carrots, runner beans and creamed potatoes, with a mouth-watering cream gateau to finish off, no one protested about an early night. Alice had taken the opportunity to ring home, and enjoyed the freedom of chatting to Leigh before her mother reached the phone, and her tone became dutiful.

As she stretched her feet down into the bed and stared into the darkness, she sensed that there was something powerful in the atmosphere, which gave her a real buzz, as she would describe it. Her heart was racing, and she tried to relax into the rather unyielding mattress, pulling up the duvet beyond her ears. She had never really enjoyed rushes of adrenalin, not like some of her friends, who could not wait for a turn on the most daring of theme park rides. She had only been persuaded once to join them, and the terror of the experience would last a lifetime in her memory. Yet, she wondered if any of them were experiencing this kind of rush. She thought at first, that the place was haunted, or was it frequented by restless spirits? She had learnt from past experience of disparagement not to voice her opinions to her peers. Only Leigh was her confidant in such matters. He had explained to her years ago when they were young children that ghosts were imprints of past energy, played and replayed in the years which followed. Whereas spirits were people who had died and passed on into a different reality, sometimes overlapping into the material world. It was all about vibrations, he had explained.

She wished that he were here with her now. She tried to visualise his face. He was growing up and altering so much. His sandy-coloured hair was darkening into what she described as 'brandysnap'. She dared not tell him that. He was very sensitive about his hair after years of teasing.

But, as she listened to the steady breathing of her friend Karen, who was sleeping soundly in the other single bed, she knew that it was nothing to do with ghosts and spirits. It was more a feeling of anticipation and that she was caught up in some kind of strange situation that was waiting for her just around the corner.

'Leigh, it really is square nine,' she whispered.

The Saturday timetable began with a discussion of the salient points of Jane Austen's novel. The students were then instructed each to write a synopsis in no more than a thousand words, which was not easy in spite of the previous discussion, but a necessary part of the transition from book to film script.

After a break for coffee, they were each presented with a copy of a script. It had been written for a dramatisation of *Pride and Prejudice*, and the class was encouraged to discuss its merits or any part of it, which they would like to amend. Towards the end of the morning session, they took turns in reading the lines.

Alice was beginning to understand that play writing was hugely different from story writing. To begin with, the dialogue must be manageable. So much had to be portrayed by actions and the tone of the voice, rather than thoughts, with affairs of the heart evident in the coy glances and moody behaviour, whilst the long descriptions, which set the scenes, characteristic of eighteenth- and nineteenth-century novels, had to be replaced with the solidity and authenticity of scenery and costume. Each aspect of the production could require many years of experience and the students began to appreciate the need for a large team of experts.

The afternoon session, where the students were introduced to the magic world of make-up and costume, appealed to everyone. They were all back in the wonderland of childhood with the dressing-up box and their mothers' forbidden creams and lipsticks. It was a licence to be 'tarty' as one of the girls said. Some of them giggled, and pulled faces, pouting their lips and making exaggerated wiggles with their hips.

A stout middle-aged lady was their teacher for the afternoon, and with the assistance of two younger women, she skilfully applied the various coats of make-up, explaining how the strong lights could draw colour from the skin and how everyone ended up looking larger than life with a mask of colour. This was particularly relevant on the stage, she explained, but even so with filming, make-up was needed to emphasise the eyes, mouths, and bone structure, and to take away any shine on the skin.

'You look remarkably like Molly Petch,' the young woman, who was applying some foundation cream to Alice's face, remarked. 'I'm Lisa by the way.'

'Who's Molly Petch?' Alice asked.

'Oh come on, Alice. Haven't you heard of her? She was in that drama about that Irish girl. Come to think of it, you are like her. Isn't she, Patsy?' Samantha Curtis raised her voice above the chatter of her companions.

'Molly Petch is taking the role of Jane Bennett,' Lisa explained. 'You would make a good understudy if looks were anything to do with it. I suppose your face is plumper. That's natural for your age darling.' She gave Alice's shoulder a reassuring squeeze. 'But then Molly is older, about twenty-six I think. They reckon that we all have a double somewhere in the world. She's got her hair cut short and of course she wears a wig for the part, but she is quite fair like you. You should see her on Monday before you go. They are filming in the drawing room with all of the Bennett family. The drawing-room scenes are being filmed here, and the ballroom ones, with some of you as extras. I'm afraid which of you gets chosen is up to the producer, but you can all get dressed up tomorrow, and hope that you catch his eye. It could even be names out of a hat, but you never know.'

They had a brief time to look at the costumes after the make-up was removed, and then went on to view the sets and be impressed by the skill of the painters and the carpenters, who could seemingly transform anything. Their guide explained that all the details had to be exactly right. One mistake could mean that a day's filming would have to be redone. 'There are a lot of eagle eyes amongst the thousands watching a television programme,' he explained. 'A car parked in the wrong place or an aeroplane going over, are hazards to watch out for. You must keep very quiet on Monday, and please do not approach the stars. Their time is expensive.'

Later that evening after a very satisfying meal in the refectory, Alice made a phone call to Willow Cottage. This time, her father answered, and she excitedly told him about the events of the day, and how she was the double of one of the stars. 'She's called Molly Petch. Have you heard of her? I haven't but apparently she has been in a film and there has been an article about her in a pop magazine. She is a good singer as well. She's Irish, so perhaps that's why we've not heard of her, but then we don't exactly keep up with the times, do we?'

She chattered on, describing the costumes and the make-up, and how much she was enjoying the meals. 'It's like being in a posh hotel. The people who live in these stately homes must have a wonderful life,' she enthused.

Simon had very little chance to comment, except for a 'That sounds good,' or 'Really!' The name Molly Petch was bouncing around in his head. Could it be her? Could it be Alice's mother?

Alice had now returned to the strange business of her uncanny resemblance to the star. 'I'll see her on Monday in the role of Jane Bennett. I wish I could get closer and speak to her, but we are not allowed to. Perhaps one of the staff can get me her autograph. Anyway, must dash. Are you all OK by the way?'

Simon barely had time to answer, before Alice yelled, 'Must go Dad,' and the phone clicked at the other end of the line. He replaced the receiver and rubbed the side of his face. It was a habit of his registering anxiety. He knew that he must not tell Marie. She would know soon enough, but it was Saturday today. She might have two more good nights' sleep before then. In any case, it could be somebody else called Molly Petch. It might be quite a common name in Ireland. Molly certainly was. Alice did not say how old she was. She would have to be quite young for the role of Jane Bennett. All he could remember from fourteen years ago was a rather scrawny looking teenager. At first, he couldn't picture her at all, but gradually, as he allowed his mind to wander, a resemblance to Alice began to filter through.

He wondered whether to tell his mother. Hannah was good at finding solutions. But he decided not to worry her. She seemed to be out of sorts these days, he thought, not physically, but she had a lost expression as though she was not happy. It was almost as though she was trying to pass the time, and filling in the gaps in her day.

He sighed. All these fretful women, he thought. Marie was becoming impossible to live with. Why wasn't she happy to give up her job at the college? She had always loved staying at Willow Cottage, but now that she was here all the time and only working part time in the garden centre, she did nothing but complain. He could not understand it. She got on well with his mother and his sisters, and enjoyed working in the greenhouse. He continually told her how much he appreciated her help, and how she was getting green fingers. He'd discussed the future major project of constructing a covered area in the sunken field next to the shrubs and trees, and she had been wildly enthusiastic. It couldn't be her age, he thought, she was only forty-three. Even he knew that that was too early for the menopause.

Alice was glad that her father had answered the phone. 'I can't seem to talk to my mother anymore,' she said to Karen, as they relaxed in their room.

'I know what you mean,' her friend replied. 'I think it's all about their lost youth, and getting wrinkles. It really irritates them to see us looking so pristine. We might be like it one day.'

'Pristine! That's a big word for you. You could be right. I'm glad I'm not the only one. Can you imagine us with wrinkles?'

They both giggled at the thought of it, and stretched their young wrinkle free bodies along their beds, before straightening their legs up into the air and doing a work out which involved a 'pedalling' exercise, ending up counting to twenty with their toes touching the bed head beyond the pillow.

'I shouldn't have had a second helping of that wonderful apple pie,' Karen groaned, as she stretched her legs back along the length of the bed. 'I'm getting a spare tyre. Still, you're a bit on the plump side according to that make-up woman.'

She laughed, and ducked to avoid the pillow, which Alice hurled across the room.

The next day began with an hour of study, followed by all the excitement of being allocated a costume for a part as an extra in the ballroom scene. Out of the footage taken, only a small proportion of it would survive the cutting room, but initially everyone had a chance to shine.

'You'll just have to wait and see, when it appears on the television next year. You may have to look hard. It could just be a fleeting glimpse, or you may be lucky and be in the limelight.' The wardrobe mistress shrugged up her shoulders and grinned broadly, exposing a large area of gum, and unwittingly providing Karen with material for a future comedy sketch, when she entertained her friends with her skills in mimicry.

The role of each extra in this scene was to stand on one side or the other of the ballroom, and appear to be in conversation. Although no speech was recorded, the girls had to behave in an excited way as they waited for the appearance of Mr Bingley and Mr Darcy. It was not easy, and involved the fluttering of fans, giggling and a little bit of jostling for a good view of the drawing room entrance.

Alice was transfixed with nervous tension. She watched as some of her companions behaved like typical socialites of the period, with no apparent fear. They peered from behind their fans and fluttered their eyelashes, mouthing words under their breaths as they had been instructed.

She had that kind of feeling, she later told Leigh, where one is standing back and viewing the scene from a distance, like looking through the wrong end of a telescope. 'It was as though I was in a different place or a different time,' she explained. 'Perhaps you were,' Leigh replied. 'Nothing is as simple as we think it is.'

'They filmed me for ages,' Melissa Blake said, as they removed themselves from all the finery, and dipped their fingers into the cold cream.

Everyone looked across at her and smiled or nodded, possibly with mixed feelings, Alice thought. She herself was in great admiration of Melissa. She appeared to have been blessed with everything that a young woman could wish for. Her skin was perfect, not even being inflicted with the dreaded monthly spots, which blighted Alice's and many of her friends' faces at 'that time of the month'. She had a slender, shapely figure, curly blond hair, was extremely clever, and excelled at sports. Now, it seemed, she was a natural at acting.

Alice rubbed the cream from around her mouth, and stared at the mirror. She narrowed her eyes at her reflection, noticing the plumpness of her cheeks and the red blemish of the threatened monthly spot.

The next morning, she awoke with the typical cramping pains of menstruation. She struggled to cope with them, managing to drink a cup of tea at breakfast, but was almost in tears when she struggled back to her room.

Karen was very concerned. 'Are you sure that's what it is? It isn't usually this bad, is it? I'm going to tell Mrs Fellowes.'

Before Alice could stop her, she was racing down the corridor towards the teacher's room, and five minutes later, after a return visit, Mrs Fellows decided that Alice should stay in bed with a hot water bottle until it was time to leave that afternoon.

'It's the best thing to do,' she assured the tearful Alice. 'It will give you a chance to get over it before our long journey home.'

Alice waited until she had gone before sitting up in bed and speaking to her friend. 'I wish you hadn't done that. Now I'll never know whether I look like Molly. See if you can get me some photographs. Look at her really hard and tell me later if you think she looks like me. You could ask Lisa, the make-up lady, to get me her autograph. Remind her about me being a "look alike".'

'Oh Alice! Look, I'm sorry I told Mrs Fellows, but you do look bad, you know. And it's not going to help being bounced up and down on a coach. A few hours lying still may just get you over it. OK. I'll do my best, but you know how sniffy they are about trying to get autographs or bothering the actors. It'll be my head on the block.'

Three hours later she returned to find Alice waiting with her suitcase packed. Her face was still pale except for the 'monthly spot', which glowed like a beacon on her chin. 'Well?' she asked.

'I saw her. You do look very like her and Lisa is going to give her your name and address as a special request from a "look alike". She does Molly's make-up, and is going to tell her about you. How about that then?' Karen's face glowed with satisfaction.

'Oh, you're an angel.' Alice clapped her hands, and then winced with pain.

It was dark by the time they reached Lincoln but Alice was still feeling very fragile and struggled to carry her case to the car park where she expected her parents to be waiting. She welcomed their dependability, and gladly relinquished the case into her father's grasp.

Her parents could not help but notice her reluctance to converse. Simon wondered whether it had anything to do with Molly Petch, and Marie began to feel irritable, asking herself what she could possibly have done this time to make Alice so moody. She doesn't deserve to be given treats, she thought. She would have something to moan about if she had had my teenage years.

It wasn't until they reached the well-lit area of the hallway in Willow Cottage, that they noticed how poorly Alice looked.

'Oh Alice, darling. You look dreadful,' Marie gasped. 'Why ever didn't you say?'

'I just wanted to get home. It's only you know what.' She mouthed the last three words turning her back on Leigh and her father. 'I could do with a cup of tea, Mother dear.'

Marie hurried into the kitchen, pleased to oblige, and Simon relaxed, feeling that his worries over the last two days were unfounded.

Molly Petch took the small, folded piece of paper out of her handbag and read the name and address. She had caught a quick glimpse of it when Lisa pushed it into her hand, with a gabbled description of one of the students who apparently was her spitting image. 'She is desperate for a signed photo. Poor kid! She didn't get to see you this morning because she was sick. I took a real shine to her. I bet you would have done.'

'Alice Clayton.' Molly mouthed the name. The address meant nothing to her, except that it was a village in Lincolnshire. Her Alice would be seventeen now. She knew that without working it out. It had to be her. It would be too much of a coincidence for someone to be so much like her that it was remarked on, and to have the name of Alice Clayton. She visualised the legal document with their three signatures: hers, agreeing to give up all legal rights to her child, and Simon and Marie Clayton's acceptance of the total responsibility for the welfare of the child. She had a copy of the document amongst the personal possessions that travelled everywhere with her when she was on tour. Once she could not find it and became hysterical with the fear of losing the last link with her child. It seemed to her that the piece of paper was her child, and at the time she could not settle to learning her lines until she had found it.

Oh! To have been so close to her yesterday and not known, she thought. How could that be? Just how strong were maternal bonds? Did Alice know that she was adopted? Does she know I'm her mother? Is that why she wanted to see me, and now wanted to make contact? They had all promised not to divulge the secret. In fact, she remembered that she had begged them not to betray her. At the time, she felt like a criminal, even though she wanted to do the best for her child and keep her out of a children's home. She still knew that she was desperate to go to drama school, and the student's grant would not have covered the expenses of a young child. It would have meant having extra jobs and then there would be the expense of childcare, and periods of time when perhaps she was working in different localities. She just could not see a good future for Alice or herself. When her grandmother died six months later, she felt totally alone, and cried for everyone she had ever loved.

Now, after a great deal of deliberation, she found one of her publicity sheets and signed her name across the bottom. The photograph was a favourite shot. It had been taken when she was twenty-two years old. She had worn her hair long at that time. It was how she preferred it, but these days a short style made it easier to cope with wigs.

'I'm in the kitchen,' Marie called, as her daughter made her usual noisy entrance, offloading her backpack onto the parquet floor in the hallway. Simon had done the school run, having business with the bank in Lincoln in the afternoon, which had allowed Marie to make an early start on the evening meal. Seconds later, Alice's face appeared through the small hatch, which linked the living room to the kitchen. It had been knocked through quite recently, one of

Simon's ideas to improve the house, and saved making a long walk with trays of crockery and leftovers after a meal.

Hannah did not approve of the change. Eating and television did not mix, in her opinion. Nevertheless, she always positioned herself close to the screen when her favourite quiz show came on between five and six o'clock.

Because the kitchen was built at a much lower level than the living room, the hatch opened through a lower shelf of a bookcase, and emerged quite high in the wall above a kitchen unit. This was an open invitation for Poppy to slide through like a snake, and a short cut for the aging cat intent on escaping from the mischievous attentions of Bobby, who was inclined to forget that he was also becoming rather long in the tooth!

Alice had quite recovered now. It was Friday again, a week since they had all set off for Dorling Hall. It was generally agreed that the long weekend had greatly enriched the students' level of understanding, and it was still the main topic of conversation.

'There's a letter for you, by the way. I can't make the postmark out.' Marie wagged a large brown envelope in the direction of her daughter's head, which filled the square hatch, reminding her of a portrait. It was a relief to see her looking so well again, with her beautiful smooth complexion and her long golden hair, which spilled through into the kitchen.

'Pass it to me then!' Alice's voice became shrill with excitement. She had begun to wonder whether Karen had really given her personal details to Lisa, although she had not liked to voice her suspicions.

Now, she extricated herself from the confines of the hatch, and ran up the gallery stairs, clutching the brown envelope. She knew it was from Molly. Who else would write to her and address it as Alice Clayton? Anything official to do with school would be prefixed with 'Miss' and would be typed. She studied the handwriting, hardly daring to open the envelope. It was artistic, she thought – rather like her writing, with a flamboyant loop to the letter 'y' and an over large 'W' in Willow.

She carefully tore the flap open and slowly drew out the flat sheet of paper. As the face came into view, she instantly recognised the familiar features. It was like looking at herself. The chin was a little more pointed and the cheeks were slightly thinner, as Lisa had said, but she could see why they had made the connection, and called her a 'Mollie Petch Look Alike'.

She did not know how to cope with this situation. Suddenly it was no longer a game, a boost to her ego. It had become personal. She knew now that she must be related to Molly Petch. But how was she related? Could she be her sister, or a cousin? Or perhaps it was even more distant. Should she show the photograph to her parents? She had told her father on the phone and he had not made any comment. Her mother had not mentioned it, so obviously he had not told her. Still, she surmised, they needn't know anything about her real family. All she knew was that her mother was too ill to keep her, and had assumed that she had died. Perhaps she had better not say anything. It had caused such a family upset when she had found out about the adoption, and had run away. She still felt ashamed about the trouble she had caused.

She eased herself up from the cushion, and went quietly down the gallery steps, and into the hall. She could hear her mother mashing the potatoes in the large vegetable pan, and crept past the half-opened door and up the main staircase to her bedroom.

'Alice,' came her mother's voice.

'Up here, Mum.' Alice put the photograph on the bed, turning it face down and partially covering it with the envelope.

Seconds later, Marie knocked on the bedroom door, and pushed it slightly open. 'Can I come in? Are you decent? What was the post? Anything exciting?'

Alice hesitated before calling out, 'It's just a photograph of one of the cast. Part of the publicity handouts. It's Mollie Petch who is playing Jane Bennett.'

She heard a gasp, and strained her ears against the silence that followed.

'Mum, are you there?' she called.

She went to the door and opened it wide. Her mother was standing holding on to the balustrade at the top of the stairs. Dark shadows emphasised her grey eyes against the paleness of her skin, and Alice noticed for the first time how tired her mother looked.

'Are you OK, Mum? You look as though you have seen a ghost.'

Marie gave a twisted little smile and nodded. 'Just a stomach upset. Something I've eaten I expect, and I swear those steps get steeper.' She was peering beyond the open door, her eyes focussing on the envelope and the white paper beneath it.

'Come and have a look.' Alice passed the photograph over to her mother. 'Did Dad tell you that they all reckoned I was a "look alike" for Mollie Petch?'

Marie shook her head.

'Honestly! He never listens, does he? Well I didn't get to see her because they made me stay in bed, so I asked Lisa, the make-up girl to get me a photo.'

'So this Mollie had nothing to do with it then? You don't want to get into trouble for bothering the stars, do you? They seem to be a bit strict about that.'

'I don't know. I gave Lisa my name and address. Perhaps she can get these publicity handouts from the office without bothering anybody.'

'Yes, I expect so.' Marie stared at the face, which was so familiar to her. Indeed a ghost from the past. 'She's very pretty,' she said.

'Yes. But she's like me, don't you think?' Alice wanted to stamp her foot with impatience.

'She certainly is,' Marie said at last, after apparently studying the photograph for a deeper impression.

'Well? What do you think then?' Alice waited hoping for some kind of explanation, but none was forthcoming. She dare not say the word 'adoption'. There seemed to be an unspoken agreement not to say the word since 'the abduction'. It was an old scar, healed over, yet always there on the surface waiting to be acknowledged.

'We're having an early meal tonight. Your dad's got a committee meeting at six. Leigh's going over to his friend's house – something to do with a shared project – and your grandma's recording for the blind.' Marie handed the photograph back to Alice. 'Don't get smitten by the acting bug,' she continued, 'I bet she's had to struggle to get anywhere.'

Alice listened to her mother's footsteps on the stairs. There was something she was not saying. Had she recognised the photograph of Mollie? Did that little intake of breath register recognition of her name or was she really in pain? Her face was blank when she looked at the photograph. Surely she should have made some comment. Alice's thoughts seemed to shoot backwards and forwards across her mind.

But nothing was said about the photograph, as they ate their evening meal around the kitchen table. Leigh was enthusing about the science project, which only his grandmother seemed to be interested in, whilst Simon appeared to be concentrating on eating his meal as quickly as possible. Marie busied herself with serving food or clearing plates. Alice wanted to say 'Mollie Petch' in a loud voice, but she instinctively knew that it would be like a bombshell. She looked at her mother. She was avoiding eye contact and, in Alice's opinion, was showing an unusual interest in the parish council meeting agenda.

It was eight o'clock when Simon returned. Alice was in her bedroom doing her homework, Leigh had rung to ask if his uncle could pick him up at ten, and Hannah was due to return from the recording studio at nine o'clock.

Alice could hear her parents' voices in the kitchen, when she crossed the landing to go to the bathroom. She did not mean to eavesdrop, although her footsteps were unusually light on the stairs. As she reached the kitchen door, she heard the name of Molly Petch. It was her mother speaking, the shrillness of her voice penetrating through the sides of the ill-fitting door.

'Why didn't you tell me that she was part of this drama group? Alice said she told you over the phone.'

Alice couldn't hear her father's muffled reply.

'Well? Are we going to tell her? She's bound to start asking questions, and why has Molly done this? She must have recognised the name, unless it was the make-up girl who sent the photo. Perhaps Molly doesn't know anything about it. After all, she was the one who insisted on it all being kept a secret.'

Alice strained to hear her father's reply, her mind racing. Her mother seemed to be saying that they had met Molly in the past, and made arrangements with her. So was she a relation? An older sister perhaps? Her heart leapt with the idea of having a sister. But why would it all be a secret?

She had to know, and turned the large brass knob in the door, pushing forward and almost falling down the steep stone steps. Her mother was sitting facing the door, her brow drawn into a tight frown. Her father turned his head to see who had come into the kitchen.

Alice waited for an explanation, and for a few seconds nobody spoke. Then both of her parents began to speak at the same time, each stopping at the sound of the other's voice. It was her father who continued.

'Sit down, my dear,' he said. 'We're going to have to tell you, even though we promised not to.'

Alice could not believe it when they explained how they had met the eighteen-year-old Molly during a visit to see Marie's sister. She had three-year-old Alice with her and was desperate to know what to do.

'She couldn't have been eighteen. She's only twenty-six now,' Alice protested. 'You can tell from the photo. She's my mother? Is that what you are saying?'

'That's not a recent photo. She was fifteen when she had you. So she'll be thirty-two now.'

'Lisa said she was twenty-six.'

'She's not going to broadcast her age, is she? Anyway, sweetheart, you wanted the truth. I don't know whether she actually knows that you were at Dorling Hall. I'm surprised if she sent you the photo. She said that she didn't want to complicate your life, and it has made it very difficult for us. But now you know, and it is up to you whether you contact her.' Marie shook her head as if in disbelief that it had come to this.

'Of course I want to contact her. I don't know how you could all be so secretive. She's probably been looking for me for years.'

Marie was about to deny that, looking across at Simon for support. He shook his head and frowned.

'Only Molly can fill in her missing years, Alice,' he said. 'We'll try to contact her at Dorling Hall, and arrange a meeting to sort all this out. Let's not get too hasty. Everything's been done with the best of intentions.'

'I'm going to bed,' Alice said.

Hannah noticed the atmosphere in the house as soon as she entered through the front door. There was a great stillness about the place as though everything was listening, she thought. The living-room door was half open, and she looked around it, noticing how the fire was low, and the curtains had not been drawn. She began to feel uneasy. Where was everybody? Had something happened? Questions began to gather in her mind as she hurried to the kitchen. She found Simon in there, dozing in the old armchair by the range. He woke with a start, and struggled to an upright position.

'Back already, Mum? Gosh! Is that the time?' Simon stood up, rubbing his eyes. 'I must have nodded off. Those council meetings are enough to send anybody to sleep. Did you have a good session?'

Hannah waved her hand. 'OK,' she replied. 'What's going on? Where is everybody? Is Marie out?'

'No. She's got one of her bad heads. Alice is doing her homework. Leigh's still out. What time is it? He needs picking up at ten. I sometimes feel that I am nothing more than a taxi service. Do you fancy a cuppa?'

Hannah gave him one of her long stares and walked over to the kettle. 'Come on, Simon. You can tell me to mind my own business if you like, but something's up. Oh, the times I do that!' She brushed her hand down her jacket where the water had jetted out from the tap.

'You silly Billy!' Simon laughed. 'I won't be a minute. I need the bathroom.'

Hannah stared after him. Now she came to think about it, there had been an atmosphere at their evening meal. Marie had been avoiding Alice. At the time she had not taken a deal of notice. Marie and Alice always seemed at loggerheads these days. It was all part of the complexities of being a woman, she thought, each approaching a turning point in their lives. She was reminded of herself when she was in her mid-teens. It was quite the norm for her to stamp off, leaving poor Aunt Kate and Auntie Ella shaking their heads and wondering whatever had become of their little angel.

Simon came back down the kitchen steps and closed the door. 'Right, Mum,' he said. 'This is the problem.'

Hannah's mind was in a whirl as she carried her milky bedtime drink up the winding stairs, which led off from the kitchen. Each night, it was like going into a sanctuary. It had been Ella's room in the past, and she had always coveted it. Leigh had shared it with Alice when he was very small, and after the deaths of Jack and Ella, Alice had moved into the room next to her parents, leaving Leigh to convert the 'kitchen room' as it was called, into a boy's domain. However, as he reached his sixteenth birthday, and his school studies began to take up much of his time during the evenings and weekends, he needed more and more space for a computer and printer as well as a large collection of books and equipment including a guitar.

Hannah had been in total agreement to a swap, and impatiently waited for Leigh to transfer his possessions into her bedroom. She no longer had any feelings of belonging in the room that she had shared with Jack for such a long time, Somehow, those days seemed to be in a previous life, and the small bedroom now wrapped around her with reassurances of sweet dreams.

She had loved decorating the walls with a pretty blue flowered paper and hanging white voile at the window, which diffused the bright sunlight and softened the hard lines of the sloping ceiling. She suspended her collection of glass crystals in a row from the top of the window frame, and on sunny days enjoyed the circles and ovals of miniature rainbows, which danced across the walls She could go into the kitchen for a cup of tea during early morning restlessness without disturbing the rest of the family, and a walk-in cupboard in the corner of the bedroom had been converted into an 'en suite', cramped but adequate. She felt that during the night hours she was in her own little house.

Now, as she got undressed for bed, she thought of Rebecca Lickis and her predictions. It was certainly an Irish connection, but it was still family, wasn't it? The clairvoyant had been quite adamant about 'her big picture', 'her dots' to join.

Alice heard the sound of her father's car, and guessed that her grandmother had retired for the night. She was fighting against tiredness as she waited for Leigh to come up the stairs. She knew that he would understand and help to put her mind into focus.

She opened her door and looked along the landing. 'Leigh,' she hissed. I've got something to tell you. Come in to my room.'

They communicated in whispers, straining to hear the sounds of Simon's bedtime routine and the clicking of the light. Leigh was excited at the revelations, but as he said, there was always a time for things to happen, and even though it may seem to be the wrong time, it was all about destiny.

Alice was not sure that she agreed with his philosophy. She was experiencing a mixture of emotions; pleasure, fear, resentment, and a sense of betrayal and rejection. She had no room in her mind for her parents' feelings. It did not occur to her that they were as confused as she was. As far as she was concerned, their role in the matter was merely a part in her resentment.

Events moved rapidly over the next few days. Marie and Simon contacted Molly Petch in order to confirm that she did send the photograph, and to ascertain her intentions for future relationships. It was a roller coaster of emotions. Molly wanted to be reunited with her daughter, Alice longed to meet her real mother, and Marie was left in a vacuum of despair. Simon found himself once more in the middle of what he described as a huge spider's web.

It was left to Hannah to be the mediator. She had long talks with Alice and with Marie, highlighting all the positive outcomes of this new chapter in their lives. She knew that Alice was struggling with that early rejection, when she was three years old, and she pointed out that nothing in life was ever simple. She painted a picture of life at the age of fifteen with a baby, education to consider, and very little support except from an aging, ailing grandmother.

'But she didn't have to get pregnant, did she? She must have known what she was doing,' Alice said during a long chat in her grandmother's room.

'We don't know the circumstances, do we? We could say the same thing about Emma. Just careless moments in one's life and very often in great innocence, and there is no turning back. Molly could have had an abortion and you wouldn't be here at all, although I think her religion would bar that. Don't let your mind dwell on it. If I could have had my mother back from the dead, I would still have loved Aunt Kate. Pure love is constant. We cannot turn it on and off. Molly has never stopped loving you. She must have longed to see you, but she sacrificed her desires for your happiness, and Marie has not stopped regarding you as her daughter. You are still very precious and you always will be.'

Alice's determination to meet Molly ebbed and flowed. 'Why did she put her job before me?' she asked Leigh. 'I must have got in her way.'

Leigh tried to reassure her as he struggled to revise for his next exams. Although he loved her company, he was finding it hard to cope with the trauma of female emotions.

At last, after numerous telephone calls, it was agreed that Alice, together with Simon and Marie, would meet Molly at a restaurant on the outskirts of Stamford. A street scene was being filmed in the town amongst the stone buildings, a favourite setting for period drama.

Molly was there ahead of them, sitting facing the door. Alice's eyes were drawn to her immediately, and she lead the way, pointing her mother out to her parents, who seemed overwhelmed by the crowded room, and reluctant to cross it. They did not recognise her at first. Her image, which had remained in their minds, was of a young girl. She looked considerably older than her publicity photograph. Her hair was cut extremely short, and, with very little make-up, she looked pale and tired.

She got to her feet, and stepped forward to greet them, shaking hands with each of them, but avoiding making direct eye contact. The conversation, which followed, was polite and strained. She hoped that the journey had not been too stressful, and Simon enquired about the filming. They agreed that Stamford was a lovely setting for this kind of drama, and talked about the next venue.

Alice did not join in the conversation. She suddenly felt that she had lost her way. Over the last week, she had imagined this meeting, visualising herself in her mother's embrace. It was such an anti-climax.

'Alice, Molly is talking to you.'

That was Marie's voice penetrating the blankness of her thoughts. She looked across at this young woman, who was her flesh and blood yet a complete stranger to her. She was asking whether Alice would like to have a holiday in Ireland when she had finished the filming. It would be in the New Year, if that was all right. Alice nodded. There was so much she wanted to ask, but it could wait. The enormity of this situation now smothered her expectations and she wanted to go home.

The usual build-up to Christmas helped to soften the tension between Simon, Marie and Alice. Hannah went on numerous shopping trips in the company of Daisy or Jane. Sally was invited and plans were drawn up for her to spend some time with her goddaughter Poppy, who she adored.

Emma had joined a local writers' and readers' group, and one of the members, a Maurice Mackinson, who impressed everyone with his knowledge of old films, English history, and 'whodunnit' books, appeared to be attracted to Daisy. She had called to see Emma on the night when the group met there, and it was noticed that she became quite 'girlish' in his company, professing a great interest in joining the readers' section.

'You never know what's in the future,' Emma commented to her mother, giving Jane and Clive a knowing wink.

Hannah stared at them uncomprehendingly it seemed. Her mind was on Molly Petch and the Irish connection.

The brief holiday in Ireland had been arranged to begin on 2nd January. It was decided that Marie would accompany Alice, and that they would fly from the East Midlands airport to Belfast, where Mollie agreed to meet them. Alice had never been in an aeroplane before. Her travels in Europe with her parents had always incorporated a channel crossing. However, in the end, it was her grandmother who was called upon to brave the hazards of flying. She had often described her return flight to Chicago, saying that she would never be nervous again, but when Marie fell down the stairs on Boxing Day, and was badly bruised, she did not immediately volunteer. At first, Simon offered to go, but everyone knew that he would rather not, and he looked relieved at Alice's suggestion that it would do Grandma good to have a change of scenery.

'You've always wanted to go to the land of your ancestry,' he said.

'Yes, but I don't know which bit, do I? My father would never talk about it, and I never knew why. His side of the family have always been a complete mystery to me. Anyway, don't forget, it's the land of your ancestors as well!'

12

"To everything there is a season, and a time for every purpose under heaven."

Ecclesiastes Chapter 3 Verse 1

Molly was waiting at the airport, and explained that there was not far to go. 'My car's a bit of a wreck,' she apologised, 'but I only need it as a run-about. I live close to the Bangor road, not far from the outskirts of Belfast.'

She had invited them to stay in her semi-detached cottage. There were only two small bedrooms, but she assured them that she often slept on the settee and they were very welcome to use both of the bedrooms. The only source of heating in the small brick cottage was a coal fire in the living room, and they sat close to the grate, enjoying a feeling of intimacy in the firelight, during the first evening of their holiday.

'Of course, I'm part Irish,' Hannah said. 'Not that I know anything about my ancestors. My father left Ireland when he was a young man. He never talked about it, except to say that he had a mother who had strange premonitions.'

'I expect that's where you get it from, Grandma,' Alice said. 'Granddad used to say she was away with the fairies.' She tapped her hand on the arm of Molly's chair to attract her attention.

Poor child, Hannah thought. She doesn't know how to address her. 'I still have a book which my Irish grandmother sent me when

I was five,' she continued. 'So my father must have kept in touch with his mother, but then the war came and everything changed.'

'What was your maiden name then?' Molly asked.

'Flynn. My father was Martin Flynn. He survived the war, although he was listed as missing during the time he spent in a prisoner of war camp. He didn't make old bones, but I did get to share some time with him when we finally got together, although, as I said, he never talked about his past, and I'd given up wanting to know, I suppose.'

'I know someone called Flynn. He lives in a kind of mansion. Well, compared to my little hovel it is. It's just down the road from me. He hasn't lived here all of his life. Apparently he went to America when he was a young man and lived the American dream. He says he has come back here to die. He doesn't seem close to that, although he must be in his eighties. He is the last in his generation. There were four brothers. Three went to the States and one went to England. They all planned to make their fortunes and...'

'Did they?' Alice interrupted.

'Well, he did. He's loaded. That's how he has bought his huge pad. You never know, Hannah, he may be a relation. I'll introduce you to him.' She giggled, and picked up the poker to give the embers a stir.

Hannah felt that familiar prickle as she lay in bed that night, thinking of the events of the day, and she told herself not to be so silly. Everything was making her prickle these days. She thought of Alice's comment about her and the fairies. 'It must be the leprechauns now,' she muttered. No doubt there were countless people in Ireland with the name of Flynn.

She pulled her knees up, drawing her feet away from the cold patch at the bottom of the bed, and wished she had brought her hot water bottle. That would be top of her shopping list tomorrow, she thought. It seemed that Molly did not possess one. They were a hardy lot, these Irish, but then we all were in the days before central heating. Willow Cottage had been exceedingly cold. She remembered how she used to shiver in front of a small electric fire next to Winston, the black Labrador when she was a child during those years of evacuation. We dressed for the cold, she reminded herself; a woollen vest, fleecy liberty bodice, winceyette petticoat, woollen jumper, serge skirt, woollen stockings, and, for outdoors, the addition of a thick coat, a hat and scarf and warm woollen mittens. It was a wonder we did not die from the heat, she told herself, after counting the layers on her fingers under the duvet.

She returned her mind to the present day, visualising the flimsy rig-outs worn by today's youth. Skirts halfway up their backsides, as Jack used to say. More like pelmets. Then of course, the next fashion could be the other extreme with clothes trailing on the ground. 'Like a blackout blind, up and down.' That was Ella's voice coming from the past. Her skirt length was constant, just below the knee and always tweed. Bless her. Hannah smiled. In spite of her occasional condemnation of modern life, Ella had kept young at heart.

Alice was also shivering with cold. Normally, her young blood coped with extremes, but now, in this strange little bedroom, where the north-westerly wind was seeking out gaps in the old window frame, she began to feel desperately homesick.

She could hear Molly downstairs in the kitchen and wondered if she was having another cigarette. She could not understand why she was so shocked to see Mollie smoking. Lots of people in her circle of friends and acquaintances smoked. It was something she had never wanted to do, but some of her friends escaped at lunchtime for a secret smoking session.

Molly had bleached her hair almost white blond since they had seen her in Stamford, and had it cut even shorter, spiking it with mousse. She had overdone it with the eye make-up, Alice thought, and her clothes were very tight-fitting. How could she give me up when I was three? The question kept repeating itself in her head.

Molly was indeed smoking another cigarette. She had tried to last the evening without one, but the stress of meeting her daughter again and conversing to the older lady who apparently used to be a teacher, had laid waste to her good intentions. She drew the smoke into her lungs, experiencing that familiar surge of pleasure as the nicotine entered her bloodstream.

'God, what a mess!' she muttered. This was not what she had wanted. She had day-dreamed of meeting her daughter again, and sometimes Alice appeared in strange night-time dreams, always it seemed disappearing around corners where she could not reach her. She should never have sent that photograph. I didn't want her life to be affected, did I, she thought? So why did I do it? I'm just a selfish little cow!

The next day, after a shopping trip to Belfast, Molly announced that she had arranged an introduction to her near neighbour, Patrick Flynn. Hannah thought of her half-brother who had the same name. Just a coincidence, she thought. Yet, in the back of her mind was the reading given by Rebecca Lickis. Both readings in fact. The Irish connection…in place already, she'd said. And it was part of her picture, her dots, which were joining up She reminded herself that she did not believe in coincidences.

The following afternoon, she stood with Molly and Alice at the front door of the large red brick house, and stared at the stone leprechaun, which sat on the side of the step, nursing a bag of gold.

A middle-aged woman answered the door.

'Hello Mrs Feeney,' Molly said. 'You're looking well.'

'I can't say the same for you,' Mrs Feeney replied. 'You need to get some food into you, and are you still smoking? I bet you are.' She made a clucking noise with her tongue, as she led them down the hallway.

Molly caught Alice's glance, and shook her head in embarrassment.

'You've got your visitors, Mr Flynn. It's young Molly and some friends.'

Patrick Flynn was sitting in a high-backed chair at the side of a large marble fireplace. Hannah liked what she saw. Although he was sitting down she could tell that he was tall and angular in build. He did not appear to have lost any hair, which was a mixture of grey and white, and was combed back from his forehead. He was clean shaven and his blue eyes were deep set and surprisingly clear for a man of his age. If Molly had not pronounced him to be in his eighties, she would have taken ten years off in her estimation.

'Excuse me if I don't get up,' he said. 'It's a painful process these days, as you may find out one day, although it comes and goes.'

'I am already no stranger to the vagaries of rheumatism,' Hannah responded. 'I'm Hannah Clayton and this is my granddaughter Alice.'

Molly heard her inner voice saying, 'No she is not.' The truth of the situation was creeping on to her by degrees, and she wanted to say that this was her daughter, and that her mother was the real grandmother. Was Alice making the same denials? Obviously there was a great bond between the two of them. But then, did she have an issue with that?

'Well, I understand that you've come a fair way from home,' Patrick Flynn was saying, 'but I can beat you with my travels. I have spent the last sixty-four years over in the United States, where I did pretty well for myself. I went with my brothers Anthony and Paul. We thought the streets were paved with gold, but we had a tough time. Still, everybody did in the 'thirties. And then the war got in the way, and we stayed on. My brothers married and had kids. I never did. I was too busy chasing that great American dream as they call it.'

'Were there just the three of you then?' Hannah asked.

'No. There was Martin. He went to England when he was eighteen. I was very young at the time. I have to admit that I can't really remember him. We seemed to lose touch with him, although I think my mother must have known where he was. She didn't say much about it.' Patrick Flynn shrugged.

'Grandma's father was called Martin Flynn,' Alice said in a loud voice. She was grinning at Hannah like the Cheshire Cat, Molly thought.

'There's plenty of them around,' Patrick said. 'Ah, well done, Mrs Feeney. Tea and scones. What could be nicer! I hope none of you are on a diet. Everybody seems to be these days. Mrs Feeney is renowned for her baking. I'm really lucky to have her here. Mrs Clayton, do help yourself.'

'No thanks. I'm not on a diet, but my digestive system is playing up.' More like butterflies in my stomach, Hannah thought. 'So did you never hear from Martin then?'

'No.' Patrick shook his head and then bit hard into the scone.

'Grandma never knew her family in Ireland,' Alice said. 'You did get sent a book by your grandmother, didn't you? She's still got it after all these years. You were five, weren't you? Her mother was called Sylvia and her father was Martin.' She turned her head from one side to the other, addressing them in turn.

Hannah almost spilt her tea in her nervousness. Alice was chattering away, saying things that she herself wanted to say, and her shoulders sank with disappointment as Patrick Flynn continued to ramble on about his adventures in America.

The fire began to induce drowsiness. Then Alice's voice and the touch of a hand on her knee brought Hannah back from an encroaching sleep state.

'He's gone to fetch some photos, Grandma. I'm sure he's related. He's got the same kind of smile as you. If your Dad was his brother, that would make him your Uncle Patrick.'

'Oh no,' Hannah protested. 'There must be thousands of Flynns in the world.'

'Here we are, look.' Patrick had returned from the other room. 'I rescued this album when I came back for Mother's funeral. That's her, bless her, and here's the four of us.'

Hannah reached for her bag and took out her glasses. She stared at the grey images of the four brothers, her eyes immediately resting on the tallest in the group. There was no mistaking her father.

Alice looked over her shoulder. 'That one looks like Leigh,' she said quietly.

Hannah's hand began to shake. 'Your brother Martin is my father,' she said, her voice choked with emotion.

'Are you sure?' Patrick was becoming very concerned and reached forward to take the photograph. 'People can look so alike, you know. Like Molly and Alice. You could easily take them for sisters.'

Alice looked across at Molly, and in that moment they both crossed over into the truth, each one recognising the strength of their relationship. There was nothing to prove or to approve of; Molly was the mother; Alice was the daughter. Nothing could change it. Now, it felt like a delicious secret to Alice, and in a strange way she seemed to be the protector. Molly looked so vulnerable with her wan complexion and rather strange hairstyle. She had such a burden of guilt, and suddenly Alice understood and visualised the agonies that her biological mother would have suffered at fifteen years of age.

Hannah was reaching into her handbag for the photograph of her parents, which she had taken out of the album before she left home, and explained that it was the only likeness that she possessed of them during those early years. Patrick shook his head, declaring that there must have been some jiggery-pokery at work. 'Strange forces have thrown us together,' he said. 'Lots of things have been happening since I got the stone leprechaun. Did you see him on the step?'

He began to explain the circumstances that led to his brother running away to England. 'For that is what he did,' he said. 'I didn't know the full story until my brothers filled in the gaps, and I, in my turn was sworn to secrecy. It won't matter now if the truth is let out, although I wouldn't want it bandied about. Apparently, he had been in a relationship with a local girl, who announced that she was pregnant, and named him as the father of her child. He denied it, and swore that they had not reached that stage in their relationship, but her father was determined that he should shoulder his responsibilities and marry her. Anyway, Martin knew that she had been seeing another young man in the village, and he left in the dead of night. When we woke up there was no sign of him, and we never saw him again. We did find out in later years that he was not the father of the child, but by then we had lost touch. Although, as you said, Alice, my mother did send your grandmother a book when she was five, so she must have known where he was. By the way, Mrs Clayton, now that you are my long-lost niece, what's your name? I'm sorry, I'm terrible with names.'

'Hannah Mary, and you're Uncle Patrick. You can't believe how good that sounds to me. And so I've got relations in America then? I can't wait to get in touch with them. It's like a fairy story. It has often been said that Dickens' plots were full of unlikely coincidences, but then what do they say about truth being stranger than fiction?'

'You've got enough cousins, and cousins once and twice removed to last you until the cows come home!'

The next hour was spent in sorting out relationships and addresses, and more photographs were revealed in the old album. Then the family bible was given an airing. Hannah was surprised to see that she was not named after her grandmother as her father had said, but her great-grandmother. Hannah Mary was written in copperplate writing on the first page of the bible, followed by the name of her daughter, Kathleen Hannah. She choked back a little sob, remembering how her father used to sing, 'I'll take you home again, Kathleen, across the oceans wild and wide…' How homesick he must have felt, she thought. Did he ever find happiness?

'What did Martin do? Did he go into the building trade? By all accounts he was a bit of a dreamer.' Patrick's voice broke into Hannah's thoughts.

'He worked in an antique shop. He was a dreamer. He introduced me to poetry and he loved old things. I couldn't imagine him working on a building site.'

'I know. Building's hard work. But then times were hard for everybody. We were living on the bread line, you know. And as for dear old Ireland, and I'll take you home again, that sentiment has come in later years.'

Hannah stared at him. Could he be reading her thoughts?

'Still, I'm happy now to be back with my roots,' he was saying. 'They would all have looked after me back in the States, I know, but we are still people, aren't we, Hannah? We still have our dreams.'

The conversation between Hannah and Patrick showed no signs of abating, and no one noticed how the light was beginning to fade until Mrs Feeney popped her head around the door.

'Did you want any more tea? Or will you wait until you have your supper?' she asked, looking pointedly at the clock on the wall.

'Oh goodness me!' Hannah exclaimed. 'Is that the time? It's almost pitch black out there. We must leave you to keep to your routine, unless you'd like to join us. I'm sure Molly can point us in the direction of a restaurant. There's a lot to celebrate. It's not every day that one finds one's family.' She hesitated, nearly saying 'and a mother', but she bit back the words. She was not sure about Molly's plans. Obviously, she had not said anything to Patrick about her relationship with Alice, merely describing her as a friend.

Patrick declined the invitation, and apologised for not seeing them to the door.

'He's got over tired with all the company,' Mrs Feeney said. 'I'll get a good meal down him, and then he will be ready for an early night.'

Another guardian angel, Hannah thought.

They hurried back to Molly's cottage, the two young ones dodging the puddles left by a recent shower, both like schoolgirls, giggling and holding hands.

Hannah's mood sobered, as she watched them running ahead. Where was life going to take them, she wondered? And what about Marie?

Rachel had dropped the twins off at the house of their mutual friend. It was only a mile away from Norbrooke, and, knowing that Marie would be fretting over the absence of Hannah and Alice, she had taken the opportunity to spend some time with her and also save herself extra mileage when it came to collecting her family later in the afternoon.

Marie was glad of the company. There was little business conducted at this time of the year. Simon was busy in the office bringing the filing and the accounts up to date, and Leigh had gone to share homework notes with one of his classmates at the other end of the village.

'It's good to be on our own,' Rachel said. 'Not that I don't get on with my mother, but for years I have felt that I am on the outside looking in. I can't accept that my father is dead. I know it's a long time but then time doesn't seem to come into it.'

Marie nodded. 'I know how you feel,' she said. 'I'm the same but then I am an outsider, aren't I? Anyway, don't get on to the time thing. It always sets your mother off. Have you noticed? She says about time being a funny thing, and then she'll be back into the realms of childhood with that old woman and her cats.' She gave a little shiver, and the hair stood up on her arms. 'Ugh,' she complained. 'Look what it's done to me. Let's change the subject. When's the big day going to be? How are Karl and Kirstie taking it? Do you think they mind that you are marrying again?'

'They're overjoyed. They think they will get me off their necks, and that Justin won't want to interfere. We're just going to have to play it by ear. Family relationships get so complicated. But of course you know that, don't you?' Rachel looked out of the window, avoiding eye contact with her sister-in-law.

Marie shrugged. 'I just don't know how to feel or what to think anymore. Simon keeps trying to reassure me but then it's all right for him. He's not the one who is at loggerheads with Alice. She was constantly in a bad mood even before this business cropped up, but he has never been in her bad books, and there is no one threatening to take his place.'

Rachel got up and reached out to Marie, and they embraced rather awkwardly, neither of them good at showing their emotions.

'Mum will sort it out. I know she wanders off into cloud cuckoo land at times, but she does seem to know about relationships. She's had a tough time of it herself when she was younger, and I know things aren't easy for her since Dad died. Don't fall out with Simon. He's a good man, better than the one I landed myself with.'

'Thanks, Rachel. It must have been very hard for you. I hope you are going to be very happy.'

Marie watched her sister-in-law driving away to pick up the twins. Talking to Rachel had been like opening a window from the outside, and looking in, she thought. She had never felt closer to her sister-in-law. Fancy, she thought, after all these years. That was the first time they had made physical contact. At that moment, Simon came into the living room, and asked if Rachel had gone. Marie nodded and put her arms around him.

'You've got me all to yourself,' she said, as she pressed her mouth against his.

Simon held her so close to him that she was soon begging him to remember her bruises. 'This must be the first time we've been on our own in months. What shall we do to celebrate?' he asked in between kissing her.

'Let's just sit on the settee and watch the box. Leigh will be back soon.'

In spite of the close contact with her husband, Marie's thoughts turned to the absent Leigh. He had tried to reassure her earlier in the day about Alice and her reunion with Mollie Petch. He was growing into such a handsome young man, with his intense blue eyes and coppery coloured hair. They're all so tall these days, she thought, visualising him standing by the kitchen table. Simon reckoned that it was caused by the hormones that were injected into the animals to make them grow quickly. She didn't know whether to agree with him but there must be some reason for so many of them being over six feet tall. 'Why do you think you met Mollie in the first place?' he'd asked. 'Alice is part of this family. It is her destiny, and you have made it happen just as if you gave birth to her. Love is the important bond, and blood to blood is not always the answer. It can cause problems. I'm studying the genetic links with diseases at the moment. You know. Where something can be inherited. That's what is so good about loving Alice. She is not related. Just keep the love going, Marie. That's easy, isn't it? Who could not help loving Alice?'

Marie remembered how he did not address her as 'Auntie'. She had noticed it before, although he still addressed Emma and Rachel with that title.

'Does Leigh call you "Uncle"?' she asked Simon.

'Now what's going on in your head? I can't say I've noticed. He's becoming quite adult, so I don't suppose it matters.'

But it would if they got married, she thought.

The flight was due in at three-twenty in the afternoon, and Simon set off in good time to meet it. His mother had telephoned on the previous evening, and he listened with increasing incredulity to her news of Uncle Patrick and a tribe of relatives in America. 'All the dots are joining up,' she'd yelled. 'Don't you think it's amazing?'

He did, and so did Marie, but Leigh just shrugged, and looked across at the Mooncat.

Hannah repeated her telephone conversation after they had settled down in the car. Alice had little to say, and Simon was happy to listen to his mother, leaving all the complications of his daughter's reactions to a later time, when Marie was with him.

It was dark by the time the car turned in to the driveway, and the lights of Willow Cottage as always were a welcoming sight. Marie stood in the doorway staring into the blackness beyond the porch light, her eyes seeking out the familiar shape of her dear daughter.

'It's good to be home. Have you missed me? It was freezing in Molly's house!' Alice flung her arms around her mother, and Marie felt the strength draining from her limbs as a huge surge of emotion swept through her.

Simon watched, relieved at this communion. He noticed how Alice was looking at Leigh over her mother's shoulder, and remembered Marie's conversation on the previous day. If they were blood cousins that would certainly have complicated things, and perhaps 'aunt' and 'uncle' would not be acceptable titles in the future He shrugged and carried the cases through into the back hallway. Everything could change, he thought. What mattered at the moment was a good meal and a cup of tea.

'The chicken smells good,' he said to Bobby, as he opened the kitchen door and went down the stone steps. Bobby stood up stretching his aging limbs, and giving his tail a slow wag. Life was back to normal, and he sank back down into his basket with a sigh of contentment, allowing the tiny kitten to curl up against his stomach. Snowy was a new member of the family, replacing old Tiger, who had died at the great age of nineteen. It was pure white, and Hannah could not resist it, although she knew that white cats had a tendency towards ear problems. It seemed to be an embodiment of the Mooncat, and soon became a well loved resident of Willow Cottage, rapidly wheedling its way into Bobby's affections.

13

And so time moved on at Willow Cottage. Hannah had established a close bond with her new-found relations through her developing computer skills, opening up her e-mails, and recounting family life. She wrote long letters to her Uncle Patrick, who preferred them to telephone conversations, savouring the words in repeated reading.

The younger generation stood on the threshold of their chosen careers. Alice did not wish to emulate Molly as an actress and pleased her grandmother by hoping to achieve a degree in English to be followed by teacher training, perhaps with an added course in drama production. Leigh lived up to the promise of dedication to healing, intent on specialising in medicine. Karl and Kirstie excelled in physical activities and resolved to set up a centre for therapy, while Poppy was an unspoilt lovely child, determined to be happy. Recently, she had developed a great interest in playing the piano, after Daisy had purchased one for the residents lounge. Arrangements had been made for a pianist to come each Thursday to entertain the elderly people with songs of yester-year, and Poppy joined them after her return from school. The pianist was also a teacher and he willingly stayed on to coach Poppy, taking no money but accepting a good meal instead.

'He's another lonely soul,' Daisy commented to Emma, and Hannah as they stood in the doorway listening. Poppy was conducting her 'choir' as she called the group of old ladies, and singing 'When Irish eyes are smiling'.

'She reminds me of Auntie Ella,' Hannah said. 'That dear lady could sing like a little bird, pure sweet notes, and she could whistle.'

Hannah, in the past, had compared Ella to a robin with her bright eyes and rosy cheeks, and here was little Poppy enchanting the world around her in the same way.

The residents had stopped singing to listen to the sweetness of her voice. 'She was born to make people happy,' Daisy said.

'Yes,' Emma agreed. 'She certainly makes me happy. Her father must have been very special.' She stared beyond the group of residents, back with her thoughts of a time before Poppy appeared in her life. She had never recalled the identity of Poppy's father, but she blessed him for his contribution to the family. She must have been attracted to him on that fateful evening, and she tried to visualise him through Poppy's bright eyes and sunny nature.

The other mid-life members of this extended family continued to weave together the threads in time and the senior members were determined not to be beaten by the infirmities of advancing age.

In June 1998 Rachel and Justin had a big wedding, with a formal reception at a Lincoln hotel not far from the cathedral. Rachel looked very elegant in a white 'two piece', her hair falling down onto her shoulders in dark curls.

'They make a handsome couple,' Sally commented to Hannah.

Hannah nodded. Jack would have been pleased. He was so worried about the breakdown of Rachel's first marriage. Justin seemed to offer such stability. She hoped he would come up to everyone's expectations. He had an academic air, emphasised by his rimless spectacles, and a rather high forehead. Rachel said that he was putty in her hands. Hannah knew that she was joking. She brushed aside the thought that some people seemed destined to be victims. Daisy was another one who worried her. This Maurice

Mackinson was very much an unknown quantity and yet Daisy was behaving like a lamb to the slaughter, she mused. She'd always said, 'Never again.' Oh well, there was always Sally. She was a confirmed spinster.

After the reception, it was a gathering of the clan at Willow Cottage made up of blood and water, Hannah commented, as Daisy was extolling the virtues of Maurice Mackinson. Uncle Patrick had made the great effort to travel over from Ireland accompanied by Molly Petch. Alice had kept in regular touch with her biological mother, treating her more like a sister, but neither of them wanted to change their lifestyles, and as Alice began to look on life beyond the emotional turbulence of those early teenage years, she understood the pain and anxiety that her adoptive mother Marie must have endured both before and after the adoption. Jack's sister was invited. Hannah could see the family resemblance and her heart ached for Jack.

Everyone commented on how happy Rachel looked, but it seemed that no one else was intent on rushing into matrimony, the bouquet enthusiastically thrown by the happy bride, reaching the gravelled driveway without being caught. Hannah looked around at all the laughing faces, hearing cries of 'Have a great time,' and 'All the best,' as the couple left for their honeymoon in Scotland. Sally was standing with Molly and Emma. The three of them had obviously bonded. Marie, standing to one side, looked a little lost, she thought. Perhaps it had been a mistake to invite Molly, but then she did accompany Uncle Patrick. Still, they could have made different arrangements. She looked across to Leigh and Alice, who were holding hands. More likely that was Marie's problem, she thought. She herself had known since they were very young, in fact at that time of Alice's abduction, that they were destined to be together, but did his parents have to die? Couldn't he have come over on a holiday? She was back with her thoughts of predestination. A sense of sadness came over her. It was at times like this that she experienced a dreadful feeling of loneliness in spite of being surrounded by all these people; a gathering that would never have happened without her existence, either through blood or through water, she thought.

She had the urge to creep into the old back kitchen, as she had done in her childhood, snuggling against Winston, the black Labrador. She jumped as a wet nose snuffled against her leg.

'Oh Bobby,' she murmured. 'How did you know?' She had always looked upon Bobby as Jack's dog, but just lately he often seemed to be somewhere nearby. The children adored him, yet, in his old age, he more often sought out the company of the senior members of the family, shying away from the exuberance of youth. Did he still miss Jack? How did dogs cope with bereavement, she wondered? He wagged his tail and pressed his flank into the side of her leg.

'How did he know what?' Simon gave her arm a squeeze. 'Come on, Mum. You look as though you need a nice cup of tea.'

She accompanied him through the back door and into the old kitchen, saying, 'Sorry to disturb you. Just going for a cuppa,' to Alice and Molly who were sitting at the old table, apparently deep in conversation.

'You must come over for a holiday again,' Molly said, 'although you seem to have got plenty to cope with. Are you going to keep it?'

'What?' Alice asked, looking away from Molly's direct gaze.

'The baby. You are pregnant, aren't you?'

'How did you know?' Alice stared at Molly, and the colour rushed to her cheeks.

'I'm your mother. Mothers know these things. So, what's going to happen about your education, the two of you? It is Leigh's child, isn't it?'

'Of course it is! I don't know what to do. I can understand how you must have felt, and I keep reminding myself that I wouldn't have been here if you had decided to have a termination. And beautiful little Poppy wouldn't have been here, if Emma had taken the easy way out. Besides, we both want to continue with it.' She stood up and scraped the chair back noisily on the quarry tiled floor as Kirsty came into the kitchen followed by Poppy.

Sally was staying at Willow Cottage for a few days, and the next morning she relaxed on her own in the kitchen after breakfast, with Emma's manuscript in front of her on the table. She had read it into the early hours of the morning, and there was only one more chapter left to read. The manuscript was entitled "I remember Mama", after the old film starring Irene Dunne. Apparently, Emma had seen the film recently on television, and had been inspired to write about her mother's life from her wartime evacuation, up to the present time. She had explained to Sally that it was not for publication, but was purely an exercise to satisfy the teacher at the writing class. Apparently they had been instructed to write about something they knew. The characters were thinly disguised, and Emma had filled in some sections with imaginative happenings.

Sally was impressed with Emma's remarkable writing skills and eagerly began to read the last chapter, recounting how Marion, the name that she had given to the mother, now widowed and in her late sixties, has met a gentleman at a fund-raising coffee morning. Emma had described him in such detail that Sally could see him clearly in her imagination; five-foot-nine, greying hair, moustache and beard, distinguished-looking, green eyes, which either twinkle with humour, or go dark with emotion, and a keen, logical mind for anything mechanical.

She gave a little shiver, even though the sun was shining brightly against the kitchen window. There was always so much going on in Willow Cottage, she thought. She had heard Alice in the bathroom trying to disguise the evidence of morning sickness, and wondered whether anyone else knew that she was pregnant. Molly had confided in her before she left, admitting that her relationship with Marie was very strained, and she had to talk to someone. Sally did not know whether Hannah had noticed the wan looks and the morning sickness, but she knew that her friend was aware of the relationship between Leigh and Alice. That was obvious to anybody who was in the same room with them.

On the previous evening, she had listened to the tape recording of the reading Hannah had had with Rebecca Lickis. All that talk about blood and water, she recalled. She felt, as she had heard

Hannah often say, that she was on the edge of understanding something profound.

'Water becomes blood…an important event'.

Hannah had not changed from when they were young, she thought. She still believed in destiny, everything planned. It was as though the whole family was caught up in a magic spell. She longed for her old friend to be happy. She knew that Hannah suffered times of great loneliness, in spite of this extended family. What had brought such a clear picture of this gentleman, as yet nameless, into Emma's mind? Was he a product of her vivid imagination, or was he really in the future? What if Emma took after her mother and had premonitions? And where did Alice and Leigh's baby fit into the scheme of things? Hannah had once said that she thought it was all about Leigh, and that she was a pawn in his destiny. But what if he was preparing the way for someone yet unborn? Blood to water. Water to blood. She shivered again, feeling the goose pimples rising on her arms, and stood up, pushing her hair back away from her face.

'Perhaps I'm away with the fairies as well!' she exclaimed loudly. 'What do you think?'

She turned towards the white pot cat sitting on the windowsill.

The Mooncat made no reply of course, but continued to stare with his big yellow eyes, across to the willow trees and into the future.